THE LAST KNOTBINDER

THE KNOT & BLADE
BOOK 1

K.K. NESS

In memory of

Sheldon

A very good boy

I acknowledge the Yuwibara people upon whose Country this book was written.

1

THE HUNTING BUGLE echoed through the trees.

Matteo scrambled up the side of a gully, tightly grasping onto ferns and decaying leaves to pull himself over the ridgeline before escaping deeper into the woods. His breath rattled in his throat. Exhaustion dragged at his limbs as he climbed over a fallen tree.

The hunting bugle rang again, closer this time. Matteo took a shuddering breath.

He'd been running for...how long? Five days? Six? Ever since he'd stumbled upon the Rhun's camp at the foot of the mountains, thinking he'd found fellow travelers on the edge of Linnia's border.

Like a damn fool, he scolded himself.

A full Rhuncavari hunting party of at least five sorcerers and five soldiers had been taking their morning ease around a campfire, slow to react in the cold first light. Matteo had managed to sprint into the woods before the first sorcerer could fling a curse at his back.

Risking a glance behind, Matteo strained to see through the foliage. He hadn't seen so many sorcerers since the Rhun first invaded his homeland of Darsha. But that was a decade ago, and he was a long way from home.

A crunch of boots in the undergrowth came from Matteo's left. He mentally cursed himself. He'd been too distracted by his thoughts to notice the Rhun's approach.

Matteo carefully slithered beneath the dark underbelly of a bush, tucking his body into a tight ball to reduce the chances of being seen.

A low warbling echoed from somewhere ahead. Matteo tried not to move, his breath stuck in his throat. The thick foliage marred his view. He shifted his gaze slowly, glancing behind.

There! A branch shivered as a shadow passed. More movement followed, now to Matteo's left and then closer still. Matteo fought not to tremble, his fingers digging into the dirt.

"Show yourself, boy," a low, masculine voice ordered nearby.

Matteo's heart skipped. He glanced sideways, suddenly spying a pair of large boots on the other side of the brush he hid beneath. How long had the Rhun been there!?

The man tapped his boot. "Surely you wish to meet your fate with fists raised rather than groveling in the dirt like a child."

Matteo carefully drew his dagger. He couldn't fight off all of the Rhun drawing near.

The man sighed. "Very well."

Matteo saw the boots move slightly as the man transferred his weight, readying to stab him where he cowered.

The hell! he inwardly snarled.

Matteo launched into the air and slammed his shoulder against the man's thighs. The man stumbled back with a startled oath but remained on his feet. Matteo rolled, raising his dagger before propelling himself up once more.

Something with orange and black wings burst in front of him, making Matteo flinch before talons scraped along his forearm. He caught sight of scales and a long, sinuous neck as a ball of flame shot past his ear.

"Dragon!" Matteo gasped.

The man spun and rammed his boot against Matteo's chest. Matteo flew backwards, hitting the ground in a wild tumble.

The man and dragon were on him before he could move, the man smacking the dagger from Matteo's grasp before slamming him hard against the mossy loam. The dragon leapt onto his legs, its weight crushing despite its smallness.

Matteo thrashed and scored a glancing punch to the man's throat, then twisted violently to wedge the dragon off. The man grabbed at his arms and trapped one in his fist. Matteo bucked in the leaf mold, searching blindly for his dagger.

The dragon left off trying to weigh down his legs and leapt at his hand. It bit hard enough for Matteo to feel teeth grind against bone.

He screamed.

The man slapped his hand over Matteo's mouth. "Shut it!" he hissed, his weight pressing hard on Matteo's chest. "You make more noise than a wounded boar." He wasn't even slightly out of breath.

Matteo sucked in great gulps of air, his muscles quivering. Hot lines of pain ran the length of his forearm while his throbbing hand remained clamped in the dragon's mouth like a warning.

With an effort, Matteo forced himself to look through

the fall of his hair to meet the man's gaze.

The man's black hair was pulled back into a braid, his green eyes shot with flecks of grey. He was tall, with muscles evident beneath a leather jerkin and breeches dyed in browns and greens to match a sun-dappled forest—nothing like what the Rhun typically wear.

"Fira can rip your arm off if she's in the mood," the man said, voice mild. "You going to keep yelling?"

Matteo carefully shook his head. Now that he'd stopped fighting, he could see the dragon was hardly larger than a housecat, with glossy black spikes running the length of her black and orange spine. She gripped Matteo's hand in her maw like a kitten with a chew toy, her golden eyes bright and tail twitching. He resisted the urge to pull free.

"Good." The man eased his grip over Matteo's mouth. "Outlanders aren't welcome in the Kingdom of Linnia. What are you doing here?"

Matteo hesitated. He had no reason to trust this man.

"I'm aware of the Rhun party who hunts you." The man gripped Matteo's chin, green eyes assessing. He seemed to take particular note of the braids in Matteo's blond hair. His mouth thinned. "That makes you either very misfortunate or a Darshian. By the look of you, I'd wager you're both."

Matteo felt his lip curl, surprised his captor was so quick to recognize his people. It meant the man had come across exiles before. "I'm Darshian. What of it?"

"The Rhuncavari are even less welcome here."

Matteo frowned at the non-answer.

"Give me your name, Darshian."

"You first, Linnian," Matteo snapped back.

His captor smirked at his attitude. "I'm Kainon Brightsong of the Dragon Plains. You're quite acquainted at the moment with my dragonling friend, Fira."

"My pleasure," Matteo gritted as blood dripped from his palm.

Kainon's smirk widened to a grin. "She must like you since you still have your fingers."

Matteo squinted at the dragonling. Twin streamers of smoke drifted up from her nostrils.

"Your name, lad, if you please, lest Fira give you one and proclaim ownership of your bloodline."

Cold flooded his guts. He didn't know if the man was telling the truth, but he couldn't risk it. "It's Matteo."

Kainon grunted. "Matteo. It's only fair to warn you there's no outrunning Fira. Nor will she appreciate the attempt."

Matteo gave him a careful look, but Kainon's attention had already shifted to the nearby trees.

"Yes, you can stop biting him now, Fira."

Fira suddenly released Matteo's hand, sending a spark of pain like a parting shot. She trotted before Kainon and faced the greenery with her wings splayed threateningly. The dark spikes under her chin bristled as she sniffed the air.

"Come now, trespasser," Kainon called out. "Ready to show yourself?"

Matteo blinked in confusion and arched his neck to peer amidst the branches.

The bushes rustled somewhere close by.

"Yes, come out," Kainon said. "The Darshian must have led you on a merry chase."

A mud-smeared Rhun soldier emerged from the trees some twenty feet away, a sword in hand.

Matteo bucked, almost dislodging Kainon.

But Kainon appeared unsurprised and unworried by the Rhuncavari soldier. The man grabbed the neck of Matteo's tunic and shoved him back down. "Steady," he said, his

5

voice dropping low. "The remaining Rhuncavari are miles out."

"You don't know that!" Matteo spat.

Kainon quirked an eyebrow. "I assure you I do. Now, don't get too excited or the poison will spread.

"Poison!"

Kainon climbed to his feet, resting his hand on the hilt of his blade.

Matteo urgently sat upright and nursed his bloodied hand close. It ached the way any animal bite would, and he felt no burn or spreading weakness. He glared up at Kainon suspiciously.

Kainon winked like it was a game.

"Hand him over, Linnian," the soldier ordered, stepping around bushes. "No need to get involved."

Kainon's humor fell away as he gave the soldier an assessing look. "Then you shouldn't have crossed the border. We don't tolerate outlanders."

The Rhun soldier sneered. "I'll be on my way once you give up the boy, dragon-lover."

Kainon's genial expression dropped as he paced forward. "I rather think not."

Matteo jumped to his feet when steel rang out. Kainon easily blocked a wild slash and swung his blade. The Rhun soldier stumbled back, the sneer slipping from his face. Kainon followed, sword grip light and ready.

"Stay there, Fira," Kainon said, his back to the dragonling who looked about to launch herself. "I have it well in control."

The Rhun spat on the ground and dashed in with a flash of steel. Kainon neatly danced sideways and parried, his braid swinging behind him like a banner. The clash of swords rang out amongst the trees as they swung and parried.

Then, without flourish or fanfare, Kainon swept his blade down and across, gutting the Rhun. The soldier's eyes bugged out, but before he could cry out in pain, Kainon moved again, beheading him in a single, economical move.

Bile flooded Matteo's mouth. He gagged.

Bending, the man wiped his blade on the dead Rhun's tunic. Then, sliding the sword into its sheath, he strode to Matteo.

"Wait—" Matteo began.

Kainon grabbed Matteo's wrist, turning his bloodied hand palm up. "Squeeze here and here. That should leach the poison out."

"I thought you were lying!"

"For Linnians, a dragon's bite is a blessing—well, from one Fira's size."

Matteo snatched his hand back and squeezed, releasing more blood. He hissed at the pain. "Now what?"

Kainon shared a look with Fira, who sidled up to the man and rubbed against his shins like a cat. "I plan to lure the Rhuncavari onto the Dragon Plains and deal with them there."

Matteo's heart stuttered. "Lure?"

The man's mouth thinned. "Outlanders aren't allowed in Linnia, Matteo, no matter the reason for being here. It goes against our treaty with the dragons." He suddenly pulled out a dagger.

"Okay, but—" Matteo stepped back, tripping on Fira who was suddenly behind him. Matteo lost his footing for a precious heartbeat.

Lightning-quick, the hilt of the dagger slammed into the side of his head, sending Matteo hurtling into oblivion.

2

MATTEO WOKE to the rustle of something moving through the branches above his head. He blinked blearily, his ears ringing. His head ached dully. Disorientated, he peered at a dragon fingerling perched atop a broad leaf a few handspans from where he lay. Its dark green scales and delicate brown talons blended so perfectly with the leaf that Matteo couldn't quite tell where the creature ended and the branch started. The fingerling gave him a curious chirp, pale eyes almost too big for its sinuous little head.

Attempting to push himself up onto his elbows, Matteo found his wrists securely bound in front of him. A burst of alarm shot through his belly. Memories of being chased by the Rhun had him casting about fearfully, but then he remembered the stranger who had captured him.

Kainon.

The man was only some ten feet away, kneeling at a stream's sandy bank while washing a small blade in the clear water. His dark hair was pulled back into a queue at the nape of his neck, revealing sun-browned skin and an open, pleasant face. He was younger than Matteo had initially taken him for, no more than thirty summers. A silvery mark flashed on his right forearm—three concentric circles with a single line running through them. It was vaguely familiar, though Matteo couldn't quite place where he'd seen it before.

Kainon didn't seem aware that Matteo was awake; instead, he appeared perfectly at ease despite the risk of the Rhun coming upon them.

But Matteo knew after ten summers of relentlessly hunting that the Rhun weren't about to quit now. He carefully tested the rope around his wrists. The dagger sheath at his hip sat empty, and Matteo silently cursed Kainon as he looked about for a sharp-edged rock or stick.

They were somewhere deeper in the valley, surrounded by giant firs, cedars and boulders. By the position of the sun, Matteo figured he'd been unconscious for half the day.

A fingerling perched atop a rock near the water's edge, its mottled purple wings fanned wide to capture the sunlight. Other fingerlings buzzed and chittered in the surrounding woodland. All seemed unremarkable.

Matteo spied a small rock beneath the shadow of a fern near his boot. The stone was small enough to fit in his palm while he discretely worked on the rope. He glanced cautiously at Kainon, who appeared lost in thought while staring at the water.

Carefully stretching his leg, Matteo hooked the rock with his boot.

He had no warning.

One moment his eyes were locked on the small rock, the next Matteo was knocked flat, the breath crushed from his lungs from the weight of a dragonling on his chest. Vibrant amber eyes glowered down at him.

This close, Matteo saw the honeycomb scales along

Fira's ribs had gleaming black flecks that fanned out into her wings. Her mantle was a series of glossy black spines matched by smaller bristles under her chin shaped into a beard. The dragonling was the biggest Matteo had ever seen, already as tall as his knee, with her features starting to show the hardness of the adult dragon she would eventually become.

Without turning from the water, Kainon said, "Fira, leave him be."

Fira looked up from her crouch on Matteo's chest and made a chirrup.

"You hunted bravely," Kainon replied mildly. "But there's a whole fish for you if you let the boy breathe."

Truly, her weight made Matteo's ribs creak. With his arms trapped under her, he had very little leverage to wedge her off.

Forked tail swishing, the small dragon appeared to consider Kainon's words before launching free like a cat after more exciting prey. Her talons left tiny pinpricks on Matteo's belly.

Matteo sat upright and sucked in a deep breath.

Kainon dried his blade before sheathing it on his belt. He stood and gave Matteo a measuring look. "Fira says you're attempt at escape is rather obvious."

Matteo scowled. "I didn't think anyone was watching." He raised his bound wrists. "Is this really necessary? I mean no harm to you or your dragon."

"Fira's hardly mine." Kainon strode toward a campfire with the dragonling trotting after him. "And no outlander may roam free in Linnia—this isn't a secret, and yet here you are."

Squatting at the fire, Kainon removed a line of skewered fish and laid them on a water-smoothed rock, absently sucking his singed fingers. The man broke apart the fish and sighed in satisfaction as steam wafted upwards.

Matteo studied the curve of Kainon's jaw and the bright green of his eyes. In Darsha, green eyes were a sign the Goddess Dar favored you as a luckbringer. "I'm not your enemy. The Rhun—"

"Will be dealt with," Kainon interrupted.

"By using me as bait!"

The man appeared unmoved by Matteo's outburst. "I know what the Rhun have done to your people, Matteo."

Matteo turned his face away, his teeth clenched. The man had no idea what he was talking about.

Screams amid fire as his mentors and fellow students were cut down by death sorcerers; the sickly glow of Rhuncavari flame blades...

He squelched the memory mercilessly.

Kainon watched him with an unreadable expression. "I can't let the Rhun roam freely in my kingdom."

"Then let me go and I'll head back to the border," Matteo said. He would have never entered Linnia had the Rhun not hounded him out of the Uhur Mountains in the first place. "I'll turn east for Erania. The Rhun will follow."

"A sound plan, if only you could outrun them," Kainon said mildly. "That soldier nearly had you."

"I'm grateful for your intervention," Matteo gritted out. He tried to twist his wrists against the rope. "I can handle the others."

"Perhaps so. One doesn't survive a decade-long Rhuncavari hunt without some level of skill." Kainon looked him over carefully. "All the same, I'd prefer a more permanent solution where there are fewer Rhuncavari in the world."

Matteo squinted at him. "It's a whole hunting party. That's too many for you to deal with."

"Let me worry about that."

Kainon was either a fool or knew something Matteo didn't. Either way, Matteo wasn't going to meet his fate quietly. "Waiting for them to show up is stupid."

The man grinned. "Agreed, but they won't be upon us anytime soon. Fira spied them ten miles west of here."

Matteo glanced between the pair. They appeared able to speak with each other.

At hearing her name, the dragonling shoved herself under Kainon's elbow, nostrils twitching toward the steaming fish.

"Yes, this one's yours," Kainon told Fira, deftly setting a fish on a rock for the creature.

The dragonling's leathery wings shivered with delight as she dived in with gusto.

Kainon waved a hand. "Help yourself, Matteo. You must be starving."

Matteo squinted as he debated whether to stay as far from the man as possible. But hunger won out and he shuffled over and reluctantly sat beside the fire.

Kainon's mouth quirked as he handed over a portion of fish. "We'd have more, but the fingerlings are rather numerous in these parts."

Matteo took the offered meal and popped a large chunk into his mouth. Crisp herbs covered the skin, and the flavorsome mix of fish, pepper and lemon burst on his tongue. He chewed resentfully.

Kainon demolished his portion in quick bites while Fira crunched loudly on the fish's head, her amber eyes closed in bliss.

"I thought dragons didn't like humans," Matteo muttered.

"Dragons tolerate us, though fingerlings are more accepting," Kainon said, stroking Fira's orange flank when she gave a voracious burp. "They hatch on the Breeding Sands and spend around fifty summers in Linnia until they're large enough to cross the mountains. Most don't survive, instead picked off by predators—even other dragons. A good thing, I suppose, since Linnia would be overrun otherwise."

"Dragons eat fingerlings?" Matteo asked, unable to mask his surprise.

Kainon grimaced. "Dragons will eat anything that takes their fancy—livestock, bandits who stray too close to the Breeding Sands or mountains."

Matteo's gaze sharpened. "Is that your plan, then? To get a dragon to attack the Rhun?"

Green eyes studied him carefully before Kainon sighed. "They wouldn't do it even if I asked. Dragons don't care about human problems so long as it doesn't affect the Treaty. They have no concern that few Darshians survived the culling ten summers ago."

Matteo swallowed against the sudden rush of sourness in his mouth.

"How did you escape?"

Shrugging, Matteo said bitterly, "They took me to be among the dead." He rubbed his chest where a Rhuncavar blade had once bitten deep. "I hid in the rubble of the knotbinder temple before I made it out of the valley. Wandered north for a time until a hedgewitch found me and took me in."

"And she kept you safe all this time?"

Matteo nodded, swallowing hard. Gnarled and surly,

Naran had taken him high into the mountains where the snow never melted. They'd lived a furtive life, foraging and trapping amidst the pines.

"She must have been quite powerful to keep you hidden from the Rhun's death sorcerers."

"Powerful?" Staring down at his bound hands, Matteo said, "I never thought so."

"If the Rhun didn't find you, it was because someone worked hard to protect you."

Matteo thought of the wards Naran had kept buried under dry herbs and ice-clear crystals. The old woman would inscribe them every day with a beady eye on the trees outside their hut. "She told me to leave the mountains if anything happened," he murmured. "When she didn't return—"

Matteo stopped, his chest aching. He'd searched the mountain pass and the river that cut a deep chasm through the rock, thinking Naran had fallen and lay injured somewhere. But when the days turned into weeks and he returned to the hut to find it ransacked, he knew he'd stayed too long.

Kainon grimaced in sympathy. "You did well to travel this far. Crossing the Uhur Mountains, even the eastern ranges, is no easy feat."

Picking at the remains of his meal, Matteo said, "Others must have made the same journey."

Kainon hesitated. "Darshians brought news from your kingdom when Rhuncavar first invaded," he allowed. "But they were not allowed to stay."

Matteo nodded, expecting no less considering his own experience of Linnian hospitality. "I need to find them."

"Let's deal with the Rhun first. There's a village about three days south of here called Briarfall. We have to cross the Dragon Plains, but things will turn in our favor once we reach the village."

Matteo resisted a snort. It appeared hardly in his favor to step deeper into Linnia. But what lay behind him was worse. He glanced down at his hands and the callouses on his fingers. If Kainon told the truth and the Rhun were ten miles away, he could bide his time.

First chance, there would be a reckoning, and Kainon would learn some things should not be bound.

3

_____

KAINON REFUSED to feel bad for the boy's plight. Linnia had always shut its borders to stop outlanders who had little understanding or care about the Treaty with the dragons. The genocide of Matteo's homeland wasn't about to change things.

But it didn't stop the niggling guilt between Kainon's shoulders as he forced the boy south through the woodlands. The boy stomped sourly behind him, pulled by a rope tied to Kainon's belt. Kainon felt the weight of Matteo's glare at the back of his head as he tugged like an irritable mule.

There was no hiding that Matteo was an outlander, not with his pale, braided hair heavily decorated with glass beads and strips of colored cloth. Kainon wondered if a Darshian knotbinder had once woven enchantments into Matteo's braids. Perhaps it was why the boy had outlived so many of his kin—and why the Rhun were so determined in their hunt.

'_He smells good,_' Fira said in Kainon's mind.

The dragonling rustled through branches and ferns as

she searched for insects and beetles to munch on. She was easy to track, her golden scales flashing in the dappled sunlight.

Kainon resisted a sigh. The whole purpose of their trek north to the base of the Uhur Mountains was to see if Fira was finally going to leave Linnia. At more than fifty summers old, Fira was long past ready to journey to the dragon lands. Like all dragons, she'd hatched in the Breeding Sands and made a slow journey north while growing from a tiny fingerling to the dragonling she was now. By her size, she should already have crossed the Uhur Mountains. And yet, she remained. It was the fourth summer she'd refused to say goodbye to Kainon.

'*We should keep him,*' Fira said as she emerged with an unfortunate lizard caught between her teeth.

'*Who? The lizard?*' Kainon replied, being deliberately dumb.

Fira rolled her golden eyes. She made a meaty slurp, and the lizard was gone.

Kainon navigated around a fallen tree, with the boy clomping resentfully behind him. '*Matteo will be out of our hands once we reach Briarfall. Then we're coming right back here.*'

'*It's not my season to cross the mountains,*' Fira declared with a sniff.

'*That's not what you said yesterday.*'

'*I know.*' Fira slinked past Kainon toward the boy, who carefully stepped out of her path. She looked up at Matteo with limpid eyes.

Kainon sighed deeply. "It's your braids that Fira wants," he told Matteo. "Dragons have a taste for magic—the rarer the better."

Matteo grimaced. "She won't try to steal my braids—" He looked at Kainon sharply. "Will she?"

"Her mischief is mostly harmless." Kainon made a shooing motion to Fira. '*It's rude to take what's not freely given,*' he admonished her. '*And no tricking Matteo into making promises he doesn't understand.*'

Fira studied Matteo as if taking his measure.

"How can she understand you?" Matteo asked.

"It's called dragon-speech. It's not as common as it once was, but there are still dragon-speakers in Linnia," Kainon said as he took his bearings amidst the trees. Pale quartz boulders indicated they were nearing the edge of the Dragon Plains.

"Do all of the dragons obey you?"

Kainon shook his head. "No matter their age, dragons won't obey anyone. All I can do is ask. The fingerlings lack the maturity to share more than vague thoughts and wants. Words are available to them when they reach Fira's age. But the bigger they get, the more painful it is to listen."

Trudging behind him, Matteo said, "I'm not sure what you mean." He sounded irritated by his curiosity.

Kainon smothered a grin. "Adults are loud." He waved his hand at the vague description. "Their presence squeezes out everything else. I avoid speaking to grown dragons—at least not with my mind."

"I heard the dragon at the Sanctuary can read the future," Matteo said.

Kainon cast a wary look upwards. The sky was clear of dragons, though it was early in the season. "Tlalam—the Sanctuary dragon—rarely speaks with pilgrims but always demands a great price. He's got little tolerance for those wanting a path to wealth, power or love. He's eaten Linnians in the past for the insult."

Matteo drew up even to him, his eyebrow raised.

Kainon grimaced. "To petition Tlalam is to forfeit all rights. A pilgrim can bring him the best jewels or the latest magic from across the seas, but Tlalam may demand a coin from a pirate ship lost at sea." He shrugged. "Other pilgrims bring incredible gifts but are denied entry. Tlalam can be equal parts mysterious and cruel."

"Is that why you're not at the Sanctuary?"

Kainon slowed and raised his eyebrow at the boy.

Matteo scowled back at him. "You said dragon-speakers are rare. I'm guessing people would pay a lot for you to get them in front of the dragon, but you're out here instead."

Kainon huffed, chagrined that the boy had the measure of him so quickly. He forced a shrug. "Tlalam knows who I am, though my duty to Fira keeps me near the mountains."

Eventually, however, Kainon knew Tlalam would demand an accounting for the seasons he'd spent avoiding the Sanctuary dragon.

Fira chirruped, twisting her sinuous neck to look up at Kainon anxiously.

'*It's worth it,*' he promised the dragonling.

By late afternoon, they came upon a rain-fed creek and followed its new path between the hills. Judging by their pace, Kainon estimated they would reach the Dragon Plains the following morning before crossing the grasslands to Briarfall two days later. After a season on the Plains, he looked forward to familiar faces and spiced ale at the inn.

Fira suddenly tensed.

'*What is it?*' Kainon asked her.

An image filled his mind of the grove where he'd first come upon Matteo. A fingerling had been inspecting the dead Rhuncavar soldier, but now a hooded figure crouched over the body. The angle was strange, as if Kainon were looking up at the stranger from within the protective shadow of the undergrowth. The hooded stranger rubbed dirt between gauntleted fingers.

'*The fingerlings say there are others,*' Fira warned.

Kainon grunted. In his mind, a rider steered her mount between the fir trees, disturbing the fingerlings in her path. He caught sight of a sword strapped to the saddlebags and a quiver set between broad shoulders before his vision swung to the sky as the fingerling took flight. By his guess, it was a full complement of Rhuncavari, and odds were that there were sorcerers in the mix, too.

Returning to himself, he saw Matteo watching him with cautious blue eyes.

"The Rhun have found the dead soldier."

Matteo's eyes widened. "How—?" He glanced at Fira.

"They'll soon realize you're no longer alone, though I doubt that will deter them," Kainon continued. "They seem uniquely determined to hunt every last one of your people."

The boy swallowed heavily. "The Rhun like to be thorough." His mouth twisted as he struggled for words. A dark, distant pain colored his eyes.

Kainon grunted. He could imagine what it must have been like for Matteo to escape the slaughter of his people. The things he must have seen...

Shaking his head, Kainon started walking again. "It was thought the Rhuncavari invaded Darsha for the land. But they've occupied your kingdom for a decade and made no real attempts to claim it. So, it's your people they want. Why?"

"You should go ask them," Matteo said, yanking the rope hard enough to make Kainon stop and turn back to face him. A streak of dirt marked the boy's cheek, giving him a petulant appearance.

Kainon grinned. "I prefer my guts inside my body."

"You've made it worse by killing one of them. They're not going to let either of us live."

Kainon grunted. "All the more reason to stick together, then."

"We've got different ideas of what sticking together means," the boy muttered. "Why do you even care that the Rhun are in Linnia? The Protectors are supposed to worry about that."

"There's a Protector outpost at Briarfall. They can deal with all of you."

Matteo gave him a black look.

The fingerlings sent Kainon an image of the Rhun picking up their trail through the trees.

Kainon turned back around and took a deep breath. "Best we keep going, hmm?"

He felt a moment of resistance against the rope before the boy trudged after him.

THEY TREKKED down the mountain trail as late afternoon cast long shadows through the trees. Fingerlings glided from branch to branch, filling the air with their little trills and warbles.

Kainon spotted the valley below, where a vast, rolling sea of grassland stretched out toward the horizon. The Dragon Plains had become his home away from the rules and obligations that haunted his life. He hoped the boy didn't signal an end to his roaming.

The trail took them alongside a fast-flowing river with rapids and waterfalls. Damp coated the rocks. Kainon knew from past wanderings that the river eventually turned mellow and calm as it meandered across the Dragon Plains below.

"Can't we stop?" Matteo asked, tugging at the rope. "We've been walking all day."

Kainon quirked an eyebrow and turned, careful not to dislodge Fira from his shoulder. Her wings fluttered as she adjusted her weight.

"You'd have better strength if you hadn't spent the day stomping and moping," Kainon pointed out to the boy.

Matteo's eyes narrowed. "I'll be more helpful the next time I'm taken captive."

Kainon smirked before casting his eyes about the trees. "It's best we keep going for a while yet. Some dragonlings like the wild rivers hereabouts and are not polite like Fira."

Matteo looked at Fira warily. Her large eyes remained on the boy as they had been for most of the afternoon. "Please don't let her eat me."

Kainon smothered a snort. "I make no promises."

Fira gave a happy chirp. She liked having a fierce reputation, even though Kainon knew she preferred to steal honey wine and snuggle under blankets like an overfed housecat.

She looked at him sideways, smoke curling from her nostrils.

'*Your secrets are safe,*' Kainon swore.

Fira settled, her tail curling around his arm.

"Why is she different from the others?" Matteo asked.

"I'm not really sure," Kainon began.

Something *thwapped* past Kainon's ear and struck the boy.

Matteo spun like a marionette, tangled in the rope before falling from the trail and into the rocks below. A yellow-fletched arrow lodged in his shoulder.

"Stay down, Matteo!" Kainon shouted as he leapt down to the rocks. He ducked low and looked upriver.

A stranger stood in the lee of a boulder with a second arrow already drawn. His tunic cut was the same as the Rhuncavari soldier Kainon had killed the day before.

The boy struggled to get up, dazed and white-faced. Blood poured from his shoulder.

"Matteo!"

The second arrow struck true, hitting Matteo in the guts. He slid deeper into the rocks with an agonized grunt.

Screeching, Fira shot upriver with her talons outstretched. The archer ducked, but not before Fira scored three bloody marks across the man's face.

She veered sharply for a fresh attack, but another stranger stepped between the boulders.

Cloaked with a grey hood, the newcomer took in Matteo lying prone on the rocks and inexplicably roared in outrage. "He's mine!" He wrested the bow from his companion and raised a fist.

Kainon took the distraction to grab Matteo and haul him upright.

Matteo screamed, cupping his hands around the arrow in his belly. The blood ran thick and hot.

Looking about desperately, Kainon knew he couldn't get the boy to safety before the Rhun got past whatever argument slowed them down. He dumped his pack on the rocks and quickly scooped Matteo off his feet. He leapt across the stones to the river.

"No, no, no," Matteo gasped, white-lipped with pain but figuring out Kainon's plan.

"Take a deep breath," Kainon ordered, hoping he wouldn't lose his grip on Matteo as he jumped into the raging water.

Cold tightened his lungs as the current snatched tight and shot them downstream. He kicked upwards, bursting through the surface.

Matteo kicked weakly before becoming a slack weight as Kainon fought to keep their heads above water. The rope tangled about Kainon's legs, and he cursed as he banged and crashed against boulders. Fira was somewhere behind them, distracted still by the Rhun.

Instinct told Kainon to fight free of the river, but they needed more distance from their enemy. Kainon did what he could to guide them downstream, gulping air and kicking desperately when the current tried to drag them into the depths. At some point, the arrows in Matteo's body snapped, leaving wooden shafts sticking through his tunic.

Eventually, Kainon kicked them free of the furious current. Gagging, water streaming from his nostrils, he sloshed through the water to the bank. He hefted the boy's slack weight across the slick rocks until he reached relative dryness beneath the trees. Panting, he pressed a finger to Matteo's throat and felt a pulse, faint and thready.

"Come on, Matteo," he whispered.

Fira crashed through branches, weighed down by Kainon's pack that she'd somehow had the nerve to grab before fleeing the Rhun. She nosed her way in and gave an excited chirrup. *'He lives!'*

"For now." Grunting, Kainon crouched to tap the boy's cheek. "Damn it, wake up, lad," he said.

The boy remained unconscious.

Muttering an oath, Kainon peeled back Matteo's tunic. The shaft in his shoulder sat high enough to have missed his heart but likely shattered bone. Dark blood pooled around the arrow lodged in his belly.

Kainon cursed under his breath. He knew a killing

wound when he saw one. He pulled a dagger from his boot and cut the rope from Matteo's wrists, cursing himself for his arrogance. The boy hadn't stood a chance.

Pale blue eyes snapped open. With a choked gasp, Matteo flailed under Kainon's hands, trying unsuccessfully to rise.

"Steady, Matteo," Kainon said, pushing him back down. "We're not about to hurt you."

The boy stared up at him in panicked confusion. "What's happening?" he croaked. "Where—?" His confusion only appeared to deepen when his gaze latched onto Fira.

"We used the river to escape the Rhun." Kainon grabbed his pack and threw a dry cloak over the shivering boy. "You're safe now. Let's see what we can do about your pain, hmm?"

Kainon carefully lifted Matteo's wet tunic again and inspected the wounds. They looked progressively worse now that the water no longer washed away the blood. He pressed a gentle hand over the lad's belly, wondering if he could get Matteo to the village of Briarfall before the pain became too much.

Dying out here was a miserable way to go.

Returning to his pack, Kainon pulled out the necessary bandages and a small jar of firemoss. The healing ointment would burn out any chance of infection and numb the worst pain. Still, it meant an uncomfortable day for them both—Kainon had every intention of getting Matteo onto a makeshift travois as soon as they finished here.

He returned to find Matteo's eyes closed, his face drawn. Kainon gently folded back the cloak to inspect the boy's belly.

Matteo came back to himself with a start. "No. I need—I

need leather," he mumbled. "Or twine. Something strong." His hands moved restlessly at his sides.

Frowning, Kainon fished through his pack and pulled out a spare shoestring. "Will this do?"

The boy nodded and took the leather with shaking fingers. He looped the shoestring together and began a strange, twisting braid.

Kainon stared in fascination, thinking Matteo was pain-addled. "Perhaps you should let me—"

A warm hum of magic brushed against Kainon's skin. He reared back in surprise.

Matteo spun the shoestring around his palm, interweaving it around his fingers before looping it together, creating an intricate, uneven knot at the tail of the leather. He shaped a second and third knot with trembling slowness until the leather took on a pale, golden glow.

By Tlalam's pointy teeth, he's a knotbinder! Kainon realized, calling him the name Darshians had once given their enchanters.

But the knotbinders were gone, having been slaughtered during the Rhuncavari invasion of Darsha more than ten summers ago. Not even the youngest knotbinders in the Temple of Dar had escaped Rhun's death sorcerers. Matteo should be dead with the rest of his kind.

With a final, intricate loop, the knots suddenly grew blinding.

Kainon squinted as spots danced across his vision. His sight cleared as the braid turned black and charred in Matteo's hand.

Matteo appeared drained, but a faint flush of color filled his cheeks.

Kainon peeled back the cloak to find smears of blood

atop unblemished skin. Even the arrow shaft was gone. Matteo observed him carefully.

"Do the Rhun know you're a knotbinder?" Kainon asked.

Matteo took a trembling breath, fingers gripping Kainon's wrist as his blue eyes darkened with fear and exhaustion. "Don't let them take me," he replied.

"I won't," Kainon promised.

Matteo opened his mouth to say more, but his eyes rolled up and his grip slackened as unconsciousness took him.

Kainon could only sit back and stare in astonishment.

4

MATTEO AWOKE to find himself slung over Kainon's broad shoulder like a sack of apples. The forest was dark and heavy, with crickets singing in the distance. Kainon must have found a new trail in the night, his steps confident through the undergrowth.

Exhaustion pulled at Matteo's limbs. His memory of weaving the knots was hazy, but a lingering tingle remained in his fingers that told him he'd drawn deep from his gift. He hadn't come so close to death since the attack on the Temple of Dar a decade ago. His luck was running thin.

The Linnian must have sensed Matteo was awake, for he paused and set him on his feet, keeping a grip on his shoulder to steady him. Though much of the man's face was in shadow, Matteo could make out the worried look as Kainon scanned his features.

"You sleep hard after weaving your enchantments, knotbinder," Kainon murmured, releasing him.

Matteo was grateful the darkness hid the heat in his cheeks. "I'm out of practice." He swallowed, feeling parched. "And nearly dying tends to make anyone weary."

Kainon grunted in wry agreement and handed him a waterskin.

Drinking deeply, Matteo noted the dragonling was nowhere to be seen. He wondered if Kainon had sent her to watch the Rhun.

Matteo looked meaningfully at his wrists. "No rope?"

"I think we're past that, don't you?"

They were certainly not friends, but Matteo owed Kainon for saving his life.

Again.

"You're still taking me to Briarfall," Matteo guessed.

The trees around them looked different and sparse, with pockets of brush making headway. The stars were bright overhead, with a few clouds trapped against the mountain peaks behind them.

Kainon's mouth thinned as he appeared to contemplate a response.

A rush of despair hit Matteo. The search for his people had already taken too long. He had to be free of Kainon before they reached the grasslands, or he'd never shake the man loose—not when Kainon had young dragons at his bidding.

"I think our odds are better at Briarfall," Kainon murmured. "Hopefully, we can get there while the Rhun are still bickering over who's supposed to kill you."

Matteo frowned.

Kainon told him about the second Rhun who'd stopped the archer from skewering Matteo a third time.

"Any idea why that fellow thinks he's entitled to your death?" Kainon asked. "You run into them before?"

"Not that I know of. Maybe it's a pride thing, considering there's not many of us left—Darshians, I mean. Not just—" he stopped.

"Not just knotbinders," Kainon finished for him.

Matteo rubbed his side, where the bruising memory of being shot still lingered. He noticed he wore a fresh tunic rather than the one torn up by the Rhun. "Thank you for saving me. You could have just left me to the river's mercy."

Kainon folded his arms. "It was my mistake for not realizing the fingerlings were tired of watching the Rhun. It was too much to ask of them." He tilted his head. "Do the Rhun know how powerful you are?"

"Power is meaningless without training," Matteo said. "I'm nothing compared to my teachers."

"And you were young when the Rhun invaded."

Too young and inexperienced to do anything about it. At seven summers old, Matteo had been skilled in the knots suited to childish ambitions and inexpert fingers. And yet, even knotbinders four times his age had been no match against the Rhun. With no teacher since then, Matteo couldn't progress to the complex enchantments he needed to fight back.

"Will you help me get to Erania instead?" Matteo asked, hating the desperation in his voice.

Kainon hesitated. "Let the Protectors deal with the Rhun first."

Matteo sighed.

"Can you walk?" Kainon asked. "We can reach the Dragon Plains by sunrise if we keep going."

With a nod, he walked beside Kainon through the scarce trees.

Dawn saw them atop a gently rolling hill, with an icy breeze rolling down the mountain peaks behind them. In the golden light, countless miles of grassland moved like waves, kicking up spores and tiny flowers that glowed like fireflies.

Matteo and Kainon traipsed into a gully dotted with blue flowers and dark green sedge.

Kainon strode as if he knew the best direction through the chin-high grass. Matteo could see little beyond more grass on the rolling hills. He wondered if the Rhun could see them from the higher altitudes. It would be easy to spot two people walking through the grass in the distance.

Snow whitened the peaks, and he wondered what it must be like for a dragon to fly over them, their wings so cold they must surely feel frozen. Matteo supposed that was why fingerlings couldn't make the journey, but he couldn't imagine it was easy for dragonlings either.

Kainon continued unconcerned.

They continued unhindered into the next day until the grass parted and suddenly finely crushed grey pebbles crunched underfoot. A graveled trail about two horses wide cut through the grass and headed south, deeper into Linnia.

Matteo paused in surprise.

Kainon had brought them directly to a trailhead, marked by a statue of a dragon curled up about itself as if sleeping.

The dragon statue came up to Matteo's hip, the damp stone grey and devoid of lichen or moss. Drawing closer, Matteo saw the serpent's eyes were half-open, decorated by glittering rubies. A sensation of being watched crept over Matteo.

"Take a rest, Matteo," Kainon said as he settled on his knees before the statue and rested his hands on his thighs. "Fira should be on her way."

Without another word, Kainon took a deep, slow breath and closed his eyes.

Matteo stared, wondering what the Linnian was doing. Praying, perhaps?

Regardless, it was his opportunity to slink back into the grass and disappear. The fingerlings might show no interest in him if he was quiet and careful enough. Fira, however, was another matter. The dragonling enjoyed the hunt.

He took a careful step backwards.

As if called by his thoughts, Fira nosed her way out of the grass at Matteo's ankle. She looked at Kainon sitting cross-legged and at peace before the stone statute. She gave a decidedly disgruntled huff.

Matteo held his breath and waited.

The dragonling wandered around the edge of the trail, sniffing the ground. Little puffs of dust followed in her wake. She reminded Matteo of a hound. Her golden eyes suddenly brightened with interest, and she launched into the grass.

An indignant squawk made Matteo straighten before a fingerling the size of his palm tumbled out of the undergrowth. It was speckled brown and grey with tiny spikes along its spine.

It spat a puff of fire at Fira, who appeared to chortle before pouncing, her talons wide enough to purposefully miss the little serpent.

The fingerling spat again and scurried into the grass.

Kainon's face remained purposefully blank as Fira leapt over him.

Matteo squinted worriedly up at the highlands, wondering again what the Rhun could see. He hoped the angry fingerling didn't start a grassfire; otherwise, they'd really be in trouble. He looked again at Kainon, who remained resolutely calm despite the uproar nearby.

Matteo took Kainon's cue and hoped they were safe enough.

Hoping he hadn't lost his best chance at sneaking away, Matteo sat on the trail and massaged his toes in his boots.

Kainon had set a brutal pace, and while Matteo had already travelled a long way, his soaked boots had hardened as they dried and now rubbed uncomfortably. He contemplated weaving a knot but resisted the indulgence. Dar would disapprove.

He settled back, watching the grass shake and shiver as Fira set about upsetting more fingerlings. He plucked a blue-starred flower by his side and considered its long stem. Bored, he gathered a small handful and made them into a chain. His magic gathered at the edge of his fingertips, but Matteo resisted the urge to create an enchantment when there was no purpose. He merely acknowledged the power and let it go.

Concentrating on tying off the end of the circlet, he whistled lowly. "Fira."

Fira stuck her nose out of the grass, sniffing.

Matteo showed her the circlet. "What do you think?"

She sniffed some more, edging forward until her golden eyes were visible.

"There's no magic in it, mind," Matteo said, wondering if Fira understood.

She fully strode out from the thick grass, her wings slightly extended.

With a grin, Matteo presented the circlet for her to smell. The dragonling flopped down and rested her head on Matteo's lap. Fira was surprisingly heavy, with her scales radiating heat. Matteo placed the flower circlet above the bony ridge of her eyebrows.

"Very pretty," he said, admiring the contrast between the blue flowers and the burnished gold of her scales.

Fira batted her eyes and tilted her head to look inquiringly at him.

"You are the most beautiful dragonling," Matteo told her.

Fira basked under the attention before wriggling upright, clambering until her foreclaws rested on Matteo's knee. Matteo gently nudged the flower circlet to stop it from sitting askew. Fira leaned forward as if to sniff Matteo's braids, and suddenly he felt snared by the gold in the dragonling's eyes.

Matteo felt drawn deep, the world quietening as if he'd dived into a golden pool. Fira's eyes seemed to swirl, carrying motes of red and orange like sparks from a fire.

Matteo edged closer, pulled deeper into the pool of light and quiet.

Kainon suddenly cleared his throat. "He's not yours, Fira," he said, voice mild.

With an effort, Matteo leaned away but felt dragged inexorably back.

Kainon gave Fira a gentle nudge until the dragonling settled on her haunches.

She blinked.

Matteo felt the world suddenly expand again. Birdlife and rustling grass filled his ears, and he sucked a cold breath deep into his chest.

"There's a difference between whimsy and a life," Kainon said to Fira, his voice gently chiding.

Matteo took another deep, shuddering breath. "What just happened?"

Kainon gave him a bemused look. "Be careful when offering gifts to dragons, Matteo. You never quite know what they will take."

Matteo blinked, looking at Fira.

The flower crown sat crooked on the dragonling's bony

eye ridges, but she held her head regally. She gave Kainon a slightly displeased side-eye.

Kainon snorted. "I mean it, my girl. A gift is sometimes just that. He hasn't promised himself or his lineage to you."

Matteo's mouth fell open in realization. "I didn't—"

"Yes, I know it's an honor," Kainon told Fira. "But don't assume. You must ask or he must outright offer. That's the way with us humans. We don't understand your ways." He stroked her flank until she settled, a disgruntled rumble coming from Fira's throat. He raised an eyebrow at Matteo. "Be careful, Matteo. A gift is never just a gift with dragons."

"But it's just a flower crown," Matteo argued, flushing slightly. "There's no magic in it."

"That doesn't matter. Fira won't forget."

Matteo wasn't sure what Kainon meant. He glanced again at Fira. Her eyes no longer drew him in, and he wondered if he'd been about to offer something he couldn't take back. He shook himself and looked at the statue. "What were you doing just then?"

Kainon rose, dusting his hands on his breeches. "Offering my thanks for the guardians of the road. It's important to acknowledge them." He hesitated. "And you never know who's watching."

Matteo looked at the statue. The red stone eyes appeared to glow.

"If the dragon lords are kind, we should reach Briarfall before sunset," Kainon said, motioning for them to take the trail as it cut south through the grass.

Fira leapt onto Kainon's shoulder, her tail swinging back and forth in apparent readiness.

Matteo walked after them, noticing how the world seemed brighter and raucous with the bickering of fingerlings just out of sight. He wondered if this was what

Kainon had meant by dragons being loud—once ensnared, they seemed to drown out everything else.

He resolved to be more careful. He had a task to complete, after all.

But he felt the weight of eyes on him and glanced behind at the statue protecting the trailhead. It stared back.

5

THEY REACHED Briarfall as the afternoon grew golden and hazy. It was a bustling village at the edge of a large ravine cut deep by a river. The scent of warm bread filled the air, accompanied by the cluck of chickens feasting on grain at the edge of the town.

Kainon noticed Matteo looking about curiously. Most buildings were squat and made of thick stone, a relic from when dragons threatened to raze Linnia to dust and ash. But now the stone buildings were peppered with hand-carved divots and niches perfect for nesting fingerlings, with some holes decorated with bright paint and others stuffed with wool and silk. Despite the cool breeze, windows remained open to allow fingerlings to come and go as they pleased, while doors had little swinging flaps that even the smallest fingerling could nudge open.

A shrine of stone and turquoise took a commanding position in front of the town hall. Kainon noted someone had left a sack of Pelannian dates for the fingerlings to take at will.

A handful of people called out in greeting to Kainon but stared at Matteo and his shock of pale, beaded hair until Kainon told him to pull up his hood.

"Where's the Protector outpost?" Matteo asked, looking about.

"We'll deal with them later," Kainon said as he steered the lad toward the Hunting Owl Inn, where a pair of fingerlings sat atop a sign of a white owl and mouse. "First, we all deserve the finest meal Briarfall has to offer."

Fira launched off Kainon's shoulder to chase the fingerlings away from their perch. *'I am returned!'*

The fingerlings scattered with outraged squawks and disappeared beneath a gap in the rafters.

Kainon resisted a snort and led Matteo around the back of the inn to a small courtyard leading to the stables.

They entered through the kitchen door into a wild mess of fingerlings scuttling over almost every surface. A handful sat on the edge of a work table, staring at the pantry. A few more fluttered near the mantle above a stone hearth, where large pots of stew bubbled above a fire. More still scampered underfoot or inspected various baskets and drying herbs strung in a line above the window overlooking the courtyard.

Kainon blinked in surprise. He'd never seen so many fingerlings inside the Owl.

It was clear that preparation for the evening had begun despite the distractions, with the main table cluttered with vegetables and steaming mince tarts.

Thia's plain, wrinkled face was fixed in a familiar scowl as she spoke to the serving girl, Jayra. "And see to it those ploughmen are out by sundown," she said as she stirred furiously at a boiling pot. "I'll not stand for men who dirty the ale room and overstay their welcome!"

Kainon caught the steely glint in her eyes and knew from long experience that Thia did not put up with duplicity.

"Perhaps I should be the one to see them out in case they want to take advantage of Jayra," Brylin offered from where she sat on a stool guarding the pantry against fingerlings. Smoke wafted from her ever-present pipe.

The serving girl deftly chopped at a hank of fresh pork, then lifted the bloodied carving knife. "I can take care of myself, mother, as you know."

A fingerling braved the length of the worktable and took a sneaky bite from a radish.

"Ha!" Jayra said, shooing the little creature. "Not again!"

Kainon walked around the worktable and helped himself to a pie. He had just enough time to duck under Thia's swatting wooden spoon.

"Off with that!" Thia exclaimed. "You'll get no welcome here after sending your critters to hound me."

Kainon quickly raised his hands. "Forgive me, my lady. The fingerlings must have quick wings to have escaped your wrath unscathed."

Thia pointed her chin toward a pink-hued fellow nesting in a straw basket by the door and said, "That one nearly lost an eye for taking a ham hock last week!"

Kainon sensed only vague contentedness and full bellies. Despite Thia's protestations, she'd taken great care of the fingerlings under her roof. "How long have they been here?"

Thia folded her arms. "They overtook the place a few days after you left for patrol."

Surprised, Kainon looked up from his regard of the fingerling. "But that was weeks ago."

"Aye. You wander too much," Thia muttered. "All that

time in the mountains. Your duties still require you to be Linnian, boy!"

Kainon rolled his eyes fondly. This was an old conversation between them.

"And who's this?" Thia asked, gaze narrowing on Matteo's hooded features. "An outlander? You know our laws better than anyone, Kainon."

Kainon waved Matteo beside him, indicating for him to drop his hood. "Matteo, this is Thia, the lady of this fine establishment. The lass beside her is Jayra, while that dour woman over there happens to be her mother, Brylin."

Brylin and Jayra gave cautious greetings.

Thia's beady look remained firmly in place. "I'm sure Kainon has his reasons for bringing you, but we've got enough trouble going on."

A familiar look of stubbornness crossed Matteo's face. "I don't plan on staying—"

"He'll be the Protectors' responsibility soon enough," Kainon said, giving Thia a look. "We've got the Rhun on our trail."

Thia's gaze only sharpened. "Is that so? There haven't been any Rhun in the Plains since the last Darshians made their way south."

Matteo straightened. "Do you know where they went?"

Thia shook her head. "They didn't stay for long, though I think a few planned to go to the royal palace in Pelan with word of what was happening in Darsha."

Matteo glanced at Kainon hopefully. "Could they still be in Pelan?"

Kainon hesitated. The likelihood was extremely slim, although the mage guild had discretion regarding appeasing the dragons with rare gifts. If the mage guild realized in time that the genocide in Darsha meant the knotbinders were all but gone, they may have hidden knotbinders somewhere in Linnia.

Kainon studied Matteo anew. It could be Matteo's fate as well, if the Protectors realized what he was. That wasn't necessarily a good thing.

"Thia, we need to do something with Matteo's hair. It's too easy for the Rhun to track him."

Thia's gaze turned knowing. "I can come up with something."

"I'm not undoing my braids," Matteo said sharply.

Kainon resisted arguing with the lad, recognizing the stubborn set of his chin. "I didn't think you would. All the same, let's try to draw less attention."

"I don't envy your timing," Brylin said. "The Protectors aren't due back from patrol for another week. Word is they got caught by snowmelt out at Ferny Crossing."

Kainon cursed. He doubted the Rhun would be so kind as to wait until the Protectors arrived, though there were people in Briarfall who he could trust.

Thia scowled. "We can handle a few scoundrels, even the sorcerous kind." Her eyes narrowed as she scrutinized Matteo's attire. "Looks like you lost everything to them."

"All but my life," Matteo said ruefully.

Thia folded her arms, her gaze measuring.

"Helping Matteo is my concern," Kainon said. "Let the mayor know I've returned. In the meantime, I'll find out what's made the local fingerlings so demanding."

Thia made a soft grunt. "That would be appreciated, dragon-speaker. Your rooms are ready, as always. Just be sure to join us in the ale room tonight," the old woman added. "It's venison stew."

Kainon smiled. "We'll be there." Pilfering another slice of mince tart, he added, "I'll show Matteo upstairs."

"Remember to open the window for that dragonling of yours," Thia called after him. "I don't want her setting fire to the upper floor again because no one thought to let her in!"

Kainon waved his hand in agreement.

Giving Matteo a wink, he led the way up the stairs near the ale room to the second floor. Kainon opened the fifth door along, ushering Matteo inside. Weak afternoon sunshine lit across the woolen rug on the floor, bouncing off the cluttered shelves that hugged all but one wall. Over-stuffed chests revealed a veritable collection of trinkets he and Fira garnered over the seasons, while a downy, dragonling-sized pallet took up much of the space in front of the hearth.

Matteo looked overwhelmed.

"It's quite safe," Kainon said, striding across the room to open the shutters. A cloak lay carelessly thrown across the desk where he'd left it. A fine layer of dust sat undisturbed save for a trail of tiny serpent feet.

Matteo glanced through to the next room, where Kainon had left more books and scrolls in haphazard piles around the large bed.

"Is this your home?" Matteo asked.

Leaning against the edge of the desk, Kainon folded his arms. "I suppose it is, though I'm not here as often as I'd like."

Matteo inspected a green ball of silken yarn left by the fireplace by a trader who had gifted it to Fira last autumn. Kainon tended not to bring folk into his rooms except for travelers seeking their ease with a brief dalliance before continuing their journey. Matteo was unexpected, although certainly the sort to draw Kainon's gaze even without the sunlight glinting off the glass beads in his pale hair.

Clearing his throat, Kainon said, "I'll have Thia organize a pallet for you. Stay up here until we get your hair sorted."

Matteo folded his arms. "I meant what I said. I won't remove my braids."

It would certainly help matters, but Kainon wasn't about to push. "We'll make it work. The less attention we draw to you, the better."

Matteo relaxed a little. "What's going to happen when the Protectors arrive?"

"You mean, are they going to use you as bait?"

"It's a fair assumption," Matteo said.

"Let's hope they can learn from my mistake," Kainon said ruefully. "I'll do what I can, but I make no promises."

Further conversation was interrupted by a polite knock on the door. It opened and Brylin came in with a platter of fruit and cheese, which she handed to Matteo. In a pot was a black liquid with an astringent smell that itched Kainon's nostrils. "Thia says to come downstairs so she can make sure it's done right."

Kainon thanked her, though Matteo looked dubious.

"No one's touching my braids," Matteo said.

"Thia will keep her hands to herself," Brylin promised, eyebrows raised in amusement. "Kainon, the mayor's already waiting for you downstairs, too."

"Tell her I'll be down in a moment."

Brylin left with a nod.

"Well, it looks like taking our ease will have to wait." Kainon handed Matteo the pot of hair dye. "Ask the stableboy to run you a bath once Thia's had her way with you. I'll be in the ale room."

Matteo put the food platter on the nearby desk just as Kainon gathered his cloak and headed for the door.

"And, Matteo, for what it's worth—" He pressed a hand over his heart and bowed his head in a Linnian gesture of greeting. "Welcome to Linnia."

MATTEO FOLLOWED the bustling sound of voices and scraping chairs down to the ale room. A handful of riders arrived, demanding food and ale as they found an empty table amongst the patrons already deep in their cups. The ale room was surprisingly large and sprawling, shaped around a bar to allow private conversations in the gloomier corners.

A hearth crackled brightly in response to the spring cool, the shutters open to allow a breeze to sweep in from the hills. Fingerlings sat on the window ledges and snatched up any insects drawn to the lanterns. Brylin and Jayra moved about the crowd with practiced ease as they unloaded trays of stew, bread and ale.

"Matteo," Kainon called out from one corner of the ale room, waving his hand. An older woman sat beside him finishing her tankard in hefty gulps while a broad-shouldered man watched.

Self-consciously running a hand across his newly darkened braids, Matteo passed Fira perched on the bar closest to the kitchen door. Her tail quivered when Thia emerged with a large tray of meat and potatoes slathered in buttery herbs.

"Don't think you're getting anything from me, you warbling wastrel!" Thia told the dragonling as she stomped past to set the tray on a nearby table where three men and a woman in traveler garb sat quietly.

Fira gave Thia an innocent trill.

"I said what I said!" Thia replied as she disappeared back into the kitchen.

Unloading empty tankards behind the bar, Jayra winked at Matteo. "Everyone knows Thia gives the best cuts to Fira," she said in a conspiratorial whisper. "Always has, ever since she showed up attached to Kainon's cloak like a burr."

The door to the kitchen banged open as Thia stuck her head out to give Jayra a beady glare.

Quickly grabbing a tray, the serving girl went to a table to clear empty plates.

Matteo crossed the ale room and sat beside Kainon. The man's companions looked at him with curiosity.

"Matteo, this is Briarfall's mayor, Risia," Kainon said, motioning to the aging woman slathering butter onto a hank of bread. "Her man is Lukas—he keeps an eye on things for the Protectors when they're out on patrol."

The red-haired man nodded. A map was spread out before him, a tankard and a sheathed dagger holding down the corners.

Wiping her mouth, Risia leaned back in her chair, tilting it at such an angle that Matteo feared it would topple. She was a stout woman with bright hazel eyes and a sun-darkened, wrinkled face. "The Rhun, is it, boy?" she said, her eyebrow quirked. "Not the sort of company we like here in Linnia."

"It wasn't my intent to bring them," Matteo said. "Kainon and Fira saved me."

Upon hearing her name, Fira raised her head from the bar and trilled at being included.

Lukas ran a quick, assessing gaze over Matteo's features.

"You might want to work on your accent, lad. Though walking through town with white hair didn't do you any favors, either."

Matteo threw Kainon a dour look. He still wasn't sure why Kainon had insisted on darkening his hair.

"What happened in Darsha was dirty business," Risia muttered. "If I could get my hands on those Rhun bastards, there'd be a reckoning!"

Matteo looked at her in surprise. "I didn't think Linnians cared about what happened outside the kingdom."

"Risia used to be a soldier in the King's army. She fought her share of Rhun on the western border," Kainon explained.

"Was enough for me to seek the quiet life here in Briarfall," she admitted. "Not that there isn't always some sort of adventure hereabouts." Risia leaned forward. "Can you tell us anything about the Rhun hunting you?"

Matteo cleared his throat. "There's not much to tell. It's a full hunting party, though Kainon dealt with one of them already."

"Any death sorcerers?"

"I-I don't know." He hoped not.

Lukas muttered, "No matter. We can't have them attacking unsuspecting folk on the road. It can't wait for the Protectors to return."

Kainon nodded. "Some fingerlings saw the Rhun past the old goatherd huts in the valley. I can't be sure where they are now."

Matteo looked at Kainon in surprise. "The fingerlings lost them?"

Kainon rubbed his chin and shrugged. "It's hard for them to stay interested, especially now that we're in Briarfall. The little ones here refuse to take up the task."

"Because they've grown fat on Thia's cooking!" Lukas said with a chuckle.

Turning to Matteo, Risia said, "You'd scarcely believe the amount these little ones can eat. I once saw a whole covey of red fingerlings take down a moose. Stripped it clean to the bone."

Matteo suppressed a shudder.

"Risia holds the dragons in great esteem," Kainon explained. "She makes a pilgrimage to the Sanctuary every few summers. Some townsfolk join her, but no one has seen Tlalam yet."

"It's likely we never will," Risia added, her disappointment tempered with acceptance. "I'm destined to see the great dragons only when they take their sacred flight to the Breeding Sands."

"You're not afraid of them?" Matteo asked curiously.

Sparing a quick look at a drowsing fingerling perched on the nearby windowsill, Risia said, "Let's say I'm deeply respectful. They've kept Linnia safe for millennia."

Kainon picked up his tankard and took a mouthful of ale. "Dragons are feared and revered in equal measure in Linnia. People like Risia are the reason why dragons choose to tolerate us."

Matteo tilted his head in curiosity.

"Pilgrims travel to the Sanctuary every season. In summer, the roads are flooded with people travelling to leave gifts during the Festival of Lights." Kainon shrugged. "For most folk, dragons are far removed from everyday life, but Tlalam was at the forging of the Treaty."

Matteo shook his head in wonder. "No one would think to invade Linnia because of the dragons."

"You have the right of it there," Kainon agreed. "If

nothing else, the dragons wouldn't tolerate us. Hence why outlanders are mostly unwelcome."

Lukas rested his elbows on the table, expression contemplative. "It's a pity the dragons aren't inclined to deal with the Rhun," he grumbled.

"It's hardly worth their attention," Risia snorted.

"No dragons needed." Kainon leaned over to tap a mark on the map. "If the Rhun continue to follow our trail, they'll come out through western pass. We can intercept them there."

"We?" Matteo repeated in surprise, looking sharply at Kainon.

Kainon hesitated. "I'm taking Lukas and some riders back to the pass tomorrow."

"Then I'm coming with you," Matteo stated.

Kainon grimaced. "It's best you stay here, Matteo. If the Rhun know what you are—" He stopped suddenly and glanced at their companions.

Risia raised her eyebrow in interest, humming.

"I mean—" Kainon began, cheeks pinkening.

Matteo resisted the urge to fold his arms. So much for secrets.

Lukas snorted. "If you want the Darshian to hide his heritage, Kainon, best remove his braids."

Scowling, Matteo gripped the green glass bead at the end of one braid. He'd no sooner be rid of his braids than the sun would stop setting.

Raising a hand, Lukas said, "You're just an exile, as far as I'm concerned, but Kainon has the right of it. Dealing with the Rhun isn't anything new in these parts. Stay here like the dragon-speaker asks."

Matteo felt his jaw tighten with stubbornness.

Lukas turned to Kainon. "Everyone will be ready to ride out at sunrise."

Kainon nodded his thanks.

Sitting back, Matteo scowled at Kainon. He wasn't some untested child; he'd travelled the ridges of the Uhur Mountains alone and survived.

Lukas turned to look meaningfully at Risia. "The evening grows long. It's time we take our leave."

Risia's eyes burned with questions as she gazed between Kainon and Matteo. But she sighed in disgust. "You have the curiosity of a turnip, Lukas."

The man nodded placidly.

"Very well," Risia muttered. Scaping back her chair, she added, "I'll have the stores in the great hall ready for you to look over when you come back tomorrow, Kainon. Can't have the little serpents dissatisfied with their spring feeding!"

Kainon nodded in thanks.

Wishing them both a pleasant meal, Risia and Lukas took their leave of the inn.

Matteo watched the mayor close the door before turning to Kainon. "First, you used me as bait, and now you want me hidden away like a child."

"I want you alive, Matteo. It proved a bit harder than I expected."

"You can't make me stay here," he muttered lowly.

Kainon gave him a steadying look. "I know, but I'm asking."

"But—"

Kainon raised his hands. "The Rhun almost killed you, Matteo—*twice*. After all that has happened for you to reach Linnia, why risk it?"

But he'd spent so long hiding from the Rhun that avoiding confrontation spoke of something cowardly.

"Fighting every wrong will just get you killed," Kainon pressed.

"I don't need you to fix my problems, Kainon."

Kainon blinked. "My obligation to Linnia has little to do with you, Matteo. It's my duty to ensure the road and Briarfall are safe."

"But—"

Thia set a plate of venison stew and vegetables before Matteo. He folded his arms as the aging woman unloaded two more meals and seated herself with a thankful groan in Lukas' empty chair.

"Go on, eat," Thia said gruffly, waving her hand. "You both look like you've spent a full season without a good meal."

Stomach heavy, Matteo nonetheless took a bite. The rich gravy carried hints of thyme.

Kainon smiled, picking up his spoon. "It smells wonderful, as always, Thia."

The innkeeper grunted around a mouthful.

Matteo swallowed, thinking over the last few days. For someone who appeared to wander the Dragon Plains for whole seasons at a time, Kainon commanded a lot of respect in Briarfall. Perhaps even authority. It certainly seemed that Risia was obliged to follow his advice.

He turned to study his companion. "Kainon, are you going back for the Rhun because you're a Protector?"

Thia stopped mid-chew, her eyes narrowing incredulously. "The boy didn't know?" she asked Kainon.

Kainon had the grace to look a little embarrassed. "We had a few distractions on the way."

"Really, Kainon?" Thia asked, her tone exasperated.

Kainon gave Matteo a chagrined look. "You're rather astute, Matteo. I tend not to bring attention to it."

Tossing her spoon into her bowl, Thia cursed under her breath. "You're the only Protector this side of the Plains right now—and the only one with a dragonling for a companion. You draw plenty of attention!"

"Someone needs to keep the bigger fingerlings in line," Kainon said mildly, though the look he sent toward Fira was warm.

The dragonling slept on the bar, her forked tail tucked against her nose.

Matteo resisted the urge to fold his arms. "But you're too young to be a Protector," he told Kainon.

"Hey, I have a few summers on you," he replied with a frown. "Think of what you've done in your lifetime."

Matteo sat back, chewing hard on a chunk of potato.

Thia studied Matteo appraisingly. "You must trust Kainon a lot to have come here with no notion of who he is."

"He didn't give me much choice." Feeling his cheeks grow warm at hearing his petulant tone, Matteo swallowed and said begrudgingly, "And he saved my life." He glanced at Kainon. "Why didn't you tell me?"

Kainon grimaced. "Not out of ill intent. Things are simpler out on the Plains. Well, most days."

Matteo nodded, though the answer didn't sit so easily.

As if reading his expression, Kainon sighed. "I was gifted to the Sanctuary when I was an infant. Considering my particular skills, becoming a Protector was always my path. Even so, I don't like to draw attention for no reason."

"Despite what he's implying, being a Protector is a great honor, Matteo—one that few achieve," Thia said. "To protect the Breeding Sands is a Linnian's highest calling."

"I didn't think dragons needed protecting," Matteo said.

"Mature dragons certainly don't. But the Sands themselves are sacred," Kainon said. "A thousand generations of dragons have hatched on the Sands—great queens and warriors, as well as dragons who are legends among their own kind. A human treading on such hallowed land is a grave insult."

Thia folded her arms. "And if given a chance, the western kingdoms would have no qualms sneaking into the Breeding Sands to steal the shells for their magic and potions. It's Linnia who'll burn for their transgression."

Matteo imagined flames eating across the grasslands and shivered.

Kainon grunted. "All the same, once everything's settled with the Rhun, we can concentrate on how to help you find your people."

Matteo almost dropped his knife. "You'd do that?"

"We'll need stealth and luck, Matteo," Kainon warned. "You will always be an outlander in Linnia, and the Treaty must come first. But I'll do my best to reunite you with other Darshians."

There was a warning in Kainon's words, but Matteo couldn't decipher where. "Thank you," he managed.

"So, I trust you won't try to follow me in the morning," Kainon pressed. "Leave the Rhun to me and Lukas."

Not for the first time, Matteo wished there were knotbindings made to hunt and attack. But knotbinders were no use in battle, even those with a gift for the darker braids.

"I'll stay here," Matteo allowed.

"Thank you, Matteo."

"Now that's settled, you can help me herd the fingerlings," Thia told Matteo. She winked. "I heard they like you."

Kainon and Thia took the opportunity to talk about the fingerlings playing siege to the Owl. Matteo sat back, watching them as his mind turned over Kainon's offer of help. He couldn't remember when he'd last heard news of other knotbinders. He'd started to fear he was among the last.

While there was still very little to go on, it was enough for Matteo to dare to hope.

6

MATTEO SAT by the window as thick grey mist sat low and heavy over Briarfall.

Across the short expanse of the courtyard, two fingerlings squabbled on the slate tiles of the stables. Their delicate wings vibrated as they hissed and postured over a dead grasshopper. The smallest fingerling, a skinny yellow creature with leaf-like wings, spat a gob of fire. The larger fingerling squawked before skittering over the arched roof and disappearing into the mist. The winner snatched up its prize and flapped away.

Three riders entered the courtyard, their hoods pulled low over their faces. Damp showed on the horses' legs and underbellies. One rider dismounted and opened the stable doors before all three travelers entered. Jayra emerged from the kitchen, calling out a greeting and following them inside.

A shift of fabric made Matteo turn to see Kainon emerge from his sleeping quarters with a pack in hand. The Protector donned wayfarer garb similar to what he'd worn when they had first met. He stuffed a water flagon from the table into his pack, humming under his breath.

Matteo suppressed a sigh. "I still think I should be going with you."

Kainon looked up from tying a bedroll, his green eyes mild. "I can't force you to stay, Matteo," he said. "But I'll feel better knowing you're safe."

Leaving the window, Matteo said, "Thia said it could take days to find the Rhun."

"We have a fair idea of where they're headed."

Matteo leaned his hip against the table. "No new sightings from the fingerlings?"

Kainon shoved a fresh tunic into the pack. "They'll grow more interested once I'm back among them." Kainon picked up a small pouch of coins. "Here, go see Risia for supplies while I'm gone. She's a mean trader but she'll give you a good price to replenish what you lost."

Testing the weight of the coins, Matteo said, "I can pay with a braid—"

Kainon raised a hand. "It's my duty as a Protector to keep the Plains safe. View it as compensation for running afoul of the Rhun."

"Saving my life is payment enough," Matteo muttered.

Kainon suddenly gripped Matteo's shoulder and gave him a steadying look. "I know it sits uncomfortably with you, especially after what befell your people and our own introduction. But you can trust me. I won't demand a braid from you."

Matteo resisted the urge to look away.

Brylin came bustling in with a bundle tucked under one arm. "Thia's found you some clothes, Matteo." She deposited her load on an uncluttered edge of the mantelpiece and pulled out a tunic and a pair of leather breeches before tossing them to Matteo. "Made of honest Linnian cloth, no less. There's more set aside for when you journey south."

Matteo thanked her, surprised by her generosity.

"It's nice to see Kainon return with good companions rather than just that bottomless pit of a serpent," Brylin observed. "You should see the condition Kainon gets into after a season on the Plains. Can barely harness two words together."

Kainon sighed as if he'd heard such judgement before. "I'm standing right here, Brylin."

"And you know I mean every word," the woman replied. "You're a good man, Kainon, but you bring us more worry than thieves eyeing off the stables."

"Speaking of horses, Matteo will need one when we eventually set off," Kainon said, folding his arms. "Take it out of my stipend, if that's alright."

"He can have the sorrel," Brylin said amiably. "She's a stocky sort but she'll handle the journey well."

Matteo looked at Kainon gratefully. "I *will* find a way to pay you back."

Hooking her thumbs in her belt, Brylin chuckled. "The Protectors send a boarding stipend to the Owl every season. A horse is barely a dent in it, considering Kainon's hardly ever here."

"Brylin's right," Kainon said with a grin. "Might as well make use of it."

"Don't forget to grab some trailbread since you're not sure when you'll be back," Brylin told Kainon. "Fira's already sniffed out the venison."

"She spent the night in the kitchen, so I'm sure she's had her snout in just about everything," Kainon observed dryly.

"We'll take it out of your stipend, too," she said cheerfully.

Kainon sighed with wry acceptance.

Brylin left, tunelessly whistling as she made her way downstairs.

"Lukas will be downstairs soon, but Fira's agreed to stay with you until I'm back," Kainon said, hoisting the pack over his shoulder.

"She has?" Matteo said, startled.

"She cares for you," Kainon replied. "Though I think it's more to do with stopping fingerlings from horning in on her territory." He gave Matteo a measuring glance. "Few Linnians gain a dragon's regard, and rarely so quickly."

Matteo flushed with pleasure. "I like her, too."

They both turned at the sound of little talons scrambling up the side of the building.

A fingerling abruptly shot through the window, hitting the opposite wall and sliding down before scurrying into the dark. Another leapt inside and tangled in Matteo's hair.

It set off a flurry of movement, with fingerlings bursting out of the shadows and attaching themselves to his clothing. His ears rang from screeches and squawks.

"Stay still," Kainon warned, even as the front of his tunic wrenched this way and that under the weight of his own swarm of serpents.

A fingerling made tiny, frantic hisses against Matteo's ear.

"Easy," Kainon murmured. "This is strange even for them." He gently dislodged a purple-flecked creature whose tiny claws punctured Matteo's tunic and scraped his ribs. The Protector murmured softly, promising safety as he grabbed a thatched basket and tipped it upside down to create a little cave. He tucked the basket under the table, tilting it slightly to allow the creatures to scurry inside.

The fingerling tangled in Matteo's hair broke free and skittered into the dark safety of the basket.

Fira shot through the window and skidded across the desk, upending inkwells and shattering glass as she hissed and cawed. She bolted into Kainon's bedroom, claws raking the floorboards as she hid under Kainon's sleeping pallet.

Matteo hesitated to follow after her.

"Don't approach Fira's lair," Kainon warned. "She might spit fire at you in her current state."

Matteo knelt beside Kainon as the last fingerling scurried under the basket. The serpents huddled close together, grunting and hissing softly. "They're frightened."

Kainon tilted his head as if listening. He shook his head. "Fira's too upset to make any sense." He gently lowered the basket and rose.

"What's scared them?"

Kainon shook his head. A distant look crossed his face as he peered out of the window. Fog still sat thick and heavy over the village.

"There," Kainon said, pointing to a whorl of spinning fog above a thatched roof on the edge of the village.

Matteo squinted.

A dark form cut through the fog. Red-tinged wings swept downward in an unrushed beat. The air vibrated as the creature glided over the edge of the village, heading north toward the Uhur Mountains.

"Dragon!" Matteo breathed. He leaned out of the window to get a better look. "How big is it?"

"An adult, by her wingspan," Kainon said tersely, hand gripping the back of Matteo's tunic as if he fought the urge to pull him back inside. "She's a red—they're small and agile, about thirty feet from snout to tail."

Matteo craned his neck, but the swirling fog had closed behind the dragon. "Has she come from the Breeding Sands?"

"I hope not. It's too early for her to have left," Kainon said. "No wonder the fingerlings are frightened."

Matteo turned to take a proper measure of his companion's expression.

Kainon appeared pale, his mouth pinched. "She either had an unsuccessful breeding or has abandoned her eggs. Regardless, it's a bad omen."

"Are we safe?" Matteo asked, his voice dropping low as he edged back from the window.

"I'm not sensing anything to worry about," Kainon said, head tilted as if listening. His frown tightened. "There's nothing we could do if she felt otherwise."

Villagers came out of their homes to stand in the street and stare up at the fog as it settled into stillness once more. The absence of squabbling fingerlings cast an uneasy silence over the village. Some people made warding signs.

Matteo glanced down to see Thia in the courtyard below with her hands on her hips. The innkeeper turned and glanced up at them, her mouth drawn tight.

Kainon sighed. "Come, let's help Thia light the incense. By midday, Briarfall will be full of prayer and songs of offering."

"Will the fingerlings be okay?"

"They'll lay low for a week at least. Fira might need a few days of protecting her hoard before she deems it safe enough to leave my sleeping quarters."

They headed out of the room, making space on the stairs

for the mist-dampened riders who silently lugged their saddlebags upstairs.

Matteo and Kainon barely reached the kitchen before the back door slammed open to reveal Jayra, white-faced and sweating.

"Kainon, come quickly!" she gasped.

Kainon gripped the young woman's arm. "What is it?"

"Lukas is bringing in travelers. There's been an attack!"

7

THEY RUSHED to the courtyard to see a horse pull up sharply in front of the stables. Kainon recognized Lukas' red hair and broad shoulders. He tightly gripped a body hunched in the saddle, while a wagon clattered around the corner behind him.

"Is that blood?" Matteo asked, squinting at a dark stain along the wagon's side. "Did the dragon attack them?"

Kainon felt his mind caught in the undertow of the adult dragon's fading presence as it flew toward the Uhur Mountains. He clenched his fists, letting the sensation of his nails digging into his palms draw him back. "No, dragons are more thorough."

Lukas pulled his horse to a halt beside them, swinging down from the saddle. With Matteo's help, he quickly unloaded his burden.

The injured woman was unfamiliar to Kainon; she was plain-faced and slim, wearing embroidered traveler garb common among the traders from the eastern cities. She gasped at being jostled as Lukas and Matteo carefully lowered her to the ground.

Thia knelt beside the injured woman. "Tell Brylin to ready hot water and salves."

Jayra rushed back inside.

Matteo looked slightly green. "Kainon, she's been stabbed."

The woman's midriff was matted dark red.

Lukas gripped Kainon's arm. "There are two more in the wagon. I found them in Henni's honeygrain crop."

The farmer, Henni, drew the wagon to a clattering halt beside them. The smell of blood wafted from beneath a bundle of blankets in the cart. The wrinkled farmer bobbed her head, the movement half-buried under the thickness of her caul.

Kainon peered into the wagon, grimacing at the two men lying supine amidst dry honeygrain chaff. He vaguely recalled the men taking their ease at a table at the Owl the previous night. "They must have left Briarfall before sunrise," he said.

"Didn't get far. Not the sort of crop I want to harvest," Henni observed, her voice like parchment.

Kainon's lips thinned. "Surely you heard something."

"Not a thing until Lukas was hollering at my door." Henni pointed a thumb over her shoulder. "The big one kept muttering about masked riders."

Peering into the cart once more, Kainon saw the man was slackly unconscious now. Blood matted his overcoat and stained the wagon floor.

Kainon motioned to Matteo and Lukas. "Let's get them inside. Gently, now. They've been through enough."

Thia threw the injured woman's arm over her shoulder and gestured at Matteo, who took up the other side. The woman groaned as they lifted her and started for the inn.

They entered the kitchen, where Brylin's upraised voice rang out with orders.

Lukas clambered up into the cart, his face grim. "Never had the Rhun attack so close to Briarfall before." He took one of the men under the arms and carefully dragged him to the edge of the cart.

With the fingerlings hiding in the town, Kainon had little to go on. "Glad you weren't set upon as well." He took the injured man's weight with a grunt. "What were you doing out that way, anyway?"

Lukas shrugged. "Spent the night competing with a covey of fingerlings over blankets and pillows. I needed the peace."

"I'll talk to them," Kainon promised.

Lukas grunted his thanks. "That dragon will have them quiet for a few days, anyway," he added.

Kainon nodded. "You saw it, too?"

"Hard to miss, dragon-speaker."

They carted the injured man across the muddy yard to the Owl. Passing through the kitchen, they entered the ale room where the woman already lay in front of the hearth. Someone had bundled a cloak under her head. Jayra crouched beside the woman, talking to her quietly. Matteo knelt beside them and tore a length of the woman's bloodied tunic.

Kainon gently lowered the unconscious man down onto the floorboards.

"I'll get the travois," Brylin said, backing away. "Won't have these poor sods lying on the bare floor."

Thia returned with a water basin, eyebrows rising as Matteo tore the cloth into three thin strips. With quick efficiency, Matteo twisted the strips into tight lines and made a double-loop knot. Grabbing one strip, he wove it between the other two strips and then repeated it thrice. A soft golden nimbus leaked between his fingers as Matteo worked.

Jayra gaped. "Knotbinder!"

Glancing up, Matteo blinked to find everyone staring. He flushed.

Kainon marched over to the windows and quickly locked the shutters from prying eyes. Nudging Lukas toward the kitchen, he said, "There's still another man in the wagon."

"I thought he was just a Darshian," Lukas murmured. "The knotbinders are all dead."

"Lukas!" Kainon hissed.

The man startled, then seemed to come back to himself. He took in the tight line of Matteo's back and grimaced. "Sorry, lad."

"I'll help you, Lukas," Jayra said, wiping her hands on her breeches as she rose. She gave Kainon a harried look before pushing Lukas from the ale room.

Thia set the water basin on a table. "I'll bring Henni into the kitchen. There's tea on the hob. I'll get a poultice ready."

Kainon murmured his thanks. Suppressing a sigh, he knelt beside Matteo. "You understand this announces you to all of Briarfall. There'll soon be tales of your existence from here to Palen. It's dangerous, Matteo."

Matteo sat back on his heels. "I can't do nothing, Kainon. It's not Dar's way."

Harder folk would have no qualms about leaving strangers to die. Kainon shook his head in frustration. There was more to worry about than just the Rhun.

"Lukas is wrong, you know," Matteo added quietly, blue eyes somber. "There are other knotbinders." He touched his darkened hair, where a blue glass bead sat within a twisted

64

braid. "They still live, Kainon. There's hope." He returned to the healing braid, tying off the end with a firm, determined tug. "I have to find them."

Blood lined the edge of Matteo's thumbnail. Kainon fought not to see it as an omen. But Matteo didn't come from a luck-born people. Getting thrown into a river could be the last time fortune turned in the knotbinder's favor.

Kainon felt the coils of responsibility wrap around him. He sighed through his nostrils. "Very well. What do you need?"

Matteo's expression eased. "Leather twine. Because they're strangers to me, the twine has to absorb their blood for a while."

Kainon nodded. "I have some upstairs."

He left Matteo and climbed the steps two at a time.

A door further down the corridor creaked open. A young woman with long, curling black hair stuck her head out. "Is everything alright?"

Kainon mustered a quick bow. "There was an incident on the road. Briarfall is safe, but it might be best to break your fast in your room."

The young woman stepped out into the corridor and clutched a shawl tight about her shoulders. "Goodness, I hope no one was hurt."

"We're tending to them downstairs."

"Perhaps I can assist," she said earnestly.

Kainon smiled. "We have it in hand, though you should delay your travel if you plan to leave today."

She nodded. "Wise advice. I'll speak with my companions." She returned to her room, closing the door.

Kainon entered his rooms and grabbed the pack he'd abandoned on the table. It still had dried mud from his journey in the Plains.

He hesitated, then went into his sleeping quarters and carefully pulled back the blankets hiding the underside of his pallet.

'*Fira?*' he called.

The darkness moved. Kainon could make the shape of Fira's snout amidst a collection of baubles and fleece blankets.

'*I'm here.*'

Tension left Kainon's shoulders. '*Are you alright?*'

'*The Old Ones are loud,*' Fira complained.

Kainon's mouth twisted. '*I know. Was she angry?*'

'*Not at me,*' Fira replied, though she hunkered deeper into the shadows. Her golden eyes glowed briefly.

'*Did she see anything before flying over Briarfall?*'

In his mind's eye, Kainon glided over a field of crushed honeygrain. Briarfall sat quiet nearby, shrouded in fog. The red dragon had flown low and hard, cutting a clear line across the fields. But the disturbed grass revealed that horses had ridden up and down Henni's farmland, almost in a search pattern. A body lay toward the center of the crop, face turned toward the sky and pale eyes unseeing. He wore similar garb to the travelers Lukas had brought to Briarfall.

Kainon cursed.

'*The Old One saw another by the stream,*' Fira said.

'*Did she see where the attackers went?*'

Fira gave a mental shrug. '*She cares only for Uhur.*' The dragonling sank lower. '*I don't like losing myself to the Old Ones.*'

'*I know,*' Kainon soothed. It was partly why they had not returned to the Sanctuary. '*Will you stay with your hoard for long?*'

Fira sniffed. '*I might.*'

'*Very well.*' Returning to himself, Kainon grabbed the

bowstrings and hurried down to the ale room. Someone had pushed chairs and tables back to allow room for three makeshift travois. Matteo was deep in his work, having moved to the unconscious man. He wove a series of knots into a new bloodied strip from the man's tunic. A line of ash covered the floor and the knotbinder's fingers.

But for all that Matteo had already completed at least one braid, the man looked worse. His skin had turned pale and sweaty, his mouth thinned with pain even in his unconsciousness. Brylin knelt beside the other travois and helped ease the woman up to allow her a sip from a tankard. She sank back down with a hiss.

"How goes it, Matteo?" Kainon asked softly, squatting.

He looked up from his work, blue eyes dark with worry. "He's got a wound that resists my workings." He lifted a wad of bandage on the traveler's arm.

Bending close, Kainon saw blood seep sluggishly from a deep puncture. The wound was already thickly crusted as if days old, with white bone visible in the depths. Dark veins of sickness surrounded the injury, the smell of rot thick in the air.

Matteo hesitated, twisting the half-finished knot between his fingers. "I don't know if I'm doing something wrong. I haven't even checked on the other man yet."

Squeezing Matteo's shoulder, Kainon said, "Lukas has everything in hand. I'm sure you're doing your best."

Matteo's expression remained worried.

"Thia knows a salve to deaden the pain," Kainon added, recognizing the astringent smell coming from the kitchen. "She'll have it ready soon. I'll come back before nightfall, okay?"

Alarmed understanding darkened Matteo's eyes. "Are you still going to search for the Rhun?"

67

"We can't leave them to attack anyone else," Kainon said. He caught Lukas' gaze and motioned with his chin toward the kitchen.

Lukas fussed with his patient's blankets before following.

They stood by the pantry, out of Thia's way as she furiously mashed herbs together at the worktable. Henni sat in Brylin's usual chair, nursing a mug between her knobby hands and looking bemused by the activity.

"Fira says there are fallen travelers still in the fields," Kainon said quietly.

Lukas swore under his breath. "This is brazen work for the Rhun."

Kainon nodded.

Thia looked up in surprise. "Fira's still able to talk after a dragon has flown? She should be a gibbering mess like the rest of the little ones. Your girl's growing strong, Kainon!"

A mix of pride and sadness settled in Kainon's belly. Fira's strength meant she could proclaim her readiness to cross the Uhur Mountains at any moment. But after so many summers together, Kainon couldn't imagine a life without the dragonling. "Aye, but for now she's bunkered down and won't be hurried out. We'll ride to Henni's farm to see if we can glean anything ourselves."

Lukas opened the door. "Let's go, Protector."

Kainon hesitated, glancing back toward the ale room. An unexpected rush of anxiety swept over him.

"I'll keep watch," Thia said as she heaped more moss into a bowl, her gaze knowing. "There'll be no harm in my house." The hard gleam of a former army captain showed in her eyes.

Kainon nodded his thanks. It had to be enough.

8

CRUSHED HONEYGRAIN ALWAYS CARRIED a cloying sweetness in the air. The stink was thickest when Kainon stood amongst the bent blue stems. He turned about in a slow circle, marking Henni's cottage at the end of the field. An unsettled quiet gripped the place, and not merely because fingerlings weren't busy with their daily mischief. Kainon sensed the fingerlings somewhere close and bundled together in a writhing mess of fear and anxiety. He should have thought to bring supplies for them. They'd likely remain fearful for days.

"Kainon, this one's still warm."

Kainon made his way over to Lukas.

The traveler lay sprawled on her back with her sightless eyes fixed on a nearby stand of grass. Heat radiated from her. The skin under her eyes and around her mouth appeared paper-thin and ash-like. Strangely, the honeygrain within touching distance had turned withered and sickly.

"They must have cut her down from behind," Lukas said, squatting to roll the dead woman over.

Kainon quickly grabbed the man's arm. "Don't touch her," he warned as cold flooded him.

Lukas threw him a startled look.

Kainon had never seen the like himself, but Protectors returning from the Rhuncavar border had spoken of it. "The Flame of Rhun has taken her."

Lukas jolted upright, face pale as he cursed softly under his breath. "A soul-stealing blade—out here? Whatever for?"

The Rhun had never bothered to cause trouble this far into the Dragon Plains. They tended not to attack Linnians unless it suited their mission. Using a flame blade on random travelers was not the Rhuncavari's habit.

Unless it was to draw out their quarry.

With a cold rush of realization, Kainon turned his gaze toward Briarfall.

Matteo...

GOLDEN LIGHT TRICKLED through Matteo's fingers as he carefully wove a knot into the softened leather twine before him, aware that his patient was watching. His gaze remained fixed upon the small cut in the woman's thigh, willing the wound to finally close.

He'd not left the ale room since mid-morning. His fingers were red raw and stiff from overuse as he wove increasingly intricate braids, seeking blindly for a solution to the impediment that stopped his healings. Brylin had spent the first candlemarks hovering nearby, lighting incense and occasionally watching as the knots flared gold and disintegrated to ash once completed. But Matteo had long since been left to do his work alone.

Matteo welcomed the challenge. For all that he'd trained in the Temple, healing didn't always come easily to him.

Perhaps if I were better trained...

But while Rhuncavar's invaders had robbed him of knowledge, they'd nonetheless made him determined to be as skilled as possible with all he knew.

With a sigh, Matteo placed a steadying hand behind the woman's leg, then centered his attention upon the pale skin above the wound. Perhaps if he flooded the surrounding tissue with health and vitality, the body's instinct to heal would take over.

The woman shivered.

Surprised, he offered her a smile. "It won't hurt."

The woman bit her lip and nodded.

Matteo set to work, waiting for the flow of golden light that slid between his fingers every time he used his gift.

A hand fell against his shoulder, giving him a shake.

"Won't be a moment," Matteo murmured distractedly, his fingers tingling as he entwined the final concentric knot. The braid blazed as Matteo set it above the wound before it transformed into ash.

The woman flinched slightly as the seeping wound remained unchanged. Matteo sat back, rubbing his eyes as he contemplated the possibility that the woman could lose the limb.

"Drink this," a familiar voice ordered. A brimming cup was thrust into Matteo's hands. Matteo blinked up, surprised to see Thia's wrinkled face.

She crossed her bony arms, her scowl deepening. "Well, don't just sit there staring. Drink! I won't have you staggering around because you're too foolish to rest. And where's Kainon, curse him? Off with Lukas, no doubt, still haring about in their hunt for enemies!" Her eyes sharpened. "I told you to drink, boy!"

Matteo felt his cheeks flush at her concern. The taste of herbs sat thick on his tongue as he swallowed, his muscles beginning to relax. He pressed his cramping hands flat against his thighs.

"Good," Thia said. "You've done more than your share. Time for a rest, I say."

The ale room was surprisingly quiet. Brylin sat on a chair, hands clasped between her legs as she kept vigil over the two injured men. Despite the heat that rolled out from the hearth, the air felt charged with cold. To Matteo's surprise, dark flooded the windows looking out into the grasslands. Evening cool now leaked through the closed shutters. He'd heard drums and chants throughout the day as the villagers sang to the dragon that had flown overhead.

A few feet away, the most grievously injured man lay on his travois, lax face pasty and sweat-sheened, his eyes closed. His breath rattled wetly in his chest. Undressing the man had earlier revealed stab wounds from both daggers and blades, all somehow missing his vital organs. Matteo saw the bandages had soaked through once again.

Matteo suppressed a shiver. "Brylin said he can't be helped," he murmured, watching.

"It'll be a mercy when he dies," Thia replied. "If a knotbinder can't turn the tide, my simple remedies certainly won't. Dark magic has a hold over him now," she added, spitting to the side.

Matteo thought guiltily of his own injuries in the mountain pass. It was sheer luck that he'd survived the encounter. Bile rose in his throat.

"Do you mind keeping an eye on her?" he asked,

indicating the injured woman. "I'm going to check how he's doing."

Thia grunted. "No one expects you to work wonders, boy."

He mustered a smile before shuffling over to the man. Touching the man's chest, Matteo found his heartbeat was rapid and thready. He peeled back the bandage on the man's arm. Black lines of sickness had spread up to his collarbone and chest. Matteo imagined it constricting the man's heart. Heat radiated off him in waves.

Matteo glanced guiltily over at the woman. If he'd learned more healings at the Temple of Dar, perhaps he'd know the knots to break the infection. It was a useless thought.

Matteo's fingers ached as he took up a discarded bit of leather.

"Please," the man croaked.

Matteo glanced up to see the injured man staring dazedly at him. Sweat peppered his forehead, his eyes glazed with half-awareness.

Matteo shifted closer and grabbed the arm that hung limply over the edge of the travois. He gently tucked it against the man's side. The man watched him with feverish intensity.

"Who—?" the man wheezed, scarcely able to talk.

"I'm Matteo. A friend. You made it back to the Hunting Owl in Briarfall. You're safe now."

The man closed his eyes and shook his head minutely. "It's no use. Dying."

Words became stuck in Matteo's throat. Silence fell over them. For a moment, Matteo thought the man had lapsed back into fevered unconsciousness, but his gaze remained firm.

"End it."

Matteo held his breath as his heart made a slow roll. "No."

"The Protectors won't do it," the man rasped. "It's not in their code. Must be you."

Matteo leaned close under the pretext of fixing the man's blanket. He hissed in the man's ear, "You don't know what you're asking!"

"No—" The man suddenly coughed, pain charging across his face. "No long death. Please…"

Matteo clenched his eyes shut. This man had no idea what it meant for Matteo to contemplate doing such a thing.

"*Please.*"

Heat burned behind Matteo's eyelids. He was weary, past all coherent thinking. But if he were in this man's position, knowing he would linger for candlemarks while fighting an agonizing, losing battle, he, too, might ask for a merciful death.

"It'll be painless," he found himself saying. "You'll find yourself in a red and gold haze. It'll smother you. Do you understand?"

The man nodded, mouth twitching into a painful echo of a smile.

Matteo took up a sweat-damp hank of the man's hair. Deep within, his gift roared to life.

"Close your eyes," he murmured, fingers looping a strand of hair around another, creating a knot that felt more inherent than any healing braid he knew. He stilled his fingers when he felt the urge to weave in a particular way that would see the man in the throes of agony. He gritted his teeth, waiting for it to pass, then continued with the braid.

Red flooded Matteo's vision. Of their own volition, his fingers threaded four strands of hair together, double-locking the knots, repeatedly looping them together until the entire braid took on a square shape.

The man's breathing became less labored. Matteo could hear it whistle through the man's lungs with less frequency. The strain slowly eased from the man's face. Matteo wove the final knot and felt the boom of power shoot through his hand, gold-laced with red.

"It's done," he whispered into the man's ear.

The man gave out a final sigh, his head turning slackly to the side.

Matteo's vision blurred. He hastily rubbed his face as the braid turned to ash, its magic spent. He had no right to feel remorse.

A hand suddenly grabbed his shoulder, squeezing.

"Knotbinders don't cause death," a familiar voice murmured.

Heart in his throat, Matteo spun to see Kainon.

The Protector examined Matteo's face, then shifted his gaze to the dead man behind him before settling on Matteo again. Kainon's expression tightened.

"But you do."

9
<hr>

KAINON URGED Matteo up the stairs and into the poorly lit corridor above. He heard Thia's voice through the thin walls and Jayra's muted tones. He pulled Matteo along, ignoring how the knotbinder stumbled in the uncertain light and ushered him into their shared quarters before closing the door and leaning against it.

He felt the press of awareness from the fingerlings hiding together in the darkness beneath the table. Fira made a chirrup from amidst the sprawling mess of oddities and trinkets under the sleeping pallet, but anxiety still outweighed her curiosity.

'*Easy*,' Kainon sent out to them all.

The fingerlings quietened. None dared emerge from the shadows.

"I can explain," Matteo said, clutching his fingers. The fire in the hearth was all but banked, casting darkness across his face.

Turning to his companion, Kainon said, "Can you? Knotbinders are known for healing and some minor enchantments, but death's no small thing."

Matteo's face grew drawn. "I only wove the knots as a mercy, I swear it."

Kainon gritted his teeth. "Truly? You're not a reaper?"

Matteo vehemently shook his head. "My word, Kainon, I'm not." His gaze fell. "I don't like to do it. But Thia will tell you the man wouldn't have survived the night."

It scarcely settled Kainon's nerves. He was not so sanctimonious as to berate Matteo for killing a man—the dragon lords knew his own hands were stained red. But he'd felt the power of that death braid. It still set his hair on end.

Matteo lifted his gaze, and Kainon saw the steely determination in his blue eyes; no doubt the same steel that had seen him traverse the Uhur Mountains with the Rhun at his heels. "I don't regret ending his suffering."

Grim, Kainon moved to the table and perched on its edge. "I want to understand, Matteo, so speak plainly."

Matteo swallowed, shaking his head. "We hide the killing braids in our lore, but they're taught just like any other braid, from knotbinder to knotbinder. Some have an affinity for them."

"Like you."

Matteo shrugged. "I learned only a little before the attack on my people." He scrubbed at his arms as if cold.

The admission sat uneasily with Kainon. One did not dally with unknown magics without bearing scars in the end. But Fira rarely misjudged a person's character and vied for Matteo's attention with a fervor usually reserved only for Kainon.

"Is this why you're so desperate to find a teacher—to learn more killing braids? You want to use them against the Rhun?"

"Sometimes," Matteo admitted, gaze dropping. "The

death sorcerers slaughtered everyone. Is it so wrong to seek vengeance?"

Kainon studied Matteo anew but couldn't find the bitter rage that so often twisted a person driven by revenge. "It's not for me to judge. But what makes you so certain any of your kind are left?"

Matteo pulled forward a braid tucked behind his ear. It was unremarkable save for the glass bead with a single dot of gold. "All knotbinders carry the *kha-shi* braid—our braid of belonging. It links us to Dar. If no one else lives to pass on the knowledge of the braids, the knots will die and turn to ash."

Kainon grunted in surprise. He wondered how many Darshians hid in Linnia with darkened hair, pretending that the braids in their hair were of no consequence. Surely they stood out like Matteo, who showed a reckless commitment to his gift.

It reminded Kainon of the danger at hand. The Rhun had announced their presence outside Briarfall, and there was only one logical reason. "What do you know of the Flame of Rhun?"

Matteo stepped back. "Death sorcerers used flame blades when they kill enchanters. I think it feeds their god, Rhuncavar." He dropped his gaze, his voice falling as he continued, "I saw them use flame blades in the Temple. No one survived."

Kainon sighed. "We found a flame-touched body in a field near where Lukas rescued the people downstairs."

Matteo's gaze snapped up to his. "Then the Rhun following me have death sorcerers. Why didn't they use a flame blade instead of shooting me?"

Kainon wondered that himself. The Rhun did not

typically make mistakes. But he remembered the man who'd been angry at the archer.

"I brought the death sorcerers here." Matteo paled in horror. "Thia—"

Kainon raised a hand. "Thia and her kin will be fine. But your work in the ale room has shouted to the world that there's a knotbinder in Briarfall."

Matteo scrubbed his hair and paced.

Kainon folded his arms and watched Matteo. He knew from experience the burden of rare gifts. Perhaps it was his turn to reach out a hand, as Thia had done for him a few summers ago. "Staying here will only give the Rhun what they want. The danger's too great—for yourself and Briarfall."

Matteo swallowed heavily. "I understand. I'll go."

"We'll find safety at Protector chapter houses. They'll keep the Rhun off our tail, but we can't dally. The nearest chapter house is a week's ride from here."

"We?"

"Certainly." Though they were strangers, the thought of Matteo meeting his fate at the end of a flame blade turned Kainon's stomach.

"What about the injured travelers?" Matteo asked.

"Briarfall will tend to them as best they can. We're not without our resources out here."

"But—"

"The Rhun are using the travelers to lure you out." Kainon studied his companion. "And likely get a measure of your power. Do they know about killing braids?"

Matteo hesitated. "It's kept secret even from other knotbinders. All Darshian children are brought to the Temple of Dar in their fifth summer and tested. The knots we choose lay out our path."

Kainon imagined innocent, blue-eyed younglings reaching for braids woven to kill. He suppressed a shudder. "Lukas is organizing riders to watch the outskirts of Briarfall. We can't let the Rhun succeed in their plan for you." He pointed to a clean pack beside the door. "Brylin brought that one up for you earlier today, though I'm sure she didn't expect you to need it so soon. Check that it has everything you need. There's extra bowstring by the chair. Be quick, we must leave now."

Matteo murmured his thanks and checked his pack. He pulled out a small blade from its depths.

"Thia has a short sword for you downstairs," Kainon said. "Have you had much practice with a blade?"

"Not really," Matteo admitted.

"Hopefully, I won't have to teach you on the road," Kainon said. "Now that a dragon's flown, Fira's instinct is to hide. We can't rely on her to track the Rhun. She'll stay in her lair for a few days."

"She'll follow us?"

Kainon glanced at the doorway of his sleeping quarters.

'I will,' Fira muttered. 'I grow strong.'

Kainon smiled. 'Never had a doubt.' Turning back to Matteo, he said. "Fira will find us when she's ready."

In the meantime, the red dragon's flight meant there would be no fingerlings to warn them, but there were other ways to look for an enemy.

Kainon and Matteo went downstairs and into the kitchen, where Brylin sorted through an array of dried herbs she pulled from a shelf. A burial shroud lay on the worktable, already seeded with tiny orange flowers. A basket of cloth sat on the cobbled floor, indicating that Brylin expected more travelers to die soon.

The absence of fingerlings underfoot left the place remarkably quiet.

"I know that face, Kainon. Leaving us now, are you?" Brylin asked as she cut the wax seal off a jar filled with firemoss.

Kainon grimaced and nodded. "We'll need to leave the travelers to your care, along with their burial."

Matteo ducked his head.

Brylin grunted. "They should have lost their battles candlemarks ago. There's a time when fighting adds to their suffering."

Matteo remained thin-lipped, blue eyes dark with guilt.

"You've done all you could and more," Brylin said reasonably, watching Matteo. "Any fool can see the risk you've put yourself in." She fetched some packets of trail bread and a sheathed sword. "You take these and keep yourself out of trouble."

Matteo fumbled out his thanks as he took the sword.

Kainon pressed a quick peck to Brylin's cheek. "Light some incense for us. We could do with some luck."

"I will. Get on with you both," Brylin muttered, though she leaned into the touch. "The night will only hold for so long." She turned to Matteo. "When it's safe and you're done with your task, boy, you come back. You'll find welcome in Briarfall."

Matteo blinked. "Thank you."

To Kainon's surprise, Thia waited for them by the stable doors. Insects buzzed about the lantern she held against her hip. On a typical night, fingerlings would have harassed her to get to the freshest bugs attracted to the light. Thia absently flicked a beetle off her tunic as they approached.

"Take the chestnut, Matteo—the one in the farthest stall," Thia said gruffly. "She's already saddled. Hurry, now."

Thia waited for Matteo to enter the stables before giving Kainon a beady look. Her eyes glittered in the lantern's light. "First, it's knotbinders, and then Rhuncavari death sorcerers."

Kainon's shoulders sagged. "Lukas has a busy mouth."

She grunted. "With good reason."

"I'm getting the knotbinder out of here," Kainon said. "With the Protectors so far away on patrol, leaving is the safest option for everyone."

"Safest for everyone in Briarfall, perhaps," Thia observed. "You're vulnerable on the road."

"I have my duty, Thia." Kainon strode into the stables, heading to the stall where his grey mare waited. She leaned her head out and nickered softly. He rubbed her silky nose before grabbing her saddle.

Thia watched him for a moment, scowling. "The Rhun aren't your only problem," she muttered. "If Tlalam has sent agents to seek you out—"

"It wasn't Tlalam," Kainon said quickly. He glanced across at Matteo, who was tying his pack to the saddle a little way down the stables. Kainon lowered his voice. "The red dragon was in flight for a different reason. I wouldn't be here if Tlalam's patience had run out."

Thia sighed, handing him the mare's bridle. "He'll make his demands, and it'll be before you're ready."

"I know," he replied softly. He slid the bit into his horse's mouth before slipping the crown of the bridge over her dappled ears. She pressed her nose against his shoulder, huffing in anticipation. "I'll be careful," he promised.

Thia sighed, frown lines deep on her brow.

Kainon grabbed her hand and squeezed. "Take care of the fingerlings for me."

"What do you think I've been doing all season?" she snapped.

Kainon grinned.

With a sniff, Thia said, "No more dallying, dragon-speaker. There's extra venison in the saddlebag for Fira when the pest leaves her hoard."

"She'll be grateful."

Thia grunted. "Return to us soon, Kainon. This was a short visit, even for you."

Kainon mustered a smile and climbed into his saddle. He nodded to Matteo, who led his horse over. Matteo bent in the saddle and pressed something into Thia's hand. Kainon saw a flash of knotted twine. It glittered like gold, carrying none of the redness Kainon had seen in the killing braid. Instead, he felt a wave of vitality wash over him just from seeing the binding.

"A well-wishing," Matteo murmured.

Thia carefully tucked it onto her belt. "Keep safe, knotbinder."

Kainon and Matteo rode out of the stables together. Kainon spared a glance at the inn, wondering when he would return. The rooms on the second floor were dark, but he thought he saw movement in the shadows.

Kainon nudged his horse into a trot and resisted the urge to look back at the stables, fearful that he would see Thia wave her final goodbye.

10

THEY RODE CAUTIOUSLY in the darkness, sticking to the road leading south from Briarfall. The moon sat behind the Uhur Mountains, the stars muted by bands of cloud. The fields around them felt eerily still to Matteo. Gone were the chitters and grass-rattling squabbles of fingerlings and the scurrying of other small creatures seeking refuge from the serpent-folk.

Matteo wondered why Kainon hadn't led the horses off the exposed road. The Protector studied the fields with a wariness Matteo hadn't seen before, his gaze sweeping across both sides of the road. He squinted as if his eyes could pierce the darkness.

The road took them past a cottage, its windows darkened. Matteo felt his gaze pulled to the field beside it. Blackened patches of scorched ground seemed to swallow the pale starlight. The air felt thick and burned the back of Matteo's throat. He'd seen such remnants at the Temple of Dar, his senses flooded by fires and screaming. People he had known his whole life had fallen beneath the glowing blades. Blood had slicked across his skin when he hid among the dead.

Matteo's heart thudded. He'd begged Dar to save him from experiencing such a thing again. But he'd brought the horror with him.

"I'm sorry," Matteo whispered. The burning in his throat turned into an ache.

"It's not you who must pay for this," Kainon said quietly with steel in his voice, slowing only long enough to make a warding sign against his chest. "They're trying to draw you out."

"It worked, didn't it?" Matteo muttered.

Kainon looked at him, keeping his voice low. "The Rhun would be waiting for us right here if that was their plan." He squinted up at the sky. "Perhaps the dragon set things awry for them as well."

"Can a dragon tell the difference between a Linnian and a Rhuncavari?"

"Dragons don't care about human squabbles so long as we serve them."

Matteo was grateful Fira wasn't yet an adult.

They neared a crossroads, where a small trail cut a silvery path through the fields heading east and west.

Kainon's horse made a sudden knicker of greeting.

Matteo stiffened.

A shadowy rider sat still and quiet at the trailhead, watching them. A saddled horse roamed behind the rider, lipping at the grass.

"Getting sloppy, Protector," Lukas grumbled. "I could hear you two from halfway across the hill."

Kainon's shoulders relaxed. "You made it here without trouble?"

"Spotted two riders in the northern hills. Be careful, Kainon. The Rhun won't stick to the roads like you."

Kainon nodded. "It's a risk we'll have to take." Glancing at Matteo, he explained, "There are fingerlings in the grass. We can't disturb their hiding place. They won't be fast enough to get out of our way in their current state."

"Whoever's on the hills, they don't care about the little ones," Lukas muttered with a soft curse. "It's a lifetime of bad fortune for killing a fingerling."

Kainon grunted in agreement. "I haven't sensed any deaths, but you'll need to walk the hills come daylight and look for injured fingerlings."

"We'll nurse them back to health as best we can," Lukas promised. He nodded his chin at Matteo. "Here, tie your pack to my spare and hand over your horse."

Matteo threw both men a curious glance.

"Your mare's got a notch on her hoof that makes her easy to track. Lukas will take her east and see if he can waylay the Rhun."

"You planned this?" Matteo asked, swinging down from the saddle and loosening his pack.

"As soon as we left Henni's cottage," Kainon said. "Lukas will head for Fowler's Ridge and meet with Jayra and a few others. The Protectors shouldn't be too far from there. They'll keep the Rhun busy."

"You just make haste for a chapter house," Lukas muttered. "The Protectors need to know about the Rhun hunting knotbinders and killing folk in our land."

Matteo mounted Lukas' spare horse, a sorrel with pale-tipped ears. He rubbed her neck in greeting.

Kainon leaned over and clasped Lukas' forearm. "Keep well, my friend."

"You, too. Both of you."

Lukas took Matteo's former horse and tied the lead to his saddle before turning about and heading down the trail at a fair trot.

Kainon steered his horse back onto the main road.

"Where are we going?" Matteo asked as they rode side by side.

"I'll get you to Pelan," Kainon promised. "It's over a month's ride from here. The Queen's Road is the safest route because several Protector chapter houses are along the way, but we risk the Rhun overtaking us." He took a measuring look at Matteo's braids. "We'll need to turn west for a time. I don't suppose you know an enchantment to waylay an adversary?"

Matteo shook his head. "Knotbindings don't work that way. They either heal or take a life. I really don't know anything else."

"Your teacher was proficient in killing braids?"

Pulling his cloak about him, Matteo said, "He was known to be a middling healer—nothing remarkable. My parents were pleased to have a knotbinder for a son, but when Kava took me on, they were disappointed."

"They didn't know?"

Matteo took in the silvery moonlight painting the fields. "No, I couldn't tell them. Darshians accept there is a time when healing braids provide no solace, but they don't know there are gentle ways to die. Killing braids are meant to end our suffering."

"But not for war?"

Matteo thought of his teacher as the Temple was overrun, how Kava had been run through even as a half-woven braid fell from his hands. "We're not much use in a fight. Weaving the knots takes time and concentration. It's so easy for it to all unravel."

Kainon tilted his head. "But what about making weavings beforehand?"

"It's dangerous. Death and sickness leach out no matter what. Perhaps it's Dar's way of ensuring no curse-weavers sweep the land."

"A sobering thought," Kainon muttered.

A horse knickered somewhere behind a hill, and Matteo craned his neck. The silvery night showed nothing beyond the gentle sway of the grasslands.

Kainon stilled, head tilted as if listening. He cursed softly under his breath.

"Has Lukas come back?" Matteo whispered.

Kainon pressed an urgent finger to his lips and motioned for them to dismount.

Matteo glanced about worriedly.

"Here," Kainon whispered, handing over the reins to his horse before edging toward a nearby stand of tallgrass. Crouching, he ushered something onto his palm before urging it onto his tunic. The Protector whispered something and more little creatures scurried out of the leaf mold.

Matteo squinted and realized Kainon had a handful of fingerlings.

"I don't know who's coming, Matteo," Kainon whispered, waving him over. "Bring the horses. Careful, now."

Matteo carefully pushed back the tallgrass before guiding the horses off the road, entering deep enough for the fronds to close in around them. Peering behind, he could barely see the road through the blades of grass.

Kainon rested his hand just behind his horse's ear and nodded to Matteo to do the same.

Both horses became still and quiet, not even flicking their ears.

Matteo held his breath as he spied a rider on the crest of

the hill some distance from the road. The rider cut across the sedges and tallgrass, taking no heed of possible fingerlings hiding amidst the greenery.

Matteo remained still, even as the breeze made the grass about him rustle and dance.

The rider paused not twenty feet from them. Matteo glanced sharply at Kainon, who pressed a finger to his lips. The fingerlings migrated to the neck of his tunic in a trembling and hissing mass. Kainon cupped his hand over them, and they seemed to settle.

Peering through the fronds, Matteo saw the rider was a middle-aged man with sharp features and a thin mouth. The man scowled deeply, his eyes fixed on the road. He pulled up, his gaze swinging from side to side over his horse, searching.

Cold flooded Matteo's gut as the man dismounted and examined something on the road before looking back the way Matteo and Kainon had come.

Matteo held his breath, hoping there were no signs he and Kainon had left the road so close by.

But the rider mounted and turned his horse about, heading back towards Briarfall. Kainon held up his hand, mouthing the word, '*Wait.*'

Matteo listened for the clop of hooves receding beyond the hill.

Kainon knelt and gently offloaded each serpent onto tiny fronds and the thick undergrowth. They protested a little, one spitting a little fireball that made Kainon snatch his hand back. Sucking on his singed thumb, Kainon eased the creature free of his tunic and set it loose.

Glancing up at Matteo, Kainon said quietly, "No Linnian would ride through the grass like that. Did you recognize him?"

Matteo swallowed hard and shook his head. "He must be one of the Rhun."

Kainon grunted his agreement. He led his horse back out onto the road.

"He's headed for Briarfall," Matteo said, hearing the worry in his voice.

Kainon nodded. "Lukas and the militia are ready, as are the people in Briarfall."

Matteo felt a rush of guilt. "We need to turn back—"

"The Rhun will eventually discover our ploy, and then all their attention will return to you, Matteo. We need to be far from here when the time comes." He mounted and turned his horse. "Let's press the advantage while we still have it."

Knowing Kainon was right, Matteo mounted and nudged his horse into a trot. He glanced nervously behind. Not for the first time, he wondered why the Rhun were so determined to see every last knotbinder killed. He'd have to ask in person to find out, and Matteo was certain he wouldn't survive the conversation.

AFTER SEVERAL DAYS on the road, the urge for Kainon to look over his shoulder grew stronger.

Fingerlings sent images of riders on the road behind them, including a familiar man with black hair and sharp features. The riders had been on their trail for the better part of a day now.

They were far enough from Briarfall that the fingerlings hereabouts were unaffected by the red dragon's flight. Instead, they were keen to show off their helpfulness to the dragon-speaker and his companion with the strange-smelling magic.

Kainon held off telling Matteo about the Rhun. There was no use warning him when the fingerlings had the matter in hand for now. But Kainon nevertheless took Matteo off the main road and onto a pilgrim road that would lead them into territory where fingerlings gathered in their hundreds.

They entered a valley of grass flattened by a passing rain shower. The air smelled damp and new, with low scudding clouds promising more rain in the afternoon.

The road took them past towering white stone monoliths perched along the crest of a hill. Fingerlings fluttered from stone to stone, nesting in tiny burrows and fissures cut into the rock. The fingerlings appeared larger than the serpents Kainon was used to, almost as long as his hand. They were startlingly bright and confident. By his judgement, they were at least twenty summers old, having hatched in the Breeding Sands and journeyed across a hundred miles of sand and forest to find safety amongst the stones.

"It looks like the bones of a dragon," Matteo observed, shielding his eyes as he squinted at the hill.

"They're called the Spines for that very reason," Kainon said. He gave the Spines a dutiful nod. Its presence hummed under his skin. Linnian scribes had long discounted the possibility of the Spines being the relic of a fallen dragon, but *something* undoubtedly lay beneath.

The pilgrim road edged around the Spines at a respectful distance.

Matteo bore a quizzical look as he stared up at the Spines. His gaze tracked the fingerlings, all bright reds and yellows and flashes of blue and purple. Some carried little trinkets and strands of horsehair pilfered from travelers and pilgrims.

"The red dragon must not have flown over here," Kainon surmised, knowing the fingerlings would be hiding otherwise. "I'd put your hood up. These folk are old enough to be disrespectful, and there's no telling what they might do for a knotbinder's braid."

Matteo gave the serpents a worried look and adjusted his hood. He seemed to notice the vast array of sharp claws and the occasional puff of smoke.

Kainon said, "The Spines are sacred, so the road's as close as anyone can get without having their breeches set alight."

"What's so special about it?"

"It's the spot where fingerlings see the Uhur Mountains for the first time," Kainon said, pointing.

Turning in the saddle, Matteo squinted at the peaks sitting low and barely visible on the horizon.

"The Plains end here, also," Kainon added, pointing to the tree line beyond the Spines. The road avoided the forest entirely and instead turned southwest. "The forest once extended far past the Spines, but dragons burned it often enough that the Plains were born. There hasn't been a burning in my lifetime, but the dragons will return here once the forest reaches the Spines."

Matteo eyed the encroaching forest. It was scarcely a hundred feet from the Spines.

'Dragon-speaker!' a distant voice called out in his mind.

An image suddenly crossed his vision of a rider with a bow raised and their eyes narrowed in concentration. Kainon had a disorientating moment of seeing himself and Matteo sitting on their horses, backs to the danger.

"Matteo, get down!"

Something whipped past Kainon's shoulder, close enough to disturb his tunic. For a heartbeat, Kainon thought a fingerling tried to hitch a ride amidst his cloak.

But a sudden, wild flurry of fingerlings burst from the grass about them in a thick cloud. Kainon momentarily lost sight of their surroundings.

The air cleared.

Five riders galloped toward them. Each rider carried shields painted stark white, framed with red and silver feathers that shivered with each powerful stride of their horses. One rider drew their bow, with an arrow aimed unerringly at Kainon.

Cold flooded Kainon's guts.

The Rhun...

Matteo turned white-faced and frozen in terror.

Kainon suddenly smacked the rump of Matteo's horse, shouting, "Ride!"

Matteo's horse leapt from the hard-packed dirt of the road toward the Spines. He kept mercifully low in the saddle. Kainon kicked his horse to follow.

The Rhun took chase, barreling down the embankment. They seemed unconcerned by the fingerlings that leapt into the air around them.

A woman jeered in the distance. "Give up the knotbinder, Protector!"

Kainon glanced back and recognized the young woman who had spoken to him at the Owl, although now she bore strange, ash-like markings on her cheeks and black feathers tied to the ends of her twin braids. Riding beside the young woman, the man they had seen on the road outside Briarfall drew a short blade, the stone on its hilt glowing a pestilent green.

"Kainon," Matteo gasped.

"I see him," he muttered grimly. Kainon cursed as their horses navigated the steep incline up to the Spines.

Matteo drew his dagger and cut a hank from his horse's mane. He quickly worked together a few knots, but his distraction caused his mount to falter.

"No time for that!" Kainon yelled.

Two Rhun riders cut across their path.

Kainon yanked on his horse's reins and ducked under a slashing blade. He pulled his sword and swung blindly, connecting against a shield. He looked up to see the thin-lipped man with circular ash symbols on his chin and forehead.

"The knotbinder dies!" the man crowed triumphantly. The hilt of his blade glowed green. "Like all the knotbinders before him!"

Kainon desperately parried, the force of the blow sending a jolt through his arm.

Blades clashed beside him as Matteo fought off the woman.

Shouts came from the Rhun as fingerlings entered the fray. A startled horse reared and kicked the air. But then the woman raised her hand and yelled a strange word. Dizziness momentarily gripped Kainon. The fingerlings scattered.

A horse rammed against Matteo's side, almost unseating him from the saddle. Kainon blindly grabbed his arm to steady him. A flash of blue and yellow whipped past his face.

Two fingerlings shot between the horses with their maws open. Great gouts of fire burst free and lit up the grass at their hooves with a whoosh.

Horses reared in terror as flames licked their bellies. The

young woman fell from the saddle and rolled frantically away.

The fire grew taller, pushing the riders apart.

Kainon looked past the flames and saw three other mounted Rhun on the road's edge, watching.

"Ride!" Kainon shouted to Matteo, kicking his mount free of the flames.

Matteo's horse leapt after Kainon. They galloped up the hill, chased by smoke and flames toward the Spines. The fingerlings let them pass between the white stones unchallenged.

The man behind them roared. "Give us the knotbinder!"

A wall of fingerlings blocked him. The man stabbed furiously at the air. The blade slashed open the wing of a blue fingerling.

A shriek cut through Kainon's mind. He lurched, sharp pain momentarily blinding him as a fingerling crashed lifeless into the grass behind him.

Outrage and vengeance gripped the fingerlings. They leapt onto their attackers, yanking hair, biting viciously at exposed necks, cheeks and bellies. The horses bucked and reared.

Shouting, the two Rhun wheeled their horses and galloped toward their companions. Fingerlings chased hard down the hill. One rider raised his bow, unleashing a flurry of arrows.

Kainon felt the deaths as sharp, hot stabs in his mind.

'*Go! Flee!*' he shrieked.

But the fingerlings paid him no mind, determined to fight. More hot spikes speared in Kainon's head until a wet pressure flooded his nose.

Kainon wiped his upper lip and came away bloody. '*Stop! You've done enough!*' he pleaded.

"Kainon!" Matteo yelled, grabbing Kainon's reins. He galloped them past the Spines and down the other side of the hill toward the forest. Smoke plumed behind them.

Kainon swayed, spots dancing before his eyes as more fingerlings died. Images of the Rhun archer grinning as he loosed another volley rocked him in the saddle. Kainon felt Matteo beside him, swearing and trying to keep him ahorse.

They galloped across the short stretch of grass and brush into the forest.

The thick canopy swallowed the sunlight and the last of Kainon's senses.

11

—————

"Your nose is bleeding again," Matteo observed. He reined his horse to a stop under the sprawling branches of an elm.

Kainon hunched in the saddle, looking pale and miserable. "It's nothing," he said wearily, wiping the blood with the edge of his cloak. He took a shuddering breath and straightened. "A small burden."

Matteo supposed it was, compared to the death of dozens of fingerlings earlier that morning. He swung down from his horse and untied his pack.

The forest around them was tangled and thick, indicating Linnians rarely traversed amongst the trees. Between the roots were little hollows and scratched-up burrows. Matteo twitched at every unexpected sound, but the Rhun had not attacked them again.

He set about grabbing firewood. They needed to pause, take stock, and get Kainon's injuries set to rights.

Kainon sighed as he slid from the saddle. "Word will spread among the serpents. Even the youngest fingerling can be vengeful." He sniffed, wiping his nose again. "That's why none are here—they're gathering at the forest's edge, hoping for their chance."

"Chance?"

"To kill the Rhun."

If only it were so easy.

Matteo flushed guiltily. He felt responsible for the dead fingerlings and the vagueness and pain that shadowed Kainon's green eyes. Pulling out the spare bowstring, he contemplated which knots would best ease the man's pain.

Large hands closed over his. "It's my burden, Matteo," Kainon murmured. "No serpent's death passes lightly."

"If you'd just let me weave a healing—"

Kainon shook his head. "I'll recover soon enough. Some of Thia's tea will suffice."

Matteo dropped his gaze to the leather bowstring. "Is it because you don't trust me?"

Kainon snorted, then winced and massaged the bridge of his nose. "I realize now that you could have killed me on the Dragon Plains if the notion took you. You said the killing braids don't work that way, but desperation and innovation make for strong bedfellows."

If that were true, Matteo would still have a kingdom to call home. His throat suddenly aching, he busied himself with pulling out a small packet of tea and organizing the fire.

Kainon dampened a cloth and wiped his face of blood. "I didn't expect the archer to aim at me this time."

Matteo poured water into a small pot and set it above the flames to boil. "The Rhun know you're a threat."

"Perhaps. I'd think it far better to take out your actual quarry, especially when you have the element of surprise." Kainon squeezed the bridge of his nose as if it pained him.

"It doesn't make sense that they would follow you from Darsha and not use the flame blade."

Matteo glanced anxiously back the way they had come. "I didn't notice," he muttered. But his scalp had tightened when he'd seen the flame blade, almost as if his braids were recoiling.

"Has it to do with the flame blade itself?" Kainon wondered. "Do they need certain conditions for the blade to feed?"

The echo of screams pulled Matteo back to the Temple of Dar. He'd seen friends fall alongside mentors. He swallowed hard.

"Did you see anything in Darsha?" Kainon prodded. "A ritual, perhaps? If the Rhun need to perform a ceremony to feed the blade, it could—"

"I hid under the bodies, Kainon. And then I ran. I just ran."

Kainon grimaced and hunched back on his heels. "I'm sorry, Matteo. I shouldn't have asked."

Matteo dropped his gaze, stirring a portion of tea into the boiling water.

He hadn't known flame blades could glow so brightly. It must have fed upon many knotbinders.

"They're never going to give up, are they?" he wondered aloud.

"The Rhun haven't taken you yet," Kainon said, his voice firming. "We'll deal with them together." The streak of blood on his cheek made it a dark promise.

Matteo wondered what had changed Kainon's mind. It wasn't so long ago that the Protector had been happy to use him to lure out the Rhun.

The tea had no medicinal properties that Matteo could

tell, but Kainon appeared to take comfort in its tepid flavor. They continued soon after.

A game trail led them deeper into the forest, where pointy-eared hares skittered in the undergrowth to avoid harassment by fingerlings. The little serpents appeared different to those in the grasslands. Their wings and tail spines were green or mottled brown and shaped like sticks and leaves.

Matteo pointed at one fingerling with horns shaped like twigs sprouting from its forehead. It hid under a fallen log, smoke curling from its nostrils as they rode past.

Kainon rallied himself with apparent effort. "It's likely never seen a human before. Fingerlings can hatch in the Breeding Sands and reach the Uhur Mountains without ever meeting a Linnian."

"Surely you jest," Matteo replied.

Kainon shook his head. "There's a large tract of land from the Breeding Sands to the mountains that's untouched so that fingerlings have an easy, unbroken journey. Very few villages or towns are on the outskirts, and the existing ones aren't allowed to grow too big. You'll see what a Linnian city is really like when we reach the coast."

They travelled east, crossing ravines and gullies where inky, dark fingerlings hid in the shadows, visible only by their brightly colored eyes. They walked their horses to avoid trampling the ones shaped like rocks and twigs that were too startled or curious to flutter out of the way. It made Matteo wonder how many fingerlings failed to survive the journey to the Plains. The eggs from which they hatched must have been tiny.

Kainon shook his head when he said as much out loud. "The size of the egg doesn't match the size of the hatchling. Dragon eggs are much bigger than their bodies need."

Matteo tilted his head, curious. "I'm not sure what you mean."

"The eggs are generally as long as your arm, but dragons are tiny when they hatch. The liquid they swim in while in the egg carries magic and potential." Kainon shrugged. "It's up to the fingerling what they do with it." He hesitated. "It's one of the reasons why the Breeding Sands are so protected. Bandits used to drain the liquid for elixirs and curses. But the magic isn't for humans, and if a dragon survived the draining, it grew sickly and deformed."

Matteo grimaced. Little wonder the Protectors had come into being when such injuries were inflicted upon a dragon's young.

If only there had been Protectors to save Darsha's young as well.

THE VILLAGE of Wolden sat a few miles from the forest's edge, perched on a river used by barges to carry goods and summer harvests from the eastern provinces to Pelan on the coast. The road forked south over a wide bridge. Kainon recalled there was a Protector chapter house in the next town of Renho.

Kainon felt a rush of relief, but he warily studied the road. The Rhun could have ridden ahead if they believed reaching the chapter house at Renho was the goal. Better that he got Matteo off the road for a night and finished their journey in daylight.

They made sleeping arrangements at an old, slightly rundown inn in the center of Wolden. Kainon slipped the stableboy a pair of coppers and asked for extra feed for the horses. He nodded to Matteo, who remained quiet with his hood up. Darkening his hair helped him escape immediate notice, but anything more than a cursory glance would show that the curve of his jaw and the shape of his eyes were not quite Linnian.

Inside, Kainon and Matteo followed the innkeeper to the second level.

"Any news of late?" Kainon asked the innkeeper as the heavy-set fellow strained his way up the stairs to the sleeping quarters.

"Nothing since last week," the innkeeper grunted. "That caused enough of a stir as it is!"

Matteo and Kainon shared a look.

"We've been on the road and haven't heard much," Kainon said, pressing a coin into the man's hand.

The innkeeper pocketed the coin without a pause. "The Protectors at Renho are all in a fuss. We had people come through saying the Sanctuary is shut."

Kainon blinked. "But Tlalam's Sanctuary never closes."

The man shrugged, pulling out a key to a door close to the stairs. He opened the room and waved them in. "Don't know what else to tell you, friend. Pilgrims have been coming through all week squalling like babes over wasted travels."

"Hardly anyone gets to see Honored Tlalam at the best of times," Kainon muttered.

The man nodded amiably. "But we all want our chance to try, eh?" He chuckled. "The Protectors still take offerings meant for the dragon, though!"

"This must have happened in the past month," Kainon murmured.

"Ever since dragons started leaving the Breeding Sands."

Kainon stilled. "What? More than one dragon has left?"

"Might be time for you to go home and see to your

basement," the man said. "War's being carried on dragon wings."

Matteo's mouth dropped but he thankfully said nothing.

"Linnia isn't at war with dragons," Kainon muttered. He'd know before anyone else.

The innkeeper shrugged. "Then where are all the fingerlings?"

Unease stirred in Kainon's belly. The man had a point. He and Matteo hadn't seen a fingerling since leaving the forest. It was almost as though the fingerlings were avoiding places where Linnians gathered.

Matteo gave Kainon a worried look but thankfully made no mention of the ability to dragon-speak. The boy waited for the innkeeper to leave, checking the corridor and closing the door. He leaned against it with his arms folded. "How bad is it?"

Kainon hesitated. "There's always a bit of worry when a dragon leaves the Sands. But if there's more than one leaving, especially before nesting season is over—that's something else." He scrubbed his chin. "Thankfully, we'll be at the Renho chapter house tomorrow. They'll have news from Tlalam."

Given Kainon's ability to dragon-speak, he feared orders would also be awaiting him to seek out Tlalam directly. Speaking with the Sanctuary dragon was an unpleasant experience, even when there was no turmoil or uncertainty. But Kainon would fulfil his duty as always.

Kainon and Matteo left the inn and headed for the market square to replenish supplies. The square was relatively quiet as stalls began packing up for the day. Kainon snaffled some apples for the horses and contemplated a pale glass bauble for Fira when she finally showed up. She had left Briarfall, but Kainon sensed her distraction. She did not travel with the urgency he'd expected. Kainon wondered if the Uhur Mountains had finally called her.

"I recognize those braids."

A stallholder sat behind a stand of wilting cabbages. He folded his arms over his skinny stomach and fixed them a winning grin.

Matteo stared at the man, blue eyes cautious.

Looking carefully at Matteo, Kainon said, "Is that so?"

The man raised an eyebrow and looked meaningfully at his stand of cabbages.

Smothering a sigh, Kainon put a coin on the stand.

The man grabbed it with surprising swiftness and tucked it somewhere in the folds of his tunic. "Aye, indeed so, my friend. A traveler passed through Wolden selling braids." He raised his eyebrows again.

The intensity of Matteo's gaze sharpened.

Seeing that he had an audience, the villager nodded. "Did braids as fancy as them in your hair, boy," he said. "Some poxy merchant paid five gold sovereigns to have her limp healed. Had it since she was a babe, no less! It was a sight to behold."

"What did the enchanter look like?" Kainon asked.

The villager grinned. "As fine a sort as yourself, good sir, for all that she hid under her cowl like a shy maid. She spoke in a whisper, but it was the soothing kind."

Kainon guided Matteo a few steps from the stall and dropped his voice. "Well?"

Matteo looked suddenly uncomfortable. "She could be a knotbinder," he hedged. "But, Kainon, we don't sell our braids. It's an insult to Dar."

"A lot has changed since the Rhun invasion. Your people

may need to choose between food in their bellies or honoring your god."

Matteo frowned. "Dar can take a knotbinder's gift for such a transgression, no matter the reason. It's one of the first things we're taught."

"Then take it as a good sign that this knotbinder can still use their gift."

Matteo hesitated before nodding. "You're right. Of course, this is what I've been looking for." He still frowned, however.

Kainon turned back to the stallholder, who craned his neck to hear. "You saw the knotbinder yourself?"

The man hedged. "Well, not me. But my cousin was there. I'm a poor farmer, you see, and have young ones to feed. Can't be wasting time watching magic tricks."

Noting the lack of dirt under the man's nails, Kainon smothered a sigh and put another copper beside the cabbages. "When were they here?"

The villager grinned. "A few weeks ago, no less. Could still be roaming these parts, though there's finer earnings toward the coast."

"Any other travelers arrive today?"

"None other than pilgrims and your fine selves."

Kainon grunted in satisfaction. He fished out a silver coin to the man and thanked him.

The man took a bite of the coin before winking. "I can tell you other comings and goings if you have a mind for it."

"If you're here in the morning, perhaps we can talk further."

The man grinned. "Certainly, good sir."

Kainon ushered Matteo away, figuring it best for them to return to the inn before he brought more attention to himself.

Matteo continued to frown in consternation as they left the market square.

"I don't get it. I thought you'd be pleased," Kainon said.

"I am, I just—" Matteo stopped, then sighed. His eyes darkened with worry. "What if I finally find a teacher and they refuse to have me as their student? I have to tell them what I can do."

Kainon squeezed his shoulder. "Don't count broken eggs before they crack. Let's celebrate instead. This is the first news we've had of knotbinders in Linnia. You'll be among them before you know it."

Matteo mustered a smile but it didn't quite reach his eyes.

Kainon squeezed his shoulder again. While he appreciated their good fortune, the thought of them going their separate ways brought an unexpected ache in his chest.

Forcing a grin of his own, Kainon promised to enjoy his time with Matteo while it lasted.

12

KAINON WOKE in the darkness that night with his arm outstretched and searching. Cold, rough-hewn blankets grazed his fingertips rather than the familiar warmth and smoothness of Fira's scaled hide. He felt no heavy press of the dragonling against his stomach or the insistent dig of her talons against his forearm. Kainon even missed the hot burps of sulphur whenever Fira breathed against his face to rouse him for food.

Smothering a sigh, Kainon pushed himself upright at peered out the shutters at the cloud-filled darkness. The dragonling's absence left a weighted silence in the room. Kainon knew he wasn't ready for their final parting. Perhaps it was even his fault that Fira stayed.

Useless thoughts.

Kainon stretched the kinks from his back and dressed before nudging Matteo's pallet with his boot. The knotbinder slept with one hand gripping a green-beaded braid.

Matteo snuffled and rolled into a ball of resentment.

"Come, it's a little ways before dawn," Kainon said, nudging his companion again. "Best time to be on the road."

Matteo muttered something low and undoubtedly foul in Darshian.

Kainon smirked. "Looks like rain, but I feel we should be at Renho by mid-afternoon," he said as if they were in mid-conversation. "The roads are well maintained hereabouts—a different story when you head further southeast. Nothing but forest trails and eventually the Breeding Sands."

Matteo pulled the blankets back. Braids were scrunched against the side of his head as he sat up. He glared about the room blearily.

"Of course, you won't have to worry when we meet with your fellow knotbinder. Cobbled roads all the way from Renho to Pelan. You can then catch a ship to wherever you want to go."

Matteo's mind appeared to awaken finally. "You'll be heading back to the Plains, then?"

Kainon couldn't mask a grimace. "I hope so, once I get the Protectors at Renho to hunt the Rhun."

Matteo tilted his head. "But the Protectors might not let you return to Briarfall because you're a dragon-speaker."

It was something Kainon didn't want to worry Matteo about, but if the Sanctuary gates were indeed closed, then momentous events were afoot. While Tlalam was often petty and cruel, his greed eclipsed all else. The dragon would not have closed the gates without reason.

"There's already a dragon-speaker at the Sanctuary. She'll know why Tlalam's annoyed and is likely soothing him as we speak." Kainon shrugged.

"Do you think it has something to do with the red dragon?"

Kainon hesitated. "I can't be sure. An unsuccessful

nesting is rare but not unheard of, but the Sanctuary gates have never been closed before."

They grabbed their belongings and left the inn. The stables had a single lantern at the door that cast dim light within. The stablehand didn't stir from the blankets in an empty stall, but Kainon set a pair of coins on the edge of her blankets before continuing.

Yawning, Matteo shuffled about the stables, giving their horses gentle pats before checking the simple braids he'd woven into their manes. He grunted in satisfaction at whatever the knots told him.

"The horses look well rested," Kainon observed quietly. "Why haven't you woven the same braid for yourself?"

Matteo shrugged. "Dar looks poorly upon knotbinders who weave for themselves."

Kainon expected the god would be more lenient considering how few of his people were left. He cast a quick, apologetic look toward the roofline.

Horses saddled, they rode out of Wolden. The wind whistled mournfully in the darkness. Kainon judged they still had around a half-candlemark before dawn.

They rode further west, with forest on one side of the road and the river on the other. A few barges sat anchored against the bank, their lanterns casting an orange glow across the inky water.

Only a handful of fingerlings braved the forest border to watch them. They blended into the branches, appearing like sticks and leaves. Kainon sensed nothing from them but vague wariness. Attempts to entice the fingerlings into observing the road for the Rhun had them disappearing into the forest with disinterest.

The road was busy with riders and wagons travelling northeast from Renho. There was an air of disgruntled disappointment among the travelers, and Kainon could only assume they were pilgrims returning from an unsuccessful journey to the Sanctuary.

Kainon and Matteo made good time and reached Renho mid-afternoon. The town bustled with activity. A shrine honoring the dragons marked the entrance to the market quarters, though no fingerlings rummaged through the offerings of bread, cured meats and trinkets. Kainon sensed the little ones nearby, but they avoided Renho as surely as they had avoided Wolden.

If Fira were here, she'd harass them into giving up why they were so unsettled, along with other handy local secrets. Kainon hadn't realized how much he relied on Fira before now.

The chapter house sat a few streets beyond the town square and towered above the squat buildings of Renho. Made of thick stone pockmarked with fingerling nests, the chapter house had fire-resistant slate for its roof, indicating it was built while the Treaty was new and tenuous.

The town square was lively, with a crowd gathered around a wagon. Kainon and Matteo edged their horses toward the crowd for a closer look.

A dark-haired woman sat on the back of the wagon, perched primly on a wooden stool with her brocaded cloak thrown over one shoulder to expose her bare shoulder and arm. Three guards waited on the cobblestones in front of her, ready to push back anyone who drew too close.

"Behold!" one of the guards yelled out. "The great healer, Mistress Bellener! Trained by the knotbinders of Darsha in their lost arts!"

Matteo gasped, leaning forward in the saddle.

"Who among you will bear witness to her power?" the guard bellowed.

Several people waved coin bags above their heads and hollered. The guard clambered onto the wagon beside the healer, gazing over the crowd before pointing.

"You there! Young girl. Come forth and be healed by the power of Darsha."

A young woman around Kainon's age stepped from the crowd, her attire marking her as a serving woman or attendant. She handed a purse of coins up to the guard, revealing horrible pink scarring up her arm. The guard inspected the contents before nodding.

The healer bowed her head to the silken ribbons in her lap. The thick folds of her cloak hid much of her workings.

Matteo arched his neck and grunted in frustration. "I can't read the braids," he whispered.

"Here, let's get closer," Kainon said, swinging down from the saddle.

They navigated through the crowd, stopping with the press of bodies halted their progress.

The knotbinder had only a handful of braids in her dark hair, nothing like the mix of beads and bindings in Matteo's. To Kainon's untrained eye, the braids themselves were simple, his gaze inclined to drift past the woman rather than be drawn closer the way he was with Matteo.

Kainon glanced uneasily at Matteo. "Keep your hood up," he warned.

Matteo threw him a startled glance but adjusted his cloak. "We have to warn her about the Rhun."

"We will."

The knotbinder appeared to finish the enchantment and motioned the young woman closer, softly instructing her to hold out her arm. With a flourish, she secured the braid around her wrist. The young woman bowed her head as if praying while the knotbinder leaned down to touch her shoulder, her brocaded cloak spilling over them both.

There was a momentary flash of yellow.

The young woman jumped back, startled, then gasped loudly. Eyes wide, she stretched out her arm, running her hand over smooth skin. "Bless the dragons!" she gasped. She turned to the knotbinder in wonder. "Oh, great lady, you've saved me!"

The woman smiled, her expression almost pious. "Hardly that, dear child," she said as she wiped ash from the young woman's wrist. "But through me, Dar has seen to free you of your burden."

The crowd erupted in cheers and pressed forward to inspect the healing. Others shouted, begging the knotbinder to heal them next.

Matteo watched, his expression souring with confusion.

"What is it?" Kainon asked over the noise of the crowd.

The guard yelled for everyone to step back and shouted that Mistress Bellener would see folk in her rooms at a nearby inn at a time of her choosing. Some waved their coin more urgently to get the knotbinder's attention.

"I don't recognize the knots," Matteo said, his voice troubled. He craned his neck for a better view.

They were perhaps three rows back from the front of the crowd. As if hearing Matteo, the knotbinder noticed them. Her expression paled before she schooled it to blankness so quickly that Kainon doubted that he saw it. But then she stood so fast that the stool toppled behind her.

The guards immediately came to attention, roughly pushing the crowd. The crowd shouted and jostled back, but the woman jumped off the side of the wagon on the other side and disappeared from view.

Matteo shouldered his way through the crowd.

"Matteo, wait!" Kainon yelled, struggling to navigate the mass of people while tracking the woman as she slipped down a side street with the head guard. If he recalled correctly, a warren of side streets and alleys lay ahead. A few dozen inns lay beyond.

"We can't lose sight of her!" Matteo yelled as he broke free of the crowd.

Kainon rushed to follow, only to be yanked back by a meaty fist grabbing his tunic.

One of the remaining guards must have noticed who had alarmed his mistress. He gave a feral grin. "Not so fast, friend."

Kainon growled. He drove his fist hard and fast into the guard's guts before slamming a second blow to his jaw. The guard staggered backwards with a startled curse and fell on his arse. Kainon let the crowd surge around him before jostling his way to the edge.

Free of the crowd, he raced past the wagon and turned the corner. He cursed at the empty street ahead of him.

Matteo was nowhere to be seen.

Cursing, Kainon stepped back onto the main street.

A trader had set up her stall as far from the knotbinder's wagon as possible. She eyed the jostling, arguing crowd with contempt while wrapping up painted baubles and wooden figurines.

Kainon approached the trader. "Good afternoon to you, honored lady."

The trader gave him a measuring look and continued packing up her wares. "I'm done for the day," she said gruffly.

Kainon nodded. "You've been here a few days, by the looks of things."

The trader grunted.

"Perhaps you would be willing to trade coin for information," Kainon said.

The trader paused, giving him a measuring look. "I'm listening."

"The knotbinder—do you know where she is staying?" Kainon asked.

The trader laughed and snatched up Kainon's coin. "That's a fool's question, my friend! Where else would she stay but in the most expensive rooms in town? You'll find her at the Golden Fowl."

Kainon murmured his thanks.

The trader looked him over curiously. "Sure you don't want some trinkets? Offerings for the dragons."

"Perhaps tomorrow," Kainon said.

She nodded in acceptance and returned to wrapping a glass orb.

Kainon hesitated. The square roof of the chapter house peeked over the surrounding buildings. He should present himself to the captain and convince them to send a patrol to the Golden Fowl. But that would take time, and a knotbinder whose location was so easily known meant danger to Matteo.

Muttering an oath under his breath, Kainon navigated the back streets until he spilled out into the merchant quarter of Renho where the better inns and entertainment houses awaited those with fat purses.

The Golden Fowl sprawled elegantly at the end of a street, its shutters painted musty yellow with shimmering, crushed shells to mimic gold.

Kainon's shoulders sagged in relief to see a familiar boy

arguing with a broad-shouldered man at the closed door.

The guard gripped Matteo's shoulder, blocking the entrance. "Private guests of Mistress Bellener only." He thrust him back.

Matteo stumbled down a step. "But she'll want to see me. Tell her I'm from Darsha."

"She won't care if you're from Tlalam's dusky balls. Shove off or I'll do it for you!"

Matteo set his jaw stubbornly.

The guard rested his hand on the hilt of his sword and grinned meanly. By his stance, Kainon judged the man was mere heartbeats from using his blade.

"There you are," Kainon said, hurriedly putting his arm around Matteo's shoulders and steering him down the two remaining steps onto the street. "I told you not to get impatient. We'll see the knotbinder soon enough." Turning to the guard, he said, "It would be in her interest to hear what we have to say."

The guard snorted. "Show your coin first. Tomorrow. She's done with you lot today."

Kainon grinned back, showing teeth. Perhaps he should have fetched the Protectors after all. "Very well." He steered Matteo about and all but marched him down the street.

"But—" Matteo protested.

Kainon ushered him further before muttering, "We're not done here." He glanced back to see the guard watching them. "I'm also curious why a fellow knotbinder has no interest in meeting you."

They reached the bend in the street and Kainon pulled them to a stop out of view. Kainon waited for a handful of heartbeats before peering cautiously back at the Golden Fowl. The guard looked bored, slouched against the entrance with his arms folded.

"I don't understand," Matteo muttered, looking around the corner of the building to glare at the guard. "Why won't Lady Bellener see me?"

Kainon shook his head. "Maybe she doesn't realize you're like her. You can't be the only outlander trying to blend in."

"She ran as soon as she saw us."

Kainon agreed it hardly made sense. "Perhaps she's just as troubled as you to be taking coin for healings." Although not too troubled considering her lodgings at one of the finer establishments in Renho.

The guard soon grew bored and went inside the Golden Fowl.

"There's our chance," Kainon said.

They strode back down the street, keeping close to the buildings. Kainon pointed to the side of the inn, where one of the shutters was slightly ajar as was customary to allow fingerlings entry. Pressing close, Kainon and Matteo took a furtive look inside. The knotbinder sat alone at one of the tables, peeling off her gloves. She looked weary and drained, like she had spent the day healing people.

"A fruitful day, my lady," the guard said, dropping a bag of coins on the table with a clunk.

She gave a wan smile. "Perhaps so, but it's time we move on."

He nodded in acceptance. "The boy followed us from the market. I forced him on but he has a certain look that could be useful to us."

The knotbinder shook her head. "We've tried that before. Darshians tend to be sticklers to the old ways."

The man grunted. "I can deal with him if you think he's trouble."

Lady Bellener appeared to contemplate it before shaking

her head. "Not with the chapter house so close. Let's enjoy one more night here."

Kainon nudged Matteo back. As they retreated, he noticed an open shutter on the second floor. A chicken coop directly under the window was just high enough for them to reach the room.

"That guard offered to kill me," Matteo hissed.

Kainon nodded. "Makes me wonder who we're dealing with."

Matteo looked at him sharply.

"It makes sense why she ran. Perhaps she realized you were a true knotbinder," Kainon muttered. "Any decent fraudster knows how to recognize the real thing."

"You don't know that," Matteo argued.

Kainon pointed at the window and the chicken coop underneath. "Shall we see for ourselves?"

Frowning, Matteo followed him to the coop, glancing about before climbing the tin roof. A chicken squawked indignantly inside but no one emerged from the inn to investigate. Kainon boosted Matteo up until he gripped the windowsill and swung himself inside.

Kainon held his breath until Matteo stuck his head out the window.

"It's clear," Matteo whispered.

Grinning, Kainon hoisted himself into the room. It appeared to be a storeroom with spare pallets, chairs, and cooking utensils.

Kainon carefully eased the door open and peered down the corridor. Footsteps creaked on the stairs as the guard trotted up with the bag of coins. The guard entered one room, whistling as he deposited it somewhere before closing the door and heading downstairs again.

They waited for the guard to begin a conversation in the

aleroom before carefully treading down the corridor. Kainon urged Matteo into the room, taking in the garishly carved four-post bed, polished dresser and washbasin. The shutters were open, taking advantage of the room being furthest from the latrine drain on the far side of the inn.

"This must be the knotbinder's room," Kainon murmured after closing the door.

Matteo did a slow turn before heading for the dresser. The drawers squeaked a little as he opened them. He glanced guiltily towards the door but no concerning noise came from the corridor.

Kainon knelt and looked under the bed, seeing nothing beyond dust and cobwebs.

"Kainon, look at this," Matteo called softly.

The boy held a bundle of braids made with ribbons similar to those used by Lady Bellener. The braids appeared half-finished with loose knots.

Matteo ran his fingers over the knots, gaze turning inward as if sensing something. "They're empty. There's no magic in them."

Kainon inspected the braids more closely. Although the differences were subtle, compared to the knots he had seen Matteo weave, these were uneven and mismatched, the tension tight in some places and loose and amateurish in others.

"Because they're unfinished, perhaps?"

Matteo shook his head. "Every knot carries power. These are untouched by Dar." He dropped the ribbons onto the dresser with disgust. "They're fake."

"But we saw the knotbinder do a healing in the square."

Matteo shrugged, expression turning bitter. "Perhaps she's a healer. That doesn't make her a knotbinder."

Kainon cursed under his breath.

"It must be why she refused to see me." Matteo's shoulders slumped.

Kainon sighed heavily. "We'll need to bring in the Protectors. There's little forgiveness for folk who prey on hope and naivety."

Something scraped against the side of the inn.

Kainon stilled, then pointed frantically at the raised bed.

Matteo shimmied underneath it, Kainon jostling in after him just as the shutters creaked open. Moments later, a pair of boots dropped down into Kainon's view. He held his breath.

The newcomer took slow, measured steps about the room. Then the intruder muttered an unfamiliar word, and the room flooded with an eerily familiar green light.

The hair on Kainon's arms rose. Beside him, Matteo stiffened.

The Rhun had found them after all.

Matteo went to pull his dagger but Kainon quickly gripped his wrist. He pressed an urgent finger to his lips.

Every instinct screamed at Kainon to move as the intruder slowly stepped toward the bed. The silence grew thick and heavy. Eventually, the intruder made their way toward the dresser. Ribboned braids fell to the floor as the intruder swept them aside dismissively.

"There's nothing here, Craise," a young woman's accented voice muttered from the windowsill. "I told you she was no Darshian."

Kainon turned his head to see a second pair of boots, these more delicate. They swung back and forward as if in boredom while the woman remained seated on the windowsill.

"And yet my blade glows," the first intruder growled.

His companion hummed softly. "It's so overfed it'd glow

if you farted."

The intruder turned to face the young woman fully.

From under the bed, Kainon saw the slight adjustment in the man's stance as if getting ready to pounce.

"Oh, relax, Craise. It'll feast on knotbinder blood again." She jumped down off the sill and stalked across the room. "The question is, will you taint your blade with anything less pure?"

"No," the man, Craise, growled.

The woman drew closer until they stood inches apart. Fabric rustled. "No?" she purred. "Are you really so certain?"

The silence grew loaded and tense. More fabric rustled before a cloak puddled to the floorboards.

Kainon grimaced, guessing where this was heading. The bed was far too close to the pair. Matteo was a solid line of tension beside him, and Kainon gripped his wrist.

"Enough, Nadiya. I'm very certain."

The young woman, Nadiya, snorted and stepped back, scooping up the cloak. "What a pity." With a sarcastic laugh, she headed back to the windowsill. "This land is so boring."

"We can't draw needless attention. We have our mission."

"You're boring, too," Nadiya muttered. "Let's not keep the others waiting."

The young woman left, barely making a sound as she navigated down the side of the building.

The man waited for a few heartbeats, slowly turning about the room again.

If Kainon didn't know better, he'd assume the man sensed them.

Matteo held his breath, one hand gripping a braid in his hair. His fingers twitched as if aching to weave.

But then the intruder stalked to the windowsill and

clambered out, boots barely scraping down the outer wall as he left.

Kainon held his breath, listening. No unusual sounds were outside; even the chickens continued their prattle unabated.

But that had been too close for comfort.

He crawled out from under the bed and motioned for Matteo to follow him down the corridor to the storeroom.

"What now?" Matteo whispered as he closed the door and crouched down to peer through the shutters. "We can't stay here."

"We wait," Kainon murmured. Judging by the orange cast of the sky, they had less than a candlemark until night. The Rhun could use the darkness to their advantage, but Kainon prayed to the dragons they had already moved on. "They know Lady Bellener's magic is a sham."

Matteo studied Kainon, thinking. "They wouldn't be able to read the knots. Only Darshians can."

Kainon shrugged. "All the same, that Craise fellow knew."

Matteo chewed on the edge of his thumbnail, eyes growing distant.

Kainon suppressed a grimace. Perhaps the Rhun had hunted so many knotbinders that they could read the braids.

They waited until dark filled the room before clambering over the windowsill and lowering themselves to the chicken coop. Kainon helped Matteo down before jumping to the cobbles.

A horse knickered, and Kainon froze. A pair of riders watched them from the shadows.

"Well, well. Looks like we caught a pair of foxes in the henhouse," a woman muttered.

13

MATTEO PRESSED his back against the wall beside the chicken coop and watched the rider warily. Kainon jumped down from the roof of the coop and took a few cautious steps with his hand resting on the pommel of his sword. The angle of the street lanterns left deep shadows across the newcomer's face. Judging by the woman's accent, she was Linnian—it was a matter of what offence she took at catching apparent thieves in the act.

The stranger pointed the tip of her sword at them. "Stay put," she ordered, then released a low whistle.

More horses approached with cautious urgency. The clattering hooves warned of perhaps a dozen riders.

Matteo held his breath. The Rhun must have found mercenaries to fill their ranks.

Black riders came from the end of the street. A band of silvery concentric circles adorned the sleeves of their tunics and trimmed their cloaks.

Kainon grunted in surprise, his grip on his sword hilt loosening. He stepped forward to meet them. "Well met,

Protector. I'm Kainon Brightsong of the Dragon Plains outpost."

The lead rider halted a few feet away and shook her head in apparent exasperation before throwing back her hood. "Kainon! As I live and breathe!"

The woman was perhaps ten summers older than Kainon, with a mop of curly brown hair, dark eyes and ready dimples. She swung down from the saddle and clasped Kainon's arm, thumb running along the silver mark on his forearm.

Protectors, Matteo realized, sagging against the building.

"Sebani," Kainon said warmly, relief clear in his voice. "It's so good to see a friendly face."

"Of course it is," she said with a grin. "I didn't recognize you without your bearded little pest. Don't tell me Fira finally crossed the mountains?"

"Not yet," Kainon said with forced lightness.

"I'm glad to hear it. But you've found someone else to cause mischief with, I see. It must be you pair frightening the wealthy neighbors." She raised her eyebrow. "You could have stopped by the chapter house before getting up to whatever this is."

"Sorry, we were distracted," Kainon said. "There are Rhun death sorcerers in Renho."

Sebani's jovial expression dropped. She made a three-fingered signal to the other Protectors. They rapidly fanned out to search the street, moving like ink in the darkness.

Sebani pointed for Kainon and Matteo to move further down the side of the inn, away from sight. "Tell me what you know, Protector Kainon," she ordered.

Kainon's spine straightened. "It's a Rhun hunting party. They've been on our trail since the Plains, and one carries a flame blade."

Sebani looked at Matteo, her eyes narrowing on his darkened braids.

Kainon turned to him as well. "Matteo, this is Protector Sebani. We've known each other since I was an initiate."

"I can't say I approve of Kainon bringing an outlander so deep into Linnia, Matteo, but well met," Sebani said, clasping Matteo's arm firmly. "I expect the pretender at the Golden Fowl is what drew you to Renho."

Matteo startled. "You know about her?"

Sebani nodded. "Bellener's braids aren't worth squat but she's a skilled healer. So be it if people want a bit of mysticism and silk with their healings."

Matteo frowned. "But Dar—"

"The Rhun know Matteo is a Darshian," Kainon said, giving Matteo a quelling look. He quickly outlined what had happened in Briarfall.

"Killing Linnians! That's bold behavior, even for Rhuncavari," Sebani muttered. "Last news we had, Darsha's people were all but gone."

"Some of us still live," Matteo muttered.

Sebani looked at Kainon for confirmation, then nodded in acceptance. "May your people find comfort in the Dragon's Embrace," she said, making a circular motion with her fingers as if in benediction.

Matteo blinked at her earnestness. "Thank you."

A Protector rode into the side street and saluted. "All clear, captain. Nothing but nosy people looking through the shutters."

Sebani nodded. "Very well, let's get our friends to the chapter house."

Stepping back onto the street, Sebani mounted her horse and then bent down, offering her hand to Kainon. He easily climbed up behind her.

Another Protector rode up to Matteo, and he planted his foot on the man's boot in the stirrup and swung up behind him.

The Protectors set off at a steady trot, hooves echoing on the cobbles. The riders drew in a tight formation around them. Matteo expected the Rhun to emerge at any moment but could not see past the Protectors.

"Our horses are back at the market," Kainon said over the jingling harnesses.

"I'll send for them," Sebani replied.

They reached the chapter house as it began to rain. The walls loomed over them, but Matteo's gaze caught on the row of dragon statues perched at random intervals along the parapet. The figures all peered down onto the road below, teeth bared. Water dripped off them, the bustling wind making an odd, whispering song through their open mouths.

The gates opened and they entered a large courtyard. Matteo drew a breath of relief. For the first time since arriving in Linnia, he felt the Rhun could not reach him. They came to a halt outside the stables.

Gripping his rider's arm, Matteo slid down from the horse.

A stableboy hurried out to take Sebani's mount while the remaining Protectors took their horses into the stable.

Kainon motioned Matteo to follow Sebani up three wide steps into the windowless main stronghold. Expecting it to be dark and damp inside, Matteo blinked in surprise to see curved inner walls with huge windows leading into an internal atrium. The atrium must have been roofed at some point, but now it was open to the rainy night. The atrium had a pond and fernery, along with an assortment of nooks, wall niches, hollows and hanging baskets meant to accommodate visiting fingerlings. The atrium was currently devoid of movement, but someone had laid out a basket brimming with cured meat and fruits at an open doorway.

Sebani led them down a hallway of closed doors before continuing up two flights of stairs to an enclosed corridor. Sebani opened a door and motioned them inside.

It was a simple room with a large desk, pale wooden waiting chairs and a couch opposite a fireplace.

Kainon slowed, giving the room an amused look. "Captain's quarters," he observed. "The tales of our misadventures seem to have been forgotten, Sebani."

Sebani sat on the edge of the desk and grinned, showing dimples that made her look only a handful of years older than Matteo. "You've been gone a while, Kainon." She motioned for them to sit. "Long enough that you failed to report the moment you arrived. Your absence from the Protectors is showing, Kainon," she chided.

He had the grace to look guilty. "I didn't mean to be waylaid," Kainon said. "We thought our search for knotbinders was over when we saw Lady Bellener."

"Sorry for the disappointment, my friend." Sebani turned to look squarely at Matteo. "There's been other fake knotbinders selling their wares. Lucrative business, the knots. The rarer something is, the more likely people are to be fooled."

"And the fall of Darsha is fresh enough that people know what was lost," Kainon agreed with a sigh.

Sebani's dark eyes turned piercing as she studied Matteo. "You've got the look of a genuine Darshian—no shame in doing what's needed to survive."

Matteo frowned. "I'm not a pretender."

Captain Sebani looked to Kainon, her gaze questioning.

"I've seen Matteo weave the knots," Kainon said with a nod. "He's an actual knotbinder."

Matteo bit the inside of his cheek, wondering if his companion would reveal the full extent of his abilities.

"Are you really?" Sebani marveled.

"Matteo barely started training when the Rhuncavari invaded," Kainon said. "He needs a teacher."

"No knotbinders passed through Renho, not even during the height of the invasion," Sebani said. "Perhaps they were discreet and didn't announce their ability for everyone to see." Her eyes narrowed as she ran her gaze over Matteo's hair. "I've seen a few fake knotbinders and how they decorate their hair with braids and beads. There's a difference when one takes the time to look."

"It's called magic, Sebani," Kainon said dryly.

She snorted. "Very well. I prefer to be certain, given how things are now. A Rhun hunting party complicates things, although they brought Kainon here, so it's not all bad."

It was Kainon's turn to frown. "How so?"

Sebani went to a cupboard and drew out a carafe of dark wine and three cups. She poured the wine, her expression contemplative. "Things have been fraught since the fingerlings left Renho two weeks ago."

"I noticed," Kainon said, accepting a cup. "They're avoiding Linnians but are too fretful to tell me why."

Sebani gave Matteo a cup of wine before taking a sip of her own. "We're hoping for news from the Sanctuary. The commander's been tearing his hair out waiting."

"We had a red dragon fly over Briarfall," Kainon said.

"Then she's another to add to our report," Sebani said with a worried sigh. She settled in one of the chairs and poked at the embers in the fireplace.

"Another?" Kainon set his cup aside and leaned forward. "How many dragons have left the Sands?"

"Perhaps a dozen." Captain Sebani stirred the coals and threw in kindling. "We dare not go in to see what's disturbed them, not without permission from Pelan, but I've patrolled the border enough to recognize a dragon with a belly full of eggs. They're not nesting, Kainon."

Kainon sank back on the couch, his expression a mix of worry and confusion. "I know."

Matteo asked, "Do the dragons nest elsewhere?"

Captain Sebani shook her head. "No. That's why it's so important to guard the Sands."

"There must be news from the Sanctuary," Kainon said.

Sebani grimaced. "Amela hasn't spoken to Tlalam in months."

Kainon looked at her sharply. "What do you mean?"

She hesitated, glancing briefly at Matteo before sighing. "I'm not privy to what was said when Amela last entered the Sanctuary, but word is that she emerged frightened. Tlalam has refused to speak further. The mage guild in Pelan has been working on a gift to appease him."

Kainon folded his arms. "If what you say is true, it'll take a fine gift to lure him out of his funk."

Sebani turned her cup about in her hands, considering. "Does Fira know anything?"

Kainon sighed. "We're quite removed from everything in the Plains, and she's still small enough that she'd rather avoid dragons. They're more likely to eat her than share their woes."

Sebani nodded, appearing unsurprised. "Let's hope Tlalam speaks soon, or you'll get sent to him with a pretty bow around your neck, Kainon."

Matteo looked sharply at Kainon.

Kainon grimaced. "It's an honor to serve," he said with an effort.

The sympathy on Sebani's face indicated she knew a little of Kainon's worries. "The commander will want to speak with you. Get yourselves cleaned up and have some rest. Let me deal with the Rhun."

A BELL TOLLED at first light.

Matteo bolted upright from his sleeping pallet, blankets tangling about his bare feet. He stumbled toward the shutters, heart clamoring. "Is there an attack?"

Kainon was already awake and pulling a black tunic over his head. "Nothing the sort," he said. "It's a call to morning prayers."

Matteo blinked, slow to take in the small quarters. It had two raised beds with a wooden chest at each end but was otherwise devoid of any comforts. He expected travelling Protectors were allocated the room during brief visits.

"Prayers?" To Matteo's understanding, Linnia had no gods.

"Protectors give honor to the dragons at dawn," Kainon said as further explanation. He hopped from foot to foot as he pulled on dark boots. Silver thread decorated the sleeve of his tunic.

"But I've never seen you do that."

Kainon gave him an amused look. "A habit I'd appreciate you keep to yourself while we're here."

"Of course," Matteo said, unquestioning. He pulled out a fresh tunic and breeches from the pack sitting atop the wooden chest. "May I come?"

Kainon smiled. "Certainly, though no one will take issue with it should you decide to stay. It can be a bit dull."

"No, I'd like to come."

"Great, but hurry or we'll be late."

Matteo dressed quickly, straightening the kinks in a braid behind his ear.

They left the room and passed the entrance to a mess hall before heading along the corridor to a new part of the chapter house. Large stone columns framed the doorway. Carvings of fingerlings adorned the stone, their tiny heads turned toward the hall. Unlike elsewhere in the chapter house, large tiles bearing blue and white patterns covered the floor. Decorative columns separated sections of the hall, with expansive, shutterless windows facing out over the atrium below. Sunrise reflected like dark pink on the still pond.

The hall was full of Protectors, but a reverent hush filled the air. A few Protectors already knelt before a small dais devoid of ornaments or statues. Instead, on a small pedestal was a carved flower shaped like a pale lotus Matteo had seen growing in the streams in the Dragon Plains. More Protectors sat behind the first in neat rows.

Matteo followed Kainon's lead and knelt on a blue and white tile. He spied Sebani a few rows ahead, her gaze on her knees, shoulders relaxed. Matteo felt strange at seeing Kainon dressed just like every other Protector.

The bell tolled again before becoming silent, and then a pair of Protectors closed the doors. Silence filled the room. Matteo glanced surreptitiously at Kainon, who gazed at the dais, his expression mild.

Guilty boredom overtook Matteo, and he resisted the urge to fidget. The Protectors around him sat in a steady and quiet reverence.

Then a soft voice in the first row broke the silence with a song filled with strange, unfamiliar words—Old Linnian, perhaps? The singing Protector paused, and the surrounding Protectors sang back. Kainon's mouth moved as he joined in.

Matteo wondered why he had never seen Kainon sing to the dragons before. Perhaps it was something only done in a chapter house.

The hall grew brighter with daylight before the bell tolled again. It clanged directly overhead, and Matteo winced, thinking fingerlings couldn't enjoy the noise.

The singing ended, and the Protectors began to rise from the tiles.

Matteo shuffled out of the way, waiting while a small group paused to speak in greeting to Kainon before leaving the hall.

Kainon motioned with his head. "Time to eat."

Matteo fell in beside Kainon. "Do all Protectors pray to the dragons like this?"

"Yes, though we call it honoring the dragons," Kainon said. He waited for the last few remaining Protectors to leave the hall. He dropped his voice. "Fira thinks it's stupid."

"Ah," Matteo said in understanding. "She prefers you honor her stomach instead."

Kainon chuckled. "You noticed."

Matteo contemplated the empty hanging baskets in the atrium. "Did you meet Fira here in Renho?"

Kainon shook his head. "Sebani and I were stationed at Bone Lake—the chapter house opposite the Sanctuary. We met Fira while patrolling the banks. She was busy divesting a pilgrim shrine of all of its honeycakes." He smiled as if remembering. "Dragonlings her size should already be beyond the Uhur Mountains, but Fira demanded a dragon-speaker as her escort. For whatever reason, Tlalam agreed."

Matteo wondered if Kainon could sense the Sanctuary dragon as well. He imagined Tlalam as a heavy presence at the back of his companion's mind.

They headed into the mess hall, where Protectors were already seated at long tables. Servants brought out plates piled high with bread and bowls of stew. No one paid them any heed as they sat at a table. Matteo glanced about but didn't see Sebani.

Kainon murmured thanks after a Protector handed him a basket with small bread rolls.

Watching him, Matteo felt a strange disconnect. Even though Kainon was a stranger to the surrounding Protectors, he belonged within the sea of black and silver.

"What is it?" Kainon asked, noticing his stare.

Matteo managed a shrug. "You're a Protector. It didn't seem real before now."

Kainon leaned back as a servant brought them steaming bowls of honeyed porridge. "There's not much use for the uniform in Briarfall." He made a show of scrunching his shoulders, the fabric holding its shape. "This one's so new, it's still stiff."

"You look like burnt bread."

Kainon laughed. "What? You never had to wear a uniform, Matteo?"

"Just ceremonial robes," Matteo said. "I was moving from my browns to blues. If things had gone as they should, I'd already be in my greys."

"The colors have meaning?"

Matteo took up a spoon and moved some raisins around his bowl. "Brown is for the first two summers of training, blue is the intermediary. All knotbinders wear those colors before we move into robes that announce our proficiency."

"And grey being?"

"Basic healing," Matteo said. He grimaced a little. "Some greys become law keepers, but most work alongside the greens—the great healers. Greys tend to be knotbinders who aren't particularly powerful. They're often overlooked."

He felt the weight of Kainon's gaze.

"I didn't know."

Matteo shrugged. "Like I said, ceremonial robes only. We tend not to announce our skills unless it's needed."

Kainon sat back, contemplative. "I wonder if the Rhun had any notion. Why else try to kill every last knotbinder?"

Matteo swallowed, noticing a heavy weight in his stomach.

Kainon grimaced. "The Rhun won't be stupid enough to take on Linnia's Protectors. You're officially too much trouble for them now."

Matteo took a deep, quelling breath. "I grateful, but what if we find other knotbinders and the Rhun kill them because of me?"

"Let the Protectors deal with them. The Rhun have killed Linnians, too."

Captain Sebani strode into the room, slowing as she gazed across the tables, searching. Seeing Matteo and Kainon, she quickened her pace.

"Commander Barner has returned," she said, motioning for them to leave their seats. "He'll see you both now."

14

KAINON HAD NEVER MET Commander Barner before. He was a spare man nearing fifty summers with hard features and mousy hair cut close to his skull. The commander sat behind a plain wooden table, with a handful of missives held down by an inkwell.

The commander looked displeased when Sebani opened the door and motioned them inside.

"Protector Kainon, I have no time for fools, but it seems today must be an exception," Commander Barner said, eyes sharp like knives.

Kainon glanced at Sebani, who settled in a stiff-backed wooden chair by the unlit fireplace. Sebani's expression was tight with warning, and she gave a subtle shake of her head.

Matteo lingered by the door, blue eyes wary.

"Sir—" Kainon began.

"I have Captain Sebani's account of why you failed to report," the commander said as he tore up a sheaf of parchment. "You're the reason we have Rhun so deep within Linnia."

Matteo gasped softly.

Kainon clasped his hands behind his back, his face carefully blank. "Sir, the Rhun continue to hunt Darshians. I hope to escort Matteo to Pelan to speak with the mage guild. There's a chance they know the whereabouts of his people."

The commander leaned back in his chair and folded his hands over his flat belly. "We received no missive from Briarfall about your Darshian or the Rhun killing our people." His brows furrowed. "It appears you've been too long from a chapter house, Protector Kainon."

Kainon stiffened. "No, sir."

"You should have sent a report rather than gallivanting all over the countryside with this supposed knotbinder."

"I *am* a knotbinder," Matteo muttered, frowning.

Commander Barner ignored the boy, his eyes stabbing into Kainon. "Captain Sebani vouches for you. It appears you have some history together."

Kainon looked sidelong at Sebani, who observed the conversation from her chair. She offered no encouragement. He quelled his annoyance that she had not warned him of the commander's mood. But it was hardly Sebani's fault Kainon had been remiss in his duties.

Clearing his throat, Kainon said, "Yes, sir. We were stationed together at Bone Lake a few summers ago."

"And then you left at the bidding of an immature dragon who is conspicuously absent," the commander said, a challenge in his voice.

"She remains in Linnia, sir." Kainon still felt their connection. Fira refused the call of the Uhur Mountains.

The commander stared unblinkingly. "It appears I must take your word on it, Protector. The dragons grow uneasy—as do we in return. Honored Tlalam is more secretive than usual, yet his future Speaker avoids his duties."

Kainon set his jaw, clenching his hands into fists behind him. "I am guiding Fira—at Honored Tlalam's bidding."

"You have an answer for everything, don't you, Protector Kainon?"

Kainon wisely held his tongue.

A knock on the door made the commander pause. A studious-looking Protector entered with some sheaves of parchment. He settled on a stool at the corner of the commander's desk, fussing with the parchment and a quill before looking expectantly at the commander.

Commander Barner leaned back, expression hard. "Protector Kainon, you will tell me everything that has transpired since meeting this Darshian."

"My name is Matteo," he growled.

The commander turned his sharp gaze on Matteo. "Another word from you, and I'll see you removed not just from my quarters but my chapter house as well." His eyes were dark with promise. "Linnia has no obligations toward your people."

Matteo frowned, his expression sour, but he wisely said nothing further.

Sweat gathering at the nape of his neck, Kainon recounted his journey with Matteo. The scribe jotted down notes, his brow furrowed in concentration. After a time, he looked up and nodded, and the conversation turned to describing the Rhun. The scribe took up drawing a fair image of each rider. The hard eyes of the flame blade bearer, Craise, stared back at him.

Weary from standing for so long, Kainon waited for a curt dismissal.

Sebani still sat in her chair, observing matters. Her expression remained grave.

The commander waited for the scribe to leave before

giving Kainon a scorching look. "It's time you return to full duties, Protector Kainon. Do you agree?"

Swallowing, Kainon said, "Yes, sir."

"You will present yourself to the chapter house at Bone Lake, and if he's amenable, you will cross to the Sanctuary and speak with Tlalam directly. You'll do everything in your power to have him appeased and get him to open the gates to pilgrims again," Commander Barner said. "And you'd better find out why the dragons are leaving the Breeding Sands."

Kainon felt a sharp tightening along his spine.

"As a dragon-speaker, you should already know the answer."

"Sir, hearing adult dragons—"

Commander Barner suddenly thumped his fist on the table. "Protector Kainon. You will fulfil your duty and learn what has angered the dragons," he ordered, voice stark. "Perhaps it's a petty dispute that has nothing to do with Linnia, but I'm not one for naivety. Present yourself to Tlalam and ask for his wisdom. Report everything immediately to the Bone Lake chapter house."

"Yes, sir." Kainon fought not to tremble. He had spent the last four summers avoiding the Sanctuary dragon. Tlalam would not be happy he had spent so long in the Plains. Although Kainon had obeyed the dragon's orders, Tlalam had undoubtedly expected him to complete them within a few short months.

"Captain Sebani and her contingent will provide an escort to ensure you arrive safely," the commander said. He smiled coolly.

"Thank you, sir," Kainon managed.

Sebani leaned forward. "What of the knotbinder, commander?"

Commander Barner smiled coolly. "Since he professes to be a knotbinder, he goes with you. Let's see if he catches Honored Tlalam's interest."

Kainon looked sharply at Matteo but bit his tongue. "Sir, I respectfully ask for a small party of Protectors to escort Matteo to Pelan instead."

"No. The boy may enjoy the company of Protectors to Bone Lake or not at all. He can choose whose attention he prefers—Tlalam's or the Rhuncavari." The commander looked at Matteo. "What say you, knotbinder?"

Frowning, Matteo opened his mouth to reply, but Kainon shook his head.

"Matteo needs to consider your offer, sir," Kainon said quickly.

The commander smiled humorlessly. "I expect so. I'll have your answer by evening, knotbinder, or the Rhun can collect you outside the front gate."

"WHAT WAS THAT ALL ABOUT?" Matteo snapped the moment they left the commander's quarters.

Kainon made a quelling motion with his hand. "Not here."

Sebani was already striding down the corridor toward her office. She opened the door and raised an impatient eyebrow.

Matteo barely stepped inside before saying, "What do you mean I need to consider? The Rhun are waiting outside!"

Sebani leaned against the door, letting out a deep sigh. "Commander Barner won't give you much choice. It's either face the Rhun or go to the Bone Lake chapter house."

"You could have warned us what was at play, Sebani," Kainon said, frustration in his voice.

"Would it have changed anything, my friend?" Sebani countered. "Linnia needs its dragon-speakers more than ever. There are only two of you, and Tlalam is not speaking to Amela. The commander was always going to order you to go to the Sanctuary."

"All the same, Matteo can't go to Bone Lake."

Matteo frowned. "Whyever not?"

"Because of Tlalam," Kainon said, tucking his chin down and frowning at the floor. "You're a tasty morsel to a dragon."

Matteo felt a rush of cold. "Tlalam's going to eat me?"

"Nothing so literal," Kainon assured him. He paused, reconsidering, then grimaced. "Well, it's doubtful. But presenting a knotbinder's braid may grant entry to the Sanctuary when nothing else has."

"The commander knows how to play Tlalam's game," Sebani said. "We need to discover why the dragons are leaving. Once Tlalam senses your magic, Matteo, he'll demand that you go to him, and Linnia will ensure it happens."

Matteo shrugged. Weaving the knots was no burden.

Kainon shook his head as if knowing his thoughts. "When Tlalam accepts a gift, it's not just the gift he takes, but the knowledge behind its creation."

Matteo stared at him.

"You give Tlalam a braid, Matteo, you'll lose the memory of how to create it again," Kainon said.

But he barely learned the foundation knots before the Rhun attacked. To lose that knowledge could mean forgetting how to weave all knots.

Swallowing, Matteo said, "I could give one that doesn't matter so much."

"Tlalam will know," Sebani murmured. She pushed off the door and made for a decanter of amber liquid. "He always knows when the cost isn't great."

The heady smell of whiskey filled the air as Sebani poured into three cups.

Matteo took his without any appetite. The braids of Dar did not lend to creativity or ingenuity. Knowledge passed from one knotbinder to another as part of honoring Dar. Bearing the power to awaken the knots was not enough. He needed a teacher.

"Will Tlalam let me ask my own question?" Matteo asked after a time.

"Like where to find your people?" Kainon said. He shrugged when Matteo nodded. "He could tell you a half-truth or speak in riddles."

"Or just take your gift because he can," Sebani muttered.

Kainon sighed. "Or that."

"But if I stay here—"

"The Rhun could succeed on their third try to kill you." Kainon swallowed a large mouthful and swore softly. "Sebani, will the commander really send Matteo out alone?"

Sebani nursed her cup. "You hold the Protectors to a high standard, Kainon. Commander Barner will do whatever best serves the kingdom, and there'll be no consequences because Matteo's not Linnian."

Kainon scrubbed his forehead. "Could you send Protectors from your contingent to accompany Matteo to Pelan?"

"I won't break orders, my friend. You know this," Sebani said gently.

Matteo folded his arms. "But there's a possibility Tlalam will tell me where to find other knotbinders?"

"That's part of his allure," Kainon muttered. "Many

pilgrims have given their lifeblood hoping that Tlalam will share his secrets."

Sebani sighed. "The commander isn't giving Matteo much choice."

Matteo shrugged. "I'm not sure if I'd choose differently anyway." He took a deep breath. "I'm coming with you both to Bone Lake."

But Kainon looked even more unhappy. "It may be all for nothing," he pressed.

Matteo shrugged in a show of carelessness he didn't feel. "Darsha's gone, Kainon. If I don't find another knotbinder, I'll have lost everything anyway."

15

THE NIGHT SETTLED into quiet but Kainon found himself unable to sleep. Matteo snored softly from beneath a pile of blankets, the top of his hair visible in the moonlight beaming through the open shutter.

There should have been fingerlings on the windowsill and in the room, the nocturnal ones fighting over insects while those who preferred sunlight jostled for warmth in the folds of Matteo's blankets.

Sighing, Kainon padded across the room before gently closing the door. He headed for Sebani's office, figuring all would be quiet inside. Entering, he stoked the coals in the hearth, thinking if Fira were here, she'd spit fire into the embers with smug aplomb. It was their longest separation since she had first scratched on his door and demanded attention. He wondered if they had already seen each other for the last time.

Kainon settled on the couch as responsibility pressed down on him. Commander Barner's words sat uncomfortably close to the truth. He'd allowed his task with Fira to drag on for more summers than was perhaps warranted. He'd made no effort to encourage the dragonling to cross the mountains. Likewise in Renho, he should have gone straight to the chapter house to report the murder of his fellow Linnians by the Rhun. After spending so long in the Plains, he'd grown lax in his duties as a Protector.

But Kainon knew the risk of re-entering a chapter house —Tlalam would call him back, and the next time he stepped into the Sanctuary, he'd never leave.

The soft snick of the door made him glance up. Sebani slipped inside, carrying two steaming mugs. "I saw the light in the hallway," she whispered.

Kainon straightened and mustered a smile. "I could use the company."

Sebani sat down beside Kainon with a sigh. "Anyone who stares into a fire so intently has troubles."

Kainon grunted and took a mouthful of spiced tea. "What news of the Rhun?"

"In the wind," Sebani said with a curse. "They blend well for outlanders."

Kainon thought of the young woman he'd spoken to at the Owl in Briarfall. She'd had no accent he could recall, but she'd been among the hunting party at the Spines. He wondered how many Rhun were already in Linnia, pretending to belong. Matteo was insistent that other knotbinders still lived. Perhaps the Rhun knew this as well.

"They won't remain hidden for long. Or is it the knotbinder?" Sebani nudged his shoulder gently. "I've never seen you willingly trouble yourself over strangers before."

Kainon nursed his cup and turned to his old friend. He hadn't known Matteo for long, though it felt like an age had passed since he threw Matteo into the river. "When was the last time you laid eyes upon a knotbinder?"

Sebani shrugged. "Can't say I ever needed their services. But you know that's not what I meant."

Kainon hesitated. "Once he's found his people, we'll part ways."

But Matteo's mild nature masked a tremendous and deadly power, and Kainon loathed to let it out of his sight until another knotbinder stood before them. It wasn't because he distrusted Matteo—far from it—but he feared what else could be drawn to the knotbinder's magic.

Sebani looked at him curiously. She eventually nodded. "You care about him."

"I do," Kainon said unbidden. "He's brave and generous to a fault. And Fira's quite taken with him."

"I bet. She hoards people rather than objects."

Kainon raised an eyebrow.

"You don't see it?" She tapped her fingertip on the rim of her cup. "Fira took you far from the Sanctuary."

"With Tlalam's blessing," Kainon argued.

"You were meant to offload the little pest in the Plains. Tlalam expected you to be gone for a season at most."

Kainon shrugged helplessly. "I'm still following Tlalam's orders. I can't force Fira to leave. She does what suits her."

Sebani gave him a contemplative look. "Would Fira let *you* leave?"

Kainon pinched the bridge of his nose. "It all seems rather moot now, doesn't it?"

Sighing, Sebani settled back into the couch. "Hopefully, Tlalam will be truthful with Matteo."

Kainon frowned. "Tlalam's cruel, but I'd never call him a liar. Even a partial truth will be enough to set Matteo's feet on the right path." Kainon would make sure of it. "What news from Bone Lake, anyway?"

Sebani stretched, spine popping. "Commander Sherin

still leads the chapter house." She looked at him sidelong, smirking a little. "She likely hasn't forgotten the last time you were stationed at Bone Lake."

Kainon cursed softly under his breath. He'd been scarcely older than Matteo was now. Being stationed so close to the Sanctuary had given him nightmares so disturbing that they caused the local fingerling population to attack the chapter house to rescue him.

"The commander won't have to deal with me for long." He hesitated. "Take care of Matteo. He'll have no one after I go to the Sanctuary."

"You speak as if Tlalam will kill you."

Kainon shook his head. "Of course not—unless a new dragon-speaker has been discovered in my absence." His stomach dropped at the thought of another child being left like an offering at a chapter house's gates.

"It's still only you and Amela."

Kainon relaxed on the couch with a sigh. "Then Tlalam will punish me for my absence. I can think of nothing worse than staying in the Sanctuary. Fira will have to make her way across the mountains alone after all."

"Perhaps Tlalam will let you remain in the chapter house like Amela. You don't need to be on the island with a dragon."

But Sebani didn't understand the pain of speaking with adult dragons, or how their presence became such a burden that Kainon sometimes couldn't lift his head from the weight of their thoughts.

"It'll be up to Tlalam," Kainon managed after a while.

Sebani patted his arm. "I'd free you of this duty if I could."

Kainon mustered a smile. It was an old conversation between them. "I know."

CAPTAIN SEBANI and twelve Protectors escorted them out of Renho as rain battered the streets. Matteo was relieved to see Sebani at the helm. She ordered the party to watch the quiet, dripping buildings as if expecting an attack. But the Rhun had disappeared like smoke.

The Pilgrim Road took them directly east into a forest with giant, sprawling trees and ferns. The road was wide and hard-packed from generations of pilgrims travelling to Bone Lake. Every few miles, a shrine decorated the edge of the road.

Matteo's gaze was drawn to Kainon dressed once more in black and silver Protector garb, sitting straight-backed and comfortable in the saddle. Surrounded by Protectors, he looked like he belonged.

As if sensing his regard, Kainon slowed his horse and drew up beside him. "The rain looks set in for the day," he said with his hood pulled low. "At least the road should have few travelers to slow us down."

The banality of the conversation surprised Matteo. "I guess so."

It settled the unease in Matteo's belly to have Kainon close. Even though he'd agreed to go to Bone Lake, Matteo was less confident he had the freedom to change his mind.

Kainon ran a critical green eye over Matteo. "You doing okay?"

Matteo nodded. "Not used to so much company," he admitted.

"Me neither," Kainon said. He stayed alongside Matteo as the rain continued to spatter over them in thick bands.

They paused around midday after letting a pair of

muddy wagons pass them. To Matteo's surprise, another six Protectors arrived from the direction of Renho.

"All clear, Captain," the lead rider said. "No one left Renho after you. Even Lady Bellener was encouraged to stay after receiving news of the Rhun."

"Excellent," Sebani said. She ordered the newcomers into formation and maintained a steady pace as thunder boomed in the distance.

Late afternoon, the Protectors set up camp with awnings in a clearing.

Matteo did his best to rub down the worst of the mud on his horse's coat, ignoring the curious gazes of the nearby Protectors. He could swear two loitered close by with little to do, and he wondered what would happen if he wandered free of the camp unattended.

"Matteo," Kainon called out, striding through the mud with a small jar half-hidden within the folds of his sodden cloak. He motioned with his chin toward the tree line.

Following, Matteo was surprised to see a little stream meandering over water-smoothed pebbles. Fat droplets of rainwater fell from the overhanging branches.

"Here, take off your cloak," Kainon said, squatting by the stream. "We don't want it stained any worse."

Matteo blinked at him.

Kainon tapped the edge of his hairline. "The rain's washed out the dye faster than I expected."

Matteo pulled forward one of his braids, seeing his hair had turned to a murky grey rather than the dark brown from that morning. "It's the knots," he said in surprised realization. "They don't like any sort of tampering."

Raising an eyebrow, Kainon asked, "Will they trust me to dye your hair again?"

"I think so," Matteo said. Out of all the people in Linnia

and beyond, he trusted Kainon. He wondered how it had happened. "It should be fine."

"Very well, then," Kainon said, green eyes bemused. He pointed to the flat rock beside him.

Matteo hung his drenched cloak over a branch and squatted with his head leaning over the stream.

Kainon opened the jar and quickly worked the bitter-smelling dye through Matteo's hair.

The braids hummed with caution under Kainon's ministrations.

"Okay?" Kainon asked, pausing.

Matteo hesitated, running his senses along the knots. The enchantments were uneasy, unused to being touched by anyone other than Matteo. But they didn't sting or zap at Kainon's hands like they would an enemy.

"It should be fine to wash it out," Kainon said.

Matteo submerged his head into the icy stream, scrubbing furiously before lifting his face and gasping from the cold. He did it again until the water ran clear over the rocks.

"It might be best you wring the water out yourself," Kainon said, amusement in his voice.

Matteo worked quickly, shuddering from the cold, his hands turning pink as he squeezed his braids.

Kainon ran a critical eye over Matteo's hair. "Well, you're no Linnian, but it'll do."

"Don't hurt yourself with your compliments, Kainon," Matteo groused.

Kainon laughed and handed Matteo his cloak.

They turned to see two Protectors a short way upstream. The pair made a poor show of aimlessly wandering the bank.

Matteo's heart sank. "They're watching me, aren't they?" he asked quietly.

Kainon scowled at the two Protectors. "Or they're keeping an eye on me," he muttered. "Commander Barner wants to be sure I get to Bone Lake." He watched the pair a moment longer before heaving a deep sigh. He appeared about to speak further when he suddenly frowned and raised a quietening hand.

Matteo slowly got to his feet and followed Kainon's gaze towards the trees on the opposite bank.

Branches cracked in the distance as if under a heavy weight.

"What is it?" Matteo whispered.

Suddenly, a gold and black dragon the size of his horse burst from the trees.

The creature was sharp-featured but ungainly like a newborn foal. It tripped over its talons as it leapt over the stream and knocked Kainon off his feet.

"Fira!" Kainon threw his arms around the dragon's neck.

The dragon made a deep-throated chitter, her spiky beard quivering. She pressed her large head up against Kainon's hand as she pressed him into the mud. Smoke plumed from her nostrils.

"So this is what you've been up to!" Kainon paused, his head tilted before nodding. "Of course, you're sore. You're ten times your size!"

Running footsteps came to a sliding stop as Captain Sebani reached them. She swore loudly. "Kainon, get up before people think you're getting eaten."

Grinning, Kainon rolled out of the mud. He and Fira were almost of a height, with Fira having the girth of a stout mountain pony. Everything about Fira was now more sinuous and solid. The scales along her flanks were the size of Matteo's palm and shimmered like bronze.

Kainon laughed, replying to something Fira said in his mind. "A cave is a good, quiet place for growing. I'm sorry I wasn't there to help."

The Protectors maintained a respectful distance, murmuring with wary amazement. A few made signs against their chests. Matteo couldn't tell if they were warding signs or genuflections.

"I didn't know dragonlings could grow so big so quickly," Matteo said, resisting the urge to touch.

Kainon shook his head in wonder as he ran his hands down Fira's neck. "Neither did I," he chuckled, scrubbing along Fira's bony jawline and the beard-like bristles under her chin.

"She's a beauty," Matteo breathed.

Fira preened, turning slightly to show Matteo her wings. New mottling of gold and yellow fanned out with fading stripes of black threaded along the wingtips. In full flight, she would look as golden as the sun.

"I have never seen anyone more glorious," Matteo told her.

"She's a wonder," Kainon agreed. "By the dragon's teeth, you've been busy, Fira!"

Sebani finally approached with respectful caution. She bowed deeply. "Honored Fira."

Fira chirped for a lengthy period, her golden eyes suddenly mournful.

Kainon let out a snort. "Fira has noticed you didn't pack her favorite jerky."

Sebani's mouth slackened before she scowled. "Why, you little—! You haven't changed at all!"

Fira hawed, acrid smoke billowing as her sides heaved,

and Matteo's eyes watered from the acrid stink of brimstone and lightning trapped beneath the branches.

Waving the smoke away, Sebani said, "Don't expect to get your fill from me. We'd empty a chapter house larder in one sitting!"

"Fira's pleased to see you as well," Kainon said to Sebani.

Sebani's scowl turned into a grin. "I worried when Kainon arrived without you, Fira. I should have known you were up to mischief."

"Is she as big as Tlalam?" Matteo asked, mesmerized by the flash of her scales when fat raindrops fell from the branches to land on her long neck.

"Hardly." Kainon fearlessly inspected Fira's talons, which appeared too large for her size. "Fira still has a lot of growing to do."

"She'll be the size of a house by the time she's finished. Then she'll give Tlalam pause," Sebani noted.

"Why didn't Fira tell you?" Matteo asked Kainon.

Kainon shook his head. "I suspect Fira didn't know. Perhaps whatever's upset the dragons forced her into a transformation to protect herself."

"That's a fun thought," Sebani said, mouth turning down.

"Or it could be her time to leave Linnia. Are the mountains calling, Fira?" Kainon asked, his voice dipping slightly with dismay.

Fira gave a dismissive chuff.

"Oh, I'm glad," Kainon said.

Fira chuffed again before ambling toward the camp.

Startled Protectors hurried out of her way as she inspected saddlebags and the large pot beside the campfire.

"Well, the pilgrims will appreciate the sight of her," Sebani said with an air of bemused resignation. She grimaced when Fira mouthed a satchel hanging from a rope, causing apples to tumble free. "That is until they lose their offerings and travel supplies as well."

Fira settled on her haunches and crunched on an apple.

"Indeed," Kainon sighed.

Fira met Matteo's admiring gaze and burped.

16

THE RAIN TRACKED east for several days, keeping pace with the Protector contingent.

It suited Kainon's mood as they drew closer to Bone Lake. A heavy presence increasingly made itself known in the back of his mind.

Tlalam...

The dragon simmered with threat and impatience at Kainon for having been gone too long. They were too far apart yet to share words, but soon Tlalam would be close enough to squash Kainon's mind like a bug.

The contingent passed a shrine adorned with azure crystals and blue glass. It marked the entrance to a small village, where blue paint decorated doorways and shutters.

Matteo leaned over his horse's neck to look more closely at the shrine. The darkest stones matched his blue eyes.

"Tlalam's a blue dragon," Sebani said to the boy. "We'll see plenty of shrines now that specifically honor him. Blue dragons are known to be steadfast and firm in their resolve."

"And prone to self-indulgence," Kainon muttered.

Sebani gave him a bemused look. "Tlalam will hear you one day, Kainon," she warned.

It was likely the least of his problems.

Sebani turned back to Matteo. "By all means, look at the offerings, but touching any is a great offence."

Fira shuffled toward the shrine, still awkward in her new size. She ignored the agitated sidestepping of the Protector's horses. Intent on inspecting each of the offerings, she nosed a jar of dried leaves shaped like tiny stars. She sneezed violently, unleashing a gout of flames that scorched the stone.

Several horses reared until the Protectors got them settled.

"She'll get us into trouble," Matteo said, rubbing his mount's quivering neck.

Kainon shook his head. "Adult dragons don't care about shrine offerings, but fingerlings like to build hoards." He sighed when Fira took a silver coin and swallowed it. "Really, girl? I don't want to hear about a bellyache later."

Chin spikes bristling, Fira chirruped, '*The little ones are fat and lazy.*' She determinedly swallowed another coin.

Relaying her words to Matteo, Kainon said to her, "They're scrawnier than you were when you showed up scratching on my door."

The next trill from Fira sounded far more petulant. She plodded away from the shrine and settled with a proprietary air beside Matteo's horse. She looked up at the knotbinder with limpid gold eyes and discreetly burped.

Matteo's eyes noticeably watered from the acrid stench, though he was too polite to comment.

Kainon smothered a grin and motioned to Sebani to continue through the village.

Passing through the main square, their presence drew

villagers from their homes and shops. Fira slowed. She basked in the gasps of awe and reverent bows from the villagers, and appeared even more pleased when a flock of chickens scattered at the sight of her.

A woman burst out of her hut, a sack in hand. She grabbed Matteo's reins. "Generous Protector, I humbly ask you give this to the honored dragon," she said, bowing deeply.

Matteo took the bag with wide eyes.

Kainon motioned the bag over. Inside were potatoes and ground roots—likely the woman's stores for the season. Kainon carefully closed the sack. "You're the one who's most generous." He grasped her hand, pressing a small pouch of copper coins.

She flushed. "No, I can't."

"You honor the dragons best by living well."

She smiled up at him. "You're a good man, and blessed to have a golden dragon for company."

Fira paused beside them, still ungainly but attempting to tilt her chin regally.

"Oh, glory," the woman breathed, hands going to her mouth. "I'll never live a finer day."

Fira's sides quivered as she held her pose, her golden eyes on some distant point as if she pondered momentous, dragonly things.

The woman bowed low as she walked backwards. "May you always grace Linnia, honored dragon."

Fira inclined her head toward the woman briefly.

The woman glanced triumphantly toward the gaggle of villagers clinging to doorways, too scared to approach the dragonling.

"Don't let it get to your head," Kainon said quietly to Fira.

Fira pretended not to hear him.

They left the village, crossing a bridge past tended fields and small vegetable plots interspersed by forest corridors left for fingerlings to gambol in. Scratches in the dirt and singed vegetation showed the recent presence of fingerlings, but none chose to reveal themselves. Kainon sensed them hiding in tree hollows and blending amongst the greenery. They avoided people in a way that set Kainon's teeth on edge.

The night's campsite was in a grove heavily carpeted in clover. The Protectors set up quickly before a pair went to the nearby stream to try their luck with fishing.

Rubbing down her horse and slipping it a sugar cube, Sebani called Matteo over.

"Did your training in Darsha include any work with a blade?"

Matteo shook his head. "Knotbinders aren't exactly useful in a fight."

Sebani raised an eyebrow before pulling out her sword. Standing beside Matteo, she showed him how to grip the hilt and test its weight.

"You hold it well enough to get yourself into trouble," Sebani noted. "Considering who hunts you, you'd do well to have some practice."

"I suppose so," Matteo said, handing back the blade.

Sebani motioned for one of the Protectors to hand over her sword. "Now's as decent a time as any, wouldn't you say?"

Matteo looked to Kainon.

Kainon shrugged. "There are worse things to learn."

Grinning, Sebani strode to a clear space along the grove's edge. "Come along, Fira."

The dragonling had been inspecting one of the tents erected by the Protectors. She made a curious trill.

Sebani shrugged as if knowing her thoughts. "Might help you get used to that big bag of bones you've grown into."

'*Sebani thinks I'm not graceful,*' Fira complained to Kainon.

Kainon huffed. '*She's not wrong.*' He sent her an image of a puppy who'd yet to grow into its feet.

She gave him a squinty look before trotting to Sebani and Matteo.

Kainon watched the trio for a short while. Sebani showed Matteo how to stand while holding the blade, taking him slowly through several defensive postures and moves. She motioned Fira closer so that she could demonstrate them faster.

Matteo hesitated. "You won't hurt Fira, will you?"

Sebani winked. "Fira's hide is too tough for that now. She's more likely to get hurt tripping over herself than from a blade."

Fira hunched down, tail wriggling in readiness to launch at Sebani.

The captain grinned and suddenly charged directly at Fira, batting away her sweeping talons before parrying.

Kainon grimaced as the sword slid along Fira's scales in a shower of sparks.

"See what I did, Matteo?" Sebani said, stepping back. "Don't get so close that you can't parry your opponent."

Matteo nodded, though he looked a little uneasy.

Noticing, Sebani said, "With me, then."

Sebani came at him with an easy lope, projecting the swing of her blade. Matteo awkwardly blocked overhead. "Stay light on your feet," the captain said. She showed her next move, her sword moving to Matteo's side and giving him time to parry. "Good! Again."

Dark blue eyes intense, Matteo ducked under the next attack and spun to block. They repeated back and forth, Sebani grinning. Training initiates had always been one of her favorite things, and Kainon recalled a walloping or two in his time.

Fira edged behind Sebani, watching with interest. She waited for Matteo to parry, forcing Sebani back a few steps before sweeping her tail behind Sebani's boots.

The captain fell backwards onto the ground with enough force to knock the air out of her lungs.

Matteo gaped in shock, sword growing lax in his grip.

A chuffing guffaw came from Fira as she bounded back.

Sebani quickly rolled to her feet. She bared her teeth in a grin. "Very well, Fira," she wheezed before straightening. She took a few deep breaths. "Let's have both of you."

Fira danced from foot to foot, making rapid, chuffing sounds as Matteo took position beside her.

Kainon hid a grin behind his hand. "Mind your size, Fira, and try not to crush Matteo," he called out.

Matteo threw him a wild look. Then he quickly raised his sword to block Sebani's downward strike. Fira took the next hit, blade skittering along her shoulder. The green bed of clover underfoot let the pair dance around each other, sharing defensive hits and parries against Sebani. Other Protectors stopped their work to watch. Golden sunlight bounced off Fira's scales as she flicked a wing to stir up bits of leaves and vegetation.

Eventually, Fira and Matteo came undone, having grown overconfident, bumping shoulders together with enough force to unbalance them both. Sebani took advantage, her sword headed for Matteo's collarbone before diverting to tap against a braid.

A sudden white light erupted from the braid. Sebani flew backwards, tumbling head over foot.

"Captain!" Matteo shouted, scrambling after her.

Sebani lay dazed, eyes vacant for several heartbeats.

Kainon skidded on his knees beside Matteo and grabbed Sebani's shoulder. "Sebani," he said urgently.

She came back to herself with a groan and grabbed her head.

Fira shoved her nose in the gap between Kainon and Matteo, sniffing loudly. She radiated a mix of curiosity and concern. A crowd of Protectors gathered around.

Sebani weakly waved them off. "I'm fine. I'll be fine. Get back to your work; don't think I didn't notice you all lollygagging about."

The Protectors retreated with a handful of grumbles.

Sebani massaged her temples, grimacing. White ash covered her cheek from the blast.

Kainon and Matteo carefully helped her sit up.

"Dragon's Teeth, Matteo, what was that?" Kainon asked.

Matteo flushed. "Dar doesn't like anyone trying to steal a braid. The knots must have misunderstood Sebani's intent." He grimaced, cheeks turning brighter. "I'm sorry, captain. I should have warned you."

Sebani made a pained, rueful huff. "Serves me right for dabbling with unknown magic. It's got quite a kick."

"Sometimes," Matteo agreed sheepishly.

Kainon wondered if the Rhun were aware of the impediment. If so, it made sense for Rhuncavar to kill every knotbinder—it was easier to destroy than coerce a kingdom capable of death magic.

"I think that's enough training for now," Sebani said dryly.

"At least for today," Kainon added, thinking that anything that increased the boy's survival against the Rhun was worth the effort.

Sebani raised an eyebrow but nodded thoughtfully in agreement. "I suppose Matteo has enough natural talent not to cut off his own foot. It's as good a foundation as any. Perhaps we can make a fighter out of you, lad."

Matteo grinned.

17

THE FOREST GREW denser as the week progressed, with the canopy of leaves so thick it blocked the sun. The few fingerlings that braved the forest's edge scattered in Fira's wake as she thumped and crashed through the undergrowth. She'd taken to hunting her own meals, and once scared a herd of deer onto the road before pouncing on one unfortunate creature.

Matteo had gawked with nauseated fascination as Fira left scarcely an antler behind in her feasting. Fira still begged for treats throughout the day, and Captain Sebani ordered the Protectors to take turns carrying the jerky bag to give Kainon some respite. The Protectors took to the task with varying degrees of eagerness and caution.

Several days of travelling surrounded by dense trees ended when the forest on one side of the road suddenly dropped away, revealing an escarpment that looked over Bone Lake.

The lake stretched a fair way to the horizon, surrounded by forest. On the shoreline, a stone tower rose above the trees, with a collection of buildings outside its walls.

But Matteo found his gaze drawn to the solitary island about a mile from the grey-pebbled shore. The Sanctuary appeared little more than a walled forest with a hill toward the center of the island.

Matteo pushed aside his disappointment. Even from their vantage point, there was nothing remarkable to be seen—no fortress or glittering pile of jewels or sight of a dragon slumbering in a clearing.

They moved down the escarpment to the shore. Gentle waves lapped amongst the rocks. The air over the water's surface seemed alive with static, making the hairs on Matteo's arms dance.

Sebani pointed to a circle of water close to the Sanctuary that appeared unnaturally still. "See there, Matteo? That's the final resting place of a dragon that dove to its death millennia ago. The water's so clear you can see its bones from the tribute barge."

There was reverence in her voice, but Matteo thought it sounded ghoulish.

Kainon was strangely silent and white-lipped on his horse, his unfocussed gaze on the Sanctuary island.

Leading their horses along the bank, they reached the chapter house. Taverns and rooming houses lined the streets, but it was surprisingly quiet. A tense heaviness gripped the air, and Matteo noticed a number of the Protectors rode with their hands resting close to their swords.

The street led them to the chapter house. Matteo heard upraised voices long before they reached the fortress walls. Turning a corner, Matteo reckoned as many as fifty people crowded close to the entrance.

A dozen Protectors watched them from the wall, seemingly unmoved by their presence.

"You deny us Tlalam!" a pilgrim shouted.

"I travelled the length of the kingdom to get here!" another complained.

"They want the dragon's secrets for themselves!"

Sebani quietly ordered the contingent to stop.

The crowd appeared increasingly angry. One woman banged her fist against the wooden gate.

"Open up! You can't send us away."

A Protector leaned over the wall to shout at them. "Curfew begins at sunset. Disperse yourselves immediately!"

A handful of people jeered.

Kainon touched Fira's golden shoulder. "This may not be safe for you," he said quietly.

Fira craned her neck, making a soft trill before taking to the air. She swooped low enough to catch the attention of the crowd.

"There!" a woman shouted, pointing frantically. "The dragons wish to speak with us."

"The dragons want the Sanctuary gate open!"

The woman's voice grew hectic. "It's the Protectors who closed it! They deny our right to speak with Honored Tlalam!"

"Protectors can't close the dragon gate," the Protector shouted over the muttering people.

More jeering rose from the crowd.

Kainon cursed softly. "We can't get in with this mob in the way." He stood up in the stirrups, trying to peer over the crowd.

One of the other Protectors on the roof finally noticed them. He turned and shouted down something that was lost the noise.

The main gate opened and Protectors spilled out like a

hoard. Fully armored as if about to go into battle, they used the butts of their spears to drive the crowd back.

Sebani kicked her mount into a trot, ordering the contingent to follow as they made for the opening. The armored Protectors quickly closed ranks behind them and hurried to slam the gates on the disgruntled faces of the crowd.

The lead rider took off her helm and wiped her sweaty forehead.

Sebani did not dismount. "Are we at siege, lieutenant?"

The lieutenant sighed wearily. "There's far more urgent matters than sulking pilgrims, Captain. We had word from Renho that a dragon-speaker was on their way. Please tell me they're among you."

Sebani motioned to Kainon.

"Good. With respect, dragon-speaker, you need to follow me now."

Matteo followed after Kainon and Sebani into the chapter house. The stone corridors were surprisingly austere, with nary a tapestry or rug to soften the coldness. Little niches and hollows allowed space for fingerlings to make their homes, but even the most popular hollows, worn smooth from lifetimes of fingerlings making their homes, sat bare. Whatever had upset the dragons was so profound that the fingerlings had emptied their makeshift homes and taken their hoards with them.

Many of the Protectors they passed in the hall looked somber or harried as if the preceding weeks had stripped them of vitality and hope.

Kainon's expression held a careful blandness Matteo hadn't seen on him before.

The lieutenant took them up a flight of stairs. Though brightly lit, the landing was quiet. She knocked gently on a door and waited. A muffled voice called out, and she opened the door.

The room held a veritable collection of scraps and oddities, with silk fabrics, glass beads and glittering hunks of metal scattered about the place like an avaricious fingerling had ratted through in search of the choicest of trinkets. It reminded Matteo of Kainon's rooms at Briarfall with Fira's little hoard under the bed.

"Commander Sherin, he's here," the lieutenant called out.

A woman dressed in Protector black and silver looked up from her seat beside an oak-framed bed wedged underneath a window. The commander was a thin woman with pale eyes and sun-darkened skin, her left eyebrow split by a scar. The shutters lay open and bathed the blankets in light.

The commander rose with an air of gravity. "Dragon-speaker. Captain Sebani. It's good to see you both returned to us."

But Matteo's eyes were drawn to the aging woman swaddled under the blankets. She was perhaps sixty summers old, her dark hair heavily seamed with grey. Her golden skin appeared weathered and sunken with illness. The only sound from her lungs was close to a rattle. She seemed unaware of her visitors, and Matteo wondered if she ever would open her eyes again.

Kainon made a choked, heartbroken gasp. "Amela."

"Now you see the enormity of our situation." Commander Sherin bowed her head somberly. "The dragon-speaker of Bone Lake has fallen."

KAINON PULLED up the stool beside the bed and grasped the woman's slack hand. "How long?" he rasped.

Commander Sherin folded her arms. "Nine days. All was well until the fingerlings took flight. Amela was in the courtyard when we heard Tlalam. I didn't know a dragon's roar could be so loud." She looked out the window as if remembering. "Then Amela fell. We've stopped the worst bleeding from her ears, but she's not roused since."

Working past the lump in his throat, Kainon asked, "Did you see Tlalam? Has he flown?"

"He's still at the Sanctuary. We'd hoped with time Amela would awaken, but..."

Amela's cheeks were sunken and grey, and a warning blue clung to her lips.

She's dying...

Unthinkingly, Kainon turned to Matteo. The boy appeared pale-faced, looking equally overwhelmed. Kainon looked away, ashamed of what he was about to ask. It wasn't his right to seek Matteo's help. "What about the healers?"

Commander Sherin shook her head. "They've tried, for certain. They're in the mess hall right now. I'm not sure what else they can do for her."

Matteo reached around Kainon to grip Amela's slack hand. A distant look passed over his eyes, with one of the braids tucked close to his ear casting a golden light. Kainon shifted, blocking Matteo from view, hoping the faint glow could be mistaken for sunlight streaming through the window.

The commander seemed not to notice.

Matteo sat back on his haunches. "I can ease the injury, but the dragon-speaker's already left her body."

The lieutenant made a warding sign behind them.

Kainon's shoulders slumped. Tlalam's bellow must have

stripped Amela of her mind, the damage far too great to recover from. Kainon squeezed the dying woman's hand. "I should have been here," he whispered.

"Then we'd have two dying dragon-speakers on our hands," Commander Sherin muttered. "There's no one left to replace you, Kainon."

Matteo looked between them grimly.

Kainon didn't dare stretch his mind across the expanse of water toward Tlalam, but the dragon felt like a mountain avalanche threatening to drag him under.

"Amela would have been working to discover why the dragons are leaving the Sands." Kainon looked about the mess of the room. "Unless she's changed her way of doing things, she always has a tome she's scribbling in."

The commander frowned. "I couldn't say, dragon-speaker."

Giving Amela's hand a final, regretful squeeze, Kainon stood. He navigated across the mess, noting a yellow gemstone on the floorboards that Fira would likely appreciate. A bookshelf held a collection of scrolls and books, with some so delicate the spine creaked when he opened them.

Matteo came up beside him and said quietly, "She doesn't suffer, but I can—"

Kainon squeezed his shoulder. "Let it be someone else's burden, Matteo. Besides, Amela could become well again."

The expression on Matteo's face told otherwise, but he did not challenge Kainon. He looked down at the book. "What's it say?"

Kainon looked at him in surprise. "It's in the Common Tongue—can you not read the letterings?"

Matteo's cheeks turned pink. "Darsha doesn't have scribes. Everything's taught through memory and action."

"So if a knowledge-keeper dies—"

"Then the knowledge is lost," Matteo said, shrugging though he couldn't hide the pain in his eyes.

It brought home the immensity of Rhuncavar's invasion of Darsha. Even if Darsha's remaining knotbinders returned to drive out the invaders, the kingdom would likely never recover.

Kainon carefully closed the book and returned it to the shelf. "I can teach you if you like."

Matteo smiled, blue eyes brightening. "I'd like that."

A shadow swooped past the window, and Kainon caught a flash of gold and black. *'Fira, you'll upset the pilgrims even more.'*

Fira felt unrepentant in Kainon's mind as she made a lazy circle about the chapter house. *'They adore me.'*

'Of course, they do,' Kainon said. *'But I'm sure the Protectors can make a clean, warm place for you in the stables and serve up a barrel or two of cured pork.'*

She gave a considering hum.

Kainon relayed their conversation to Commander Sherin.

"I'll see to it, commander," Sebani said before ordering the lieutenant to follow her downstairs.

Commander Sherin peered out the window as Fira landed in the courtyard below amid shouts of astonishment. "My last report indicated your dragon wasn't so big."

"Not my dragon," Kainon said reflexively.

Commander Sherin threw him a wry look. "More yours than anyone else's, dragon-speaker."

Kainon resisted the urge to scowl. Some Protectors mistook friendship with dragon-kind as ownership, treating the little serpents like pets. They didn't understand that fingerlings eventually grew into their own minds and remembered how they were treated.

Though Fira had never explicitly spoken about her experiences in Linnia, her general disinterest in the Protectors was telling. As it was, she put up with Kainon's responsibilities as a Protector with a level of boredom that indicated she would not always be so patient.

Kainon opened a wooden chest, seeing a few loose sheafs of paper. He quickly scanned them, finding them to be Amela's musings on the seasonal dietary changes of fingerlings. He dropped them back into the chest.

"There's nothing here," he said. It was quite unlike Amela.

The commander approached the bookshelf, running her hand along a few books. "The dragon-speaker hasn't been acting unlike herself in recent months. Quiet. Secretive. Spending time on the banks, just watching the island."

Kainon frowned at her. "Did Amela speak to you about her worries?"

"None that I can recall," Commander Sherin said. She sighed regretfully. "I let Amela be when perhaps I should have pushed her a little." She looked at the bed. "We've known each other a long time, well before you were stationed here, Kainon. I'm certain she's glad you've returned."

Kainon glanced at Amela also. The woman was unrecognizable. She'd taught him how to modulate his mind's voice when speaking to fingerlings, how to project a firm and kind manner to the mischievous ones, and how to coax the frightened and scrawny serpents who showed up begging in winter. Kainon remembered Amela taking one look at Fira when the dragonling first settled on Kainon's shoulder and laughing in delight.

"Perhaps Amela left something in the vault," Kainon murmured, recalling the storeroom that held the best gifts from Pelan meant for Tlalam.

The commander hesitated. "Maybe. As I said, Amela spent many days outside the chapter house. After you've settled, I'll get a servant to take you to the vault. You're welcome to take your old room next door. I'll arrange for your companion to billet with a few Protectors."

"Matteo and I stay together." It came out unbidden. Kainon felt his lips thin in an effort to stop himself from speaking further.

Commander Sherin raised an eyebrow. "Very well. I won't deny my curiosity." She appeared to fully study Matteo for the first time. "Commander Barner provided an interesting report on you, Matteo of Darsha."

Kainon felt his spine tighten.

The commander smiled. "But we can speak of it later. Take yourselves to the bathhouse while servants freshen your quarters. Amela and her vault will still be here when you get back."

18

KAINON TROTTED down the stairwell with Matteo at his side as they made their way past the mess hall. Though there was little conversation, the sound of the crowd beyond the walls grew louder. A side door showed a path leading to the bathhouse, with the stables just behind it. Kainon hesitated, sensing Fira's contentment radiating from the stables before he steered Matteo downstairs to the underground level.

The air felt cool and damp, with the stones stained white after centuries of holding back the water from Bone Lake.

Matteo slowed at the last step, peering down the short corridor to the single door. "Kainon, what are we doing here?"

Kainon shouldered open the wooden door to the vault. "With all respect to the commander, the sooner we find Amela's journals, the quicker we discover what's happening."

Matteo trailed in after him and made an audible gulp.

Although the vault wasn't particularly impressive in size, it was brimming with dragon gifts. Kainon glanced over it all as if seeing it for the first time with Matteo.

Small podiums held the most dangerous magical gifts, some enclosed within glass or metal bars to ensure no one accidentally touched them. Against one wall were bolts of the finest cloth from the kingdom and beyond, while a long table held a bevy of gold and jewels laid out on silken cushions like a dragon's hoard.

There were no windows in the vault. The only light came from the sconces that initiate Protectors maintained daily as a symbol of connection between Linnia and the dragons.

The only way in or out of the vault was through the thick oak door, which bore warding spells around its edges to stop the most adventurous fingerlings from sneaking inside. Kainon didn't want to think of the chaos that would ensue if a fingerling took off with something dangerous.

"Be careful not to get too close," Kainon warned as Matteo inspected a glass globe with blue light dancing within. "Some of these things have teeth."

Matteo raised an eyebrow. "Why keep them here, then?"

Kainon shrugged. "Tlalam has eclectic tastes. One day he might want a collection of the bawdy sonnets from the pirate kingdoms, and the next day demand a cursed coin that strips a person of their youth."

Matteo took a careful step back. "Shouldn't it all be at the Sanctuary?"

"It was Amela's role to sense what would most appeal to Tlalam, rather than risk presenting gifts the dragon thinks is beneath him. Amela represents Linnia, so she must carefully consider her choices." Kainon browsed the shelves, seeing nothing of note, though there were far more items than he was used to seeing in the vault.

He shook his head. Amela would not have changed so

much in four summers to have ceased her journaling. She'd hidden them, but why?

Pressure built behind Kainon's eyes. He rubbed them and glanced at Matteo, remembering a more significant concern. Perhaps something here would soothe Tlalam and make Matteo's offer of a braid redundant. But Matteo was a curiosity, and if there was one thing Kainon knew about Tlalam, it was his thirst for rare gifts.

Kainon's one solace was that Matteo would be safe here at the chapter house with Sebani while he curried favor with the dragon.

The pressure in his head grew worse. He pinched the bridge of his nose, but the sensation grew worse.

"Kainon, your nose is bleeding," Matteo said, alarm in his voice.

He wiped the wetness above his lip and came away with blood. The pain in his head grew suddenly monstrous. He lurched toward the door. "We have to..." he gasped in realization. The room wavered and spun. "Out. Matteo, *out!*"

Matteo hurriedly threw Kainon's arm about his shoulders before bodily heaving him out of the vault. They stumbled upstairs, where the brightness from the windows seared Kainon's eyes.

He blearily looked into the mess hall as they passed. Protectors sat about talking or mending clothes, oblivious to any threat. "Everyone outside!"

They staggered along the corridor and down the stairs. Matteo kicked open the door.

The sharp sunlight in the keep made Kainon groan. His joints felt like ash.

"What is it?" Matteo asked, his voice panicked.

A terrible roar filled the air.

The sun was suddenly blocked out by a massive shadow. A sharp gust of wind kicked leaves and dust into the air.

Kainon blinked rapidly, his head exploding with pain. Dark green and silver scales filled his vision. Then there were black eyes and stained teeth, a long sinuous neck and silvery belly. Nasty hooks as long as Kainon's forearm spread from the dragon's wingtips.

'*Fira, don't come out here!*' Kainon yelled, pushing his mind with an effort toward the stable. Fira was just large enough for adult dragons to view her as a threat.

Mercifully, Fira hunkered in a stall, not yet strong enough to quell her instincts to hide.

The green dragon hovered above the courtyard, its wingbeats strong enough to topple barrels.

'*Thieves!*' it shrieked.

Kainon fell to his knees in agony.

Shouts and cries came from within the chapter house and the pilgrim camp.

'*Tiny, stinking thieves!*"

Kainon could feel her intent, the air changing as she drew in a large breath, fire gathering in her massive belly.

Matteo braced in front of Kainon as if to take the first blow.

'*Wait,*' Kainon pleaded. '*We live to serve you.*'

The green dragon startled at his voice, her wingbeat changing. Her rage burned through his mind like hot coals through parchment.

'*Tlalam's toy,*' she sneered in recognition. '*You will fix it.*'

'*I will,*' Kainon swore desperately, though he hardly knew what he promised.

She lifted her head and unleashed a gout of flames that roared over the parapet of the chapter house. More shouting filled the keep as Protectors dove out of the way.

'*Tell me what I must do,*' Kainon pressed.

The green dragon's talons twitched with the desire to rend and tear.

Another presence suddenly stretched out with cruel fingers from the Sanctuary. The weight of its presence all but crushed Kainon's mind.

Tlalam...

The green dragon jerked as if buffeted by an unseen wind. She resisted for a few wingbeats before shrieking her anger. Wheeling away from the keep, she glided over the pilgrim buildings toward the forest. Kainon tracked the dragon's rage in his mind, muscles trembling. The Uhur Mountains called her.

"Kainon," Matteo gasped. He gripped Kainon's shoulder tightly, blue eyes dark with worry.

"It's fine. We're safe," he managed. The cobblestones under Kainon's knees seemed to buck and roil. The sun's heat on his back felt too much, his head growing heavy.

Matteo caught him. "You're badly hurt."

He managed a wincing smile. "The price of talking to dragons. It'll pass."

But the second presence had yet to recede. It burned through Kainon's mind, sifting through his memories like it was its birthright.

'*Honored Tlalam,*' Kainon sent with an effort.

The dragon seemed to gloat at his pain. '*Welcome home, dragon-speaker.*'

Kainon let the darkness reach up and embrace him.

19

———

Kainon woke to sunlight warming him through swaddling blankets. The smell of fresh hay, horses and leather filled his senses. Squeezing his eyes shut, he waited for the lancing pain in his head to begin.

To his surprise, it was little more than a dull memory. He gazed up at the sturdy rafters of the stables, wondering.

A hand fell against his shoulder, and Kainon blinked at Matteo's concerned face. Worry bruised his eyes, his skin pale and drawn as if he had been lost in a thrall of his own dragon-borne nightmares. A quick glance at his fingers revealed them covered in ash.

"You shouldn't have—" Kainon began, realizing what Matteo had done.

Matteo shook his head. "I had to. You nearly died." He blinked and quickly glanced away, but Kainon saw the unease welling in his eyes. Ducking his head, Matteo busied himself by fussing with the blankets. "Whatever you said must have satisfied the dragon," he continued. "We've not seen it since."

Kainon shook his head, knowing there was little they

could do if the green dragon chose to turn its rage on Bone Lake once more.

Matteo sat back, his gaze seeming to measure Kainon carefully. "How do you feel?"

"Like I've been torn apart and put back with a few parts missing," he said with a rueful smile.

In truth, Kainon knew he was in far better condition than he had any right to be. Not even the royal healers of Pelan could have had such success with his battered mind, mending thought and spirit as easily as one might repair a torn tunic. It served only to confirm that Matteo was far beyond gifted.

"Can you get up? Commander Sherin has called a meeting with the Protectors. She wants you there even if your brain is dripping through your nose—her words."

Propping himself on his elbows, Kainon was astonished at how little the world spun. Judging from how the green dragon ripped through his mind, Kainon suspected he shouldn't have woken at all.

He scrubbed his scalp, startled when he came up against resistance in the form of a braid. He pulled it forward, examining the intricate knots. They vibrated with warmth and subtle power. On closer inspection, he noticed a thick strand of dyed brown hair interwoven with his own darker hair. Soon it would turn blonde and be impossible to ignore.

Matteo flushed. "Injuries of the mind aren't familiar to me. I had to be certain it'd work."

"Thank you, Matteo," Kainon said with feeling.

Fira poked her nose over the stall door, sniffing. She looked him over curiously, slitted eyes narrowing. '*She hurt you.*' Her mind darkened. '*Tlalam, too. I'll remember their transgressions for all time.*'

'*Indeed.*'

She looked at the braid in his hair and brightened. '*Do you think Matteo would make magic for me if I was hurt?*'

The obvious calculation in Fira's question made Kainon snort. '*Let's not find out, hmm?*'

Fira rumbled but wasn't quite agreeable.

Kainon sifted through a jumble of pained memories. '*The green dragon thinks something was stolen. Did you get any idea what she meant?*'

Fira sunk into herself, with just her snout visible over the stall door. '*Too big and loud. Would have munched and crunched.*'

Kainon felt his innards tighten in sympathy. '*You were wise to stay hidden.*'

Pushing himself upright with an effort, Kainon waited for the inevitable dizziness but it didn't come. He quickly hid his astonishment, not wanting Tlalam to become more aware of Matteo.

Matteo was suddenly up close. "Does your head hurt?" he asked, running a quick, assessing glance over Kainon.

Kainon smiled slightly. "I'm doing well, thanks to you, Matteo."

Matteo nodded, though the worried, searching look didn't leave his face.

Sebani met them in the courtyard. She noted the braid in Kainon's hair, her eyebrows rising. "You gave us a scare, Kainon, swooning like that. But you've always been lucky with the company you keep." She smiled at Matteo. "We owe you a debt, lad."

"I'm glad I could help," Matteo replied.

Sebani motioned with her head. "Come along. The commander sent me to fetch you both."

"Good, I'm afraid this can't wait," Kainon said.

The commander was in a private dining room not far

from the mess hall. Five other Protectors Kainon didn't recognize were already seated at the table, though there was no food or drink on offer.

Commander Sherin waved them to take up the empty seats closest to her. "Kainon, I feared you were lost to the same illness as Amela."

Kainon cupped his hands on the table. "I'm recovered from my injury, commander."

The commander looked speculatively between him and Matteo. The tip of one of Matteo's braids was already turning blond again.

"Excellent. There are several theories afoot, but I expect you're best to answer what the dragon was up to," Commander Sherin said. "If I didn't know better, I'd think it wanted to set fire to the chapter house."

"Aye, instead, there's a mile of scorched trees to the north of here," a grizzled Protector with mismatched eyes said. "We have the dragon-speaker to thank for sparing our skins."

There were murmurs of agreement about the table.

Kainon raised a hand, knowing they had little time for congratulations. "She called us thieves, commander," he said.

Sebani inhaled sharply. Two other Protectors seated at the table murmured to each other.

Commander Sherin's eyes narrowed. "Then she's mistaken. The Protectors are above reproach."

Kainon tilted his head in thought. "I'm unsure if she was talking specifically about Protectors or Linnia in general."

"The dragon gave no indication of what she thinks was stolen?" the commander asked.

"I'm afraid not. Although there was a hint of silver to her belly. She's carrying an egg."

Commander Sherin leaned back in her chair, frowning. "This isn't news, Kainon. We're aware some dragons aren't nesting."

He hesitated before asking, "Have we withheld anything in the vault that Tlalam has expressed interest in? I've been gone these past four summers, but I don't recall the vault being quite so well stocked back then."

The commander's expression turned cool. "Speak very carefully, dragon-speaker, lest you make unwarranted accusations."

Kainon blinked. "That's not my intent, commander."

She frowned at him contemplatively. "You can figure out whether there's anything Tlalam fancies when you visit him at the Sanctuary."

Cold flooded Kainon's guts. "Commander?"

She smiled. "Now that you've recovered, I'll order the bargemen to be ready tomorrow."

Swallowing, Kainon said, "It'd be good to find Amela's journals first, commander. She may have discovered something about what's disturbed the dragons."

"I rather think not; Amela would have spoken to me about it," Commander Sherin said.

"Yes, commander."

She turned to Matteo. "Darshian, I appreciate what you've done for our dragon-speaker. Linnia's not your kingdom, however, we'd be grateful if you accompanied Kainon to the Sanctuary."

Kainon cut in before Matteo could respond. "Forgive me, commander, but Matteo must stay at the chapter house."

Matteo looked at him in dismay. "Kainon—"

"And why is that?" Commander Sherin said, ignoring the boy.

Holding the commander's gaze, Kainon said, "We don't

know Tlalam's mood; having an outlander set foot in the Sanctuary could be an insult."

"Insult?" Matteo muttered, cheeks flushing.

"The Treaty is Linnia's responsibility," Kainon continued. "We can't have an outlander traipsing about with no understanding of how to respect the dragons properly."

Commander Sherin tapped her nails on the table. She studied him, her expression carefully bland. "Commander Barner warned in his report that you may resist using every advantage, Protector Kainon."

Kainon struggled against the urge to argue otherwise.

The commander's gaze slid to the braid in Kainon's hair. "At this stage, I'm willing to accommodate you, if only because you're Amela's former student. But don't test my patience, dragon-speaker."

"Yes, commander."

She studied him a moment longer. "Very well. The knotbinder can stay here for now. I suggest you prepare yourself for tomorrow, Kainon. If Tlalam's mood improves, you should outlive the day."

20

MATTEO STRODE OUTSIDE AFTER KAINON, feeling his cheeks burn with anger. "What's your problem, Kainon?"

The Protector paused on the steps, taking a deep breath. The rapid beating of drums reverberated beyond the walls, combined with raucous singing and the tinkling of bells. Matteo wondered what it meant but was too mad to ask.

"I don't expect you to understand," Kainon said tersely, heading across the courtyard to the stables.

Matteo matched his gait. "Damn right, I don't!" He gritted his teeth as they entered the stables, and Kainon made for the oversized stall Fira had claimed for herself. "You said I was disrespectful!"

"That's *not* what I said, Matteo."

Matteo scowled. "What, then? Why don't you trust me?"

The stableboy saw their approach and set aside his curry combs and discretely went outside.

They paused at Fira's stall, where she lifted her head out of a nest of hay, chirruping and huffing with urgency.

Kainon raised a hand to quieten her before scritching around her chin beard.

Matteo folded his arms, feeling hurt close his throat. "You said you'd help me petition Tlalam."

"I did."

"Then what's changed? Have I done something wrong?"

Kainon sighed and turned to meet his gaze. "No, Matteo, far from it."

Matteo could only scowl in confusion.

"My injuries weren't solely from the green dragon. Tlalam wanted to hurt me, Matteo." Scrubbing a hand over his face, Kainon said, "I can't expose you to the same risk."

Matteo shuffled his feet. "I didn't know." He suddenly felt foolish.

Kainon grimaced. "It's not—there are few people I would count as friends, and most of them are back in Briarfall. I don't trust easily, and in truth, I've had little need. You're very unexpected, Matteo."

Feeling a rush of relief, Matteo said, "I trust you, too."

"Then let me travel across the lake to Tlalam alone this time. Once I know it's safe, I'll bring you across. But I don't trust him to treat you well because of your association with me. He's vindictive right now, not only because I've been away for four summers. Let me discover what is going on." Kainon looked at him earnestly. "Will you trust me and wait just a little bit longer? I swear I'll do everything I can to help you get the answers you need."

Matteo swallowed. It felt like a lifetime since he left Darsha, and while he understood Kainon's reasons to delay, it still chafed. There could be other Rhun hunting parties in Linnia. Matteo had to find and warn other knotbinders before it was too late.

"How long must I wait?" he asked.

"I can't say. Dragons don't view time as we do."

Matteo appreciated Kainon's honesty but despaired at

the prospect of waiting while the dragon-speaker curried Tlalam's favor.

"And before you suggest it, don't offer a braid until you stand before Tlalam yourself. Take this time to carefully consider what to ask him, as he may purposely misunderstand."

Matteo resisted a sigh. It had taken no small effort to heal Kainon from what the green dragon had done to his mind. "Is it safe for *you* to go to the Sanctuary?"

Kainon gave a faint smile. "I'll be careful."

Matteo scowled at the non-answer. He wanted to challenge Kainon further, but the feverish drumming and shouting outside the chapter house proved distracting.

Kainon seemed to notice and latched onto it. "The pilgrims are celebrating. It's a great privilege to stand under a dragon's shadow."

"They don't realize we were all nearly roasted?"

"It's better this way. Come along and see."

Matteo frowned.

Kainon waved at Fira, who seemed disinclined to investigate. She burrowed back into the straw until only the tips of her wings were visible.

Leaving the stables, they crossed the courtyard and climbed the stairs to walk along the stone parapet and look over the pilgrim buildings. They had a clear view over the shore of Bone Lake, where pilgrims either knelt or danced with hands raised to the sky as they moved to a steady beat. A robed man had a pipe that created a low, whooshing sound each time he blew out his cheeks. It reminded Matteo of the sound of a dragon in flight.

The lake was still and quiet, the only movement being a band of mist close to the island.

Captain Sebani was already on the wall. Dressed in

leather armor and a matching helm, she looked more like a soldier on patrol than a Protector.

Kainon had no qualms coming up beside Sebani. He leaned against the stone wall.

"Everything well?" Captain Sebani asked, not taking her gaze from the celebrating pilgrims.

"It will be," Kainon said.

Sebani raised an eyebrow, looking between Matteo and Kainon before nodding. She pointed with her chin at the pilgrims. "Damned fools don't know how close we came. They have no idea about the constant negotiations we must make with dragons just to survive."

Matteo gave the captain a curious look.

Noticing his regard, Sebani's expression eased and she winked. "Reverence and respect, Matteo. That is how we protect Linnia's future."

Movement out on the water dragged Matteo's gaze back to the mist.

"Strange that Fira isn't down there amongst the pilgrims," Sebani noted. "They'd pamper the fickle beast as if she were the last dragon in Linnia."

"I think the green dragon frightened her," Kainon said.

"What about Tlalam? Does he blame her for your absence?" Sebani asked.

Kainon grimaced. "He's ignoring Fira for now. Possibly because she's still too small to be a threat, or maybe because she'll be a full gold once she matures."

Matteo tilted his head. "What does that mean?" He recalled Sebani mentioning something about Tlalam's coloring. "Is she royalty?"

The captain snorted. "Don't let Fira hear you say that."

Ignoring Sebani, Kainon said, "Gold means Fira's guided

by destiny. Once she's completed her purpose, the color will fade to black."

Matteo glanced down at the stable roof in wonder. "I had no idea."

"Fira doesn't know what her great purpose is yet. Which she uses to her advantage," Kainon added dryly.

In sudden understanding, Matteo said, "That's why Tlalam let you escort her to the Uhur Mountains."

"Yes, although I fear he won't be so accommodating in the future."

TLALAM'S ROAR brought Kainon to his feet before he was fully awake.

Every inch of his skin pebbled in fright. He stared about the darkness of the room and saw Matteo stir fitfully. He swallowed against the rush of sourness in his mouth.

'Dragon-speaker,' Tlalam hissed in his mind.

Kainon felt the weight of the dragon's rage build as another roar gathered deep in Tlalam's throat.

"No!" he gasped

Tlalam bellowed, the roar so loud that the shutters trembled.

Matteo launched off the pallet, tripping over himself in panic.

Kainon grasped both sides of his head, expecting terrible pain, but nothing came. He panted, his breath short in his lungs as golden light leached from the braid in his hair.

"Tlalam's attacking you!" Matteo gasped.

The enchantment in the braid held firm rather than turning to ash. It glowed brighter, its magic far from spent.

Realization suddenly struck Kainon, and he bolted to Amela's room. The aging dragon-speaker appeared sunken and frail under the blankets. The shutters were wide open, showing moonlight on the lake.

Kainon skidded to a halt beside Amela and gripped her hand. Rapid footsteps behind him showed that Matteo followed.

The boy put his hand on Amela's chest and waited for long heartbeats. "She breathes, Kainon."

Kainon sat back in relief.

Fire lit up the northern side of the Sanctuary island. Pilgrims gathered on the shore, pointing and exclaiming.

Kainon stretched his mind toward the island. '*Please*,' he begged. '*Spare Amela.*'

A spike of interest came from Tlalam as if the dragon was surprised Kainon could still form words.

Kainon realized his mistake just as another terrible roar shook the chapter house. Nervous screams rang up from the pilgrims as they scattered toward the buildings lining the shore.

Kainon threw himself over Amela ins some futile attempt to protect her. The pressure in his head built, but the pain was unable to find purchase, instead skimming like a pebble skipping across the lake's surface.

Blood dribbled out of Amela's nose.

'*Honored Tlalam*,' Kainon sent out with effort. '*I beg that you let her live.*'

Matteo pushed him aside, rapidly weaving something into Amela's hair. He winced as the dragon roared again. The braid unraveled between his fingers, and Matteo cursed under his breath. "Dar, protect us all," he whispered, trying again.

Each knot turned to ash scarcely moments after Matteo

finished weaving them. His hands glowed, leaking magic even as the shutters shook from the dragon's next roar.

Kainon realized then it was too late.

Amela's eyes were open and vacant, her chest unmoving. In the stables, Fira released a low keen.

Kainon sank to the floorboards. Tears burned behind his eyelids.

"I'm sorry," Matteo said, voice heavy with regret. "The knots won't hold."

Kainon nodded, knowing it wasn't his fault. There wasn't a magic in all of Linnia that could stand against a dragon's attack. Whatever strange alchemy kept himself alive surely couldn't last.

Before he could brace himself, Tlalam's heavy presence rammed into Kainon's mind again, searing through his memories and discarding them like worthless debris. Bile rose in Kainon's throat as he tried to fight off the creature. The dragon seemed to find something that stirred his greed.

Tlalam's voice swept through like an icy wind. *'Bring me the knotbinder.'*

21

THE BARGE SAT MOORED on the shore, guarded by two Protectors who owlishly blinked with the weariness of a long night spent watching raucous pilgrims. One gave Kainon a nod as he and Matteo neared the barge. Behind the chapter house, dawn was little more than uncertain greyness through the mist.

Most pilgrims had retired to their tents or other accommodation in town, though a few still wandered the shoreline or dozed on the pebbled banks.

Fira loitered on the rocks, her expression crestfallen. '*Tell Tlalam you're mine, Kainon,*' she complained.

'*I'll convey the sentiment,*' Kainon said, rubbing her shoulder.

He found it curious Fira had made no demands on Matteo. The knotbinder would likely weave Tlalam a braid —he carried a pack with strips of leather and silk ribbon for that very purpose—but Fira hadn't wheedled so much as a knot of well-wishing from Matteo as they prepared for the journey across Bone Lake.

'*I'm not Tlalam,*' Fira said, revulsion in her tone. She'd

liked Amela well enough, especially after the dragon-speaker showed her the secret passage to the chapter house's kitchens. Fira swiveled her head to blink at Kainon. *'He'll eat me if I come with you.'*

Kainon nodded. *'Will you wait for us here?'*

She eyed the pilgrims on the shore, her golden eyes gleaming. *'I can.'*

Sebani stood in quiet conversation with the bargeman. Mist rolled around the barge, having grown thick during the night. Dew made the floor and railing slick and cold.

Matteo looked over Bone Lake with interest. It worried Kainon how quickly the boy had accepted the turn of events. He feared Matteo didn't quite understand what he stood to lose in his quest to find other Darshians.

Tlalam's gloating presence cast a deep pall over everything.

Smothering a sigh, Kainon motioned to Matteo to step onto the barge. He felt determined not to look out over the water.

"Time to go," Sebani said quietly.

The bargeman unhooked the rope and gently pushed the barge away from the shore. Immediately, a gentle current gripped the vessel and pulled them toward the center of the lake.

Some believed the current was due to the magic leaching from the dead dragon's bones. Very little was known about the dragon beyond that it had fallen to its death in a storm. Dragons rarely spoke of the dead except in tales of extraordinary heroism and misdeeds. Tlalam had only spoken of Linnia's reverence to Bone Lake with bemused disdain, leading Kainon to assume that the fallen dragon was notable only because of where it had died.

Kainon glanced back at Fira back at the shore. Even on a

grey morning, she gleamed.

Matteo leaned over the railing and gazed into the clear water, where pebbles gave way to sand and submerged tree trunks.

"Careful," Kainon murmured. He didn't want to discover what would happen if the boy fell into the depths.

Matteo gave him a curious look but trustingly stepped back.

Closer to the Sanctuary island, the water grew dead still, without so much as a ripple caused by their approach. The barge slowed, released from its mysterious current. They drifted to a stop, the barge rocking gently from side to side before settling.

Matteo leaned over the rail. "I can see the bones," he said, voice reverent. "They're bleached white."

Sebani pressed a hand to her heart. "Nothing touches the bones. Not fish, not algae, not Linnians."

"It's why we have a chapter house here," Kainon said quietly. "There are folk beyond Linnia who see great value in the bones."

Sebani's mouth curled. "Aye, they'd boil them like in a stew and leach out all that makes them magical." She looked ready to spit but fortunately refrained. "A person could get very rich by stealing from dragons—if they live long enough."

A rumbling came from the depths of the water. Kainon glanced about, but no one else seemed to hear it. It grew in intensity, and he held his breath.

'*Give him to me...*'

Kainon stepped away from the railing, heart in his throat.

'*A princely gift.*'

Kainon swallowed, his gaze drawn to Matteo. His braids

were bright even in the uncertain light.

Kainon closed his eyes. "No," he whispered.

'Lower him to the depths. I will repay thee gladly.'

Kainon felt pressure in his mind. He pinched the bridge of his nose, sniffing.

Matteo frowned. "Kainon?"

He mustered a smile. "It's nothing," he said.

Matteo gave him a measuring look, eyes falling on the enchantment in Kainon's hair. The braid was intact, but Kainon wondered if Matteo could sense it at work.

"All is well," Kainon promised.

Matteo's fingers twitched as if with the urge to create another braid, but he trustingly nodded.

Kainon breathed a little easier. *'Matteo's not yours to have,'* he pushed out with his mind.

'Matteo. Matteo. Matteo.'

The knotbinder suddenly glanced at the water, frowning.

The mist coalesced around them and pushed against the barge. The vessel rocked from side to side hard enough for everyone to cling to the railings.

Sebani cursed and grabbed a hook. She leaned over the edge of the barge and splashed the hook about. The barge rocked again. Matteo gripped the railing as the barge pitched and yawed.

'I hunger! Feed me!'

Sebani gave a triumphant shout, fishing a rope from the water.

"Quickly!" Kainon ordered, bodily shoving Matteo along the barge.

They grabbed the rope from Sebani and heaved. The barge fought them for a few heartbeats as if held in a terrible grip.

They heaved again, and suddenly they were free. The barge skimmed along the water, away from the bones, heading rapidly towards the island.

They hit the shore with a gravelly hiss. The wooden ramp hit the ground with a thump, and the bargeman all but tumbled out in his rush to be free.

"Out, my friends," Sebani said, her voice shaky. "Quickly. We've upset it."

"Him," Kainon managed. "The bones are from a male."

Sebani stared at him for a moment before nodding. "Very well. Let's not anger *him* further. Go, Matteo. Grab your things before the lake ensnares us again."

They quickly jumped onto the pebbled shore.

"Has that ever happened before?" Matteo asked, blue eyes wild as he took backward steps toward the trees, his eyes on the water.

"The barge tends to get stuck over the bones," Sebani conceded with a mild shrug. "We usually drop a gold coin to appease it."

Matteo stared at the quietening water. "I didn't see anything but the bones."

Sebani nodded. "No one's entirely sure where the coins go."

"A dead creature's hoard," the bargeman muttered, making a sign of protection.

"Enough of that," Sebani ordered. "We stay put until the dragon-speaker and his companion return."

Kainon smothered a grimace. He turned to gaze up at the stone wall visible through about a hundred feet of trees and vines. Linnia built the wall following the Treaty when bandits were drawn to the island by stories of a dragon hoard ripe for the taking.

Kainon had never paid much attention to the Sanctuary

gates, having never seen them closed before. The gate was silver, with whorls and inscriptions delicately inscribed across the metal. There appeared to be no pattern or reason to the markings, but Kainon knew Tlalam would never accept the gates if they did not contain some rarity or magic.

He and Matteo stood together before the gate.

"We come at your behest, Honored Tlalam," Kainon called out. "We respectfully request an audience with you."

Kainon held his breath, mentally bracing himself for Tlalam to scorch his way into his thoughts. Long heartbeats passed.

The gate groaned before being pushed open by unseen hands. Sebani and the bargeman knelt on one knee with their heads bowed. A forest awaited within, eerily quiet and devoid of fingerlings. The path ended a scant few feet beyond the gate. Kainon knew they would have to forge their own way to Tlalam.

Matteo looked expectantly at Kainon.

"Carefully, Matteo. Don't let him trick you into giving promises you can't keep," Kainon warned.

"I understand," he replied.

"We'll be waiting, my friends," Sebani promised.

Hoping it was enough, Kainon motioned Matteo to enter the Sanctuary.

An eerie stillness gripped the forest. It should have been alive with raucous little serpents. The gnarled tree trunks held time-smoothed hollows and nests, the earth a warren of holes leading to underground burrows. Amidst the roots, Kainon spied glittering gems and flashes of gold and silver. Evidence of bickering between fingerlings showed on scorched rocks and charred branches.

But Kainon heard nary a skitter of talons on stones or

slithering in the leaf mold. A lone bird let out a cautious trill in the distance as if unsure of its welcome.

Kainon frowned, scanning the tree canopy. "Tlalam must have sent the fingerlings away," he mused. "Or it's too dangerous for the little ones to stay. Tlalam's moods are legendary for a reason."

Matteo swallowed uneasily.

Despite the absence of a path, Kainon strode unerringly amidst the trees and crossed a stream sprouting from a fissure within the rocks. Abandoned treasures littered the earth, some tarnished with age and neglect.

Kainon grew increasingly worried. "Each fingerling's hoard is hard-won. They wouldn't have abandoned them lightly."

"Are any still here?"

Kainon shook his head. "Not one. Though I can't tell where they have gone."

Eventually, the trees parted to reveal a clearing where a temple awaited. It was startlingly austere, made of pale stone and bereft of sculptures or decorative etchings. No fingerlings had burrowed into the stone to make themselves a little cave, and no lichen or moss dared make purchase on the outer walls.

Kainon eyed the five steps leading into the temple with an air of resignation.

Much of the temple bore no roof. The sun baked the white stone, with heat radiating in waves. Nervous sweat gathered along Kainon's spine.

At the far end of the temple was an alcove, the shadows within deep and ominous.

'*My wayward Speaker,*' Tlalam hissed in welcome.

22

THE DRAGON STEPPED out from the alcove.

Matteo resisted the urge to retreat. He and the dragon's head were of equal height. Tlalam was predominately deep indigo, but some of the individual scales on his neck were patchy and muddied to a pale grey. He was bereft of chin spikes like Fira, but two great horns rose from the back of his head. He lumbered out as if the movement was an effort, his round belly scraping across the tiles. To Matteo's untrained eye, Tlalam's wings appeared withered with disuse, and he wondered if the dragon had even flown in the last century.

The dragon turned his head, and Matteo caught sight of a snaggletooth—on a fingerling, it would have looked charming, but there was nothing sweet or endearing about Tlalam.

Kainon's expression was tight, green eyes slightly distant, and Matteo knew he spoke with the dragon. He felt the hot sting of the knots in Kainon's hair working hard.

Tlalam rumbled after a time. "I will indulge you,

dragon-speaker," he growled, his voice a rasping hiss. "And allow the pilgrim to converse with me."

Matteo's mouth fell open.

"Thank you, Honored Tlalam," Kainon said, bowing deeply. "I live to serve your people."

A low, stuttering huff came from the dragon, and Matteo realized it was laughter. "Do not play with words, boy. I know whose company you keep."

Matteo stiffened, wondering if Tlalam somehow knew about his killing braids.

"Fira is of the Catsyn line, and your close cousin," Kainon countered. "It's my privilege to accompany her."

"I know who she is," Tlalam growled. "Just as she knows my wishes."

Kainon bowed again. "Of course, Honored Tlalam."

"I do not care for her defiance, Linnian. She is to make the great flight soon," Tlalam announced.

Matteo risked a glance at Kainon.

Kainon turned pale but nodded stiffly. "I'll convey the message, but we're here as a matter of urgency," he said. "We humbly ask for your wisdom."

The dragon's tail swished across the tiles in agitation. "I grow weary of Linnians and your begging," Tlalam announced.

Kainon said, "Perhaps our gift will be worthy of your time, Honored Tlalam."

The dragon's great slitted eyes did not so much as blink in interest. "Bring it forth, Speaker. I will decide if it is worthy of me."

Kainon urged Matteo a few steps closer. "Carefully, Matteo," he murmured under his breath.

Taking a quelling breath, Matteo crossed the heated tile

floor, his gaze drawn almost helplessly to the dragon's snaggle tooth.

Tlalam rumbled. "I smell no mastery upon you, pilgrim. Anything you provide is an amateur's gift."

Matteo froze.

The dragon swung his massive head toward Kainon, hissing. "How dare you think this worthy of me, Speaker."

Kainon remained unflinching. "He bears the magic of a dying people," he stated. "You know how many of his people are left."

"I suppose."

"Even now, his enemies hunt him," Kainon pressed. "It's possible no knotbinder will ever stand before you again."

The dragon gave a low hiss.

Swallowing to clear his throat, Matteo said, "But I seek to find a new teacher, honored dragon." He resisted promising to encourage them to seek their own answers from the Sanctuary dragon.

Tlalam unleashed a dark chuckle. "I know your potential, pilgrim. What you seek is closer than you think."

Matteo stepped forward, hope choking his words.

"Where might he find his people, Honored Tlalam?" Kainon asked.

"There is a price, dragon-speaker," Tlalam warned. "But I do not think that is the most pressing question you bring to me," he added, his voice sly.

"Not a question, Honored Tlalam," Kainon said. "It appears we have disrespected your people. Linnia seeks to make amends."

The dragon chuckled. "Do you, now? I suspect you will not like what is asked of you in return."

Kainon's brow furrowed. "Honored Tlalam—"

"I grow bored of you, Speaker, and have nothing to soothe me," Tlalam warned with a hiss.

Kainon glanced urgently at Matteo.

Slipping the pack off his shoulder, Matteo knelt and fished out a handful of silk ribbons. He debated momentarily, letting his palm skim across them before the inkling to choose the black ribbons called to him. Making a braid without an intended person was difficult and inherently doomed to fail, but creating a killing braid to give to a dragon seemed like folly. He glanced hesitantly up at the dragon, gaze catching on a handful of scales that were murky with age. Kainon had promised no human magic could kill a dragon, but he didn't know if a Darshian knotbinder had ever tried.

"I want what feeds a prideful god, pilgrim," the dragon said. "I care little for what brings you shame."

Matteo blinked up at the dragon, thinking. He instead chose a handful of deep blue ribbons that Kainon had insisted he bring amid mutterings about Tlalam's vanity. He thought of the Day of Testing in his village, when all Darshian children in their fifth summer take up leather twine tied to a newel post and make a knot in honor of Dar. Matteo remembered stepping free of the crowd of onlookers when the knotbinder called his name. His fingers had ached with cold as he'd gripped the wet leather, but then he'd closed his eyes and allowed golden warmth to bloom for the first time.

"Yes," Tlalam hissed, drawing close. His brimstone breath soured the air.

Matteo let his fingers weave the first knot and then a handful more his teacher had imparted upon him. An ache caught in his throat. Darsha had been a kingdom of magic nestled amongst mountains and frozen streams. The Rhun had taken that from him, and he still didn't know why. He wondered if he would ever understand.

"Be sure of your gift, pilgrim," Tlalam warned.

Matteo opened his eyes and studied the braid, feeling the knowledge of his homeland and the knots of Dar melding together. He nodded shakily. "I'm certain."

Tlalam's head slid sinuously into view. His snaggletooth was almost as long as Matteo's forearm. The dragon's tongue scooped up the braid into his mouth.

Tlalam bit down.

Agony suddenly ripped through Matteo. Screaming, he fell to his knees. In his mind, something bright and golden snapped, disintegrating like ash in the wind.

Kainon gripped his shoulder and squeezed hard. He pulled him out of easy reach of the dragon.

Panting, Matteo turned his hands over, staring at his fingers and their strange emptiness. They twitched, but the knowledge of how to turn the knots was missing. He choked down a cry of anguish.

With a satisfied rumble, Tlalam said, "Now we may discuss the consequences of your transgression, dragon-speaker."

His emerald eyes narrowed with dark promise.

KAINON'S SPINE tightened in warning. He sensed Tlalam's mood change now that the dragon had what he wanted. "I stand before you to understand and make amends, Honored Tlalam. But will you not first grant Matteo his answer?"

"I will speak no more of a dying magic," Tlalam announced coldly.

Matteo gasped, face pale and drawn. "But—"

"Your dissatisfaction means nothing, pilgrim!" Tlalam roared, causing the slate roof of the alcove to quiver. "You come with your platitudes and groveling in the company of this dragon-speaker. He means something to you?"

Matteo stumbled back a pace, his blue eyes bright with confusion. "I—yes."

"So you share in the transgression!"

Tlalam reared back, spiked tail snapping back and forth, uncaring of the temple columns. He smashed through them, stone and wooden beams crumbling and shattering about him.

Kainon and Matteo scrambled back, barely escaping the debris.

"What transgression?" Kainon called up.

Tlalam rose to his full height. The sedentary years in the temple had done him little favor. Bloated on the easy pickings of pilgrim offerings, he could barely stand under his weight, leg muscles trembling. His underbelly had likely not seen sunlight in a lifespan and was now the color of moist fungi.

Kainon pushed down his disgust before Tlalam could sense it. "A dragon flew across Bone Lake. She carried an egg that won't be laid in the Breeding Sands. You must know why!"

"Oath breakers," Tlalam hissed, his voice rumbling through the temple.

'*Liars and traitors,*' Tlalam spat in Kainon's mind.

Kainon gripped the sides of his head as Tlalam's voice stabbed through him.

'*Are all dragon-speakers so perfidious?*'

"There are no others," Kainon gasped as the pressure built in his head. "You saw to that yourself." He clenched his eyes shut, stumbling. Something hot and wet gathered on his upper lip. He wiped it free to discover blood. He feared his ears bled, too.

"Kainon!" Matteo hissed, his grip keeping Kainon upright.

"You think we didn't know," Tlalam hissed. "We have watched since the first offence. No more!"

Kainon fell to his knees. "Please," he gasped. "What transgression?"

Tlalam roared, the sound like a giant sword cleaving Kainon's mind in two. Blood dripped from Kainon's eyes. The shredding pain took his breath and reduced his world to a single hot ember of agony.

I'm dying, he realized.

Matteo fell beside him, frantically gripping a thick lock of Kainon's hair as if to braid it. "I don't know how!" he choked out.

Matteo's hand brushed against the braid woven at Bone Lake. It burst to life in a blast of light.

Soothing coolness washed over Kainon's mind like a foaming ocean tide, washing clean the hot embers burning through his mind. He gulped, breath shuddering, his lungs loosening. His vision cleared to see Matteo hovering over him, blue eyes confused and wondering.

"I don't understand," Matteo whispered.

Kainon swallowed. He hadn't the strength to explain that Tlalam had taken Matteo's knowledge, not the power within him.

Tlalam suddenly loomed into view.

Kainon shoved Matteo out of the way. He shakily pushed himself to his knees. "Turn your anger on me, mighty Tlalam," he said raggedly, arms raised. "I beg you spare the knotbinder."

"*No,*" he hissed. His mind scraped against Kainon's but found no purchase.

Kainon bowed deeply, forehead pressing against the hot tiles. "I humbly beg the chance to make this right."

"You and the knotbinder."

Kainon raised his head in confusion.

"The Treaty is a shell of what it once was. The Great Razing will be upon Linnia if you fail. Our patience has ended."

Fresh terror gripped Kainon's guts. The Great Razing would burn all of Linnia to ash. The Treaty had been the only thing to stop it millennia before.

"I am sworn to prevent the Great Razing, as all Protectors are," Kainon managed, voice hoarse. "What must I do—"

"I weary of your blathering. I have spared you both. Your redemption lies in sand and water."

Kainon hesitated, glancing at Matteo. He stood pale and shaking with blood smeared on his palms. "The knotbinder will need to know how to weave the knots if he's to serve you well," Kainon said.

"Does he?" Tlalam replied darkly. The dragon turned his attention to Matteo, smoke curling from his maw. "Your magic sits so sweetly in my belly, knotbinder. Be careful you don't reside there, also."

"Yes, Honored Tlalam," Matteo replied, face drawn.

Swiveling his head back to Kainon, Tlalam said, "You will not enjoy so comfortable a fate, dragon-speaker, should you fail us. I will char off every limb until you are but a nub, and you shall sit upon the walls of Pelan as it burns."

Bile rose in Kainon's throat. "I understand."

"Stupid human. I don't think you do."

Tlalam raised his snout to the air and suddenly leapt.

The powerful beat of his wings disgorged more debris, momentarily blinding Kainon. When his vision cleared, Kainon saw Tlalam high above them, taking slow, laborious wingbeats as he turned north to the Uhur Mountains.

23

THEY CLIMBED over crumbling stones and smashed columns to escape the ruined temple.

Matteo numbly slid down a large slab of marble. His hands felt numb and strange, the familiar warm hum of magic gone. Dar must surely despise him for trading his gift to a dragon who treated it like sweetmeats.

He stumbled, fearing the ache in his throat would never leave.

"Touch nothing," Kainon cautioned, steering Matteo from a bolt of cloth so dark it seemed to swallow all light.

Unable to help himself, Matteo looked at the callouses on his thumbs. Soon enough, they would fade. His breath hitched. "You tried to warn me," he rasped.

Dust on Kainon's face gave him a mournful look. "You can't blame yourself for having hope."

"But we learnt *nothing*," Matteo said, his throat tightening with despair.

Kainon slowed to a stop, green eyes careworn as he turned Matteo to face him. "Tlalam doesn't lie." He gripped both of Matteo's shoulders. "He said what you want is nearby."

"But Tlalam said that before I gave him the braid!"

"Aye, but that doesn't make it any less true." Kainon's eyes grew earnest. "Take heart, Matteo. There are other towns along the Pilgrim Road, and your teacher is likely at one of them. They're likely only days away. Tlalam confirmed there are still knotbinders in Linnia."

Matteo swallowed heavily, unable to shake the despair that swelled up whenever he looked at his hands. There was a stillness about them as if a life had ended. "They won't want me, Kainon," he whispered. "I have nothing to offer."

Kainon squeezed his shoulders. "That's not true. You need only look at me—you saved me from sharing Amela's fate."

Matteo shrugged helplessly. "I don't know what I did," he admitted.

"It's because your magic isn't gone. You can learn to weave the knots again."

"I hope so," Matteo said.

They entered the forest. Birds chattered and trilled as if knowing a great predator had left.

Kainon wiped the blood from his ears with the edge of his tunic.

With an effort, Matteo forced himself to think of what else Tlalam said. "Tlalam threatened you with the Great Razing."

Kainon nodded. "Linnia came close before Tlalam convinced the other dragons to agree to the Treaty. Should they decide to raze Linnia, nothing will survive." He climbed over a fallen tree. "I'm sorry Tlalam has tangled you up in this."

But Matteo had grown used to a fate that was not his own. "He gave us little to go on."

Grimacing, Kainon said, "I have to assume Tlalam doesn't want Linnia destroyed, or he wouldn't have tasked us with stopping it." He looked skyward, squinting in thought. "Perhaps we should head for Pelan and see the written Treaty itself. Dragons and mages created it—maybe there's something in the pages that can guide us."

Matteo shrugged. "He said something about sand and water—was he talking about the Breeding Sands?"

Kainon grunted. "You may be on to something there. The Treaty lets dragons and humans peacefully share this land, except for the Sands," Kainon continued. "No one may enter."

"Has someone stolen a dragon's egg?"

Kainon shook his head. "We'd already be dragon fodder if that was the case." He nodded, suddenly more resolute. "We should get back to the chapter house and warn the commander of our quest."

They navigated the forest, trekking the stream that led towards the gate.

Matteo wondered if journeying to the Breeding Sands would take him from the one chance he had of finding his teacher. He bit his lip, recalling Tlalam's threat of being eaten. "What does it mean that Tlalam left?"

Kainon shook his head, the purpose in his eyes cooling. "I don't know. There's always been a dragon at the Sanctuary."

Matteo caught flashes of the outer wall through the foliage. He slowed at the sound of upraised voices beyond the trees.

"It's the pilgrims," Kainon said, pausing to listen.

"They must have crossed Bone Lake," Matteo said. He

wondered if the submerged bones gave the pilgrims a difficult time as well.

"Tlalam's departure will have upset them." Kainon gave Matteo a thin-lipped look. "The Protectors may need our help."

They reached the gate to see pilgrims clamoring for a view. A contingent of Protectors guarded the gates, stopping any pilgrim from entering the Sanctuary. Sebani stood at the helm with her spear pointed toward the crowd.

To Matteo's alarm, Fira was drawn to the island as well. The dragonling looked to have been thrust behind the Protectors, her tail spikes bristling with agitation.

"There they are!" a white-haired man shouted, pointing over the Protectors to Matteo and Kainon. "Traitors!"

Matteo froze, startled.

"You angered Tlalam!" another pilgrim hollered, her face red with outrage. "He abandoned the Sanctuary because of you!"

"Look! Tlalam tried to smite them for the insult!" the first man shouted, waving frantically at the blood on Kainon's tunic.

Kainon blinked in astonishment before nudging Matteo backwards. "Perhaps we should retreat."

The crowd heaved forward, shoving against the barrier of Protectors. The Protectors held firm against the first wave. More pilgrims surged up from the shore, shouting questions about Tlalam's whereabouts. A handful of pilgrims sat on the barge and wept in anguish or terror.

Fira stood up on her hindquarters behind the Protectors to watch the crowd with alarmed curiosity.

"Look how they stop us attending to the next Sanctuary guardian!" a new voice shouted, and attention turned to Fira.

"They want the dragon for themselves!"

"The Protectors broke the Treaty!"

"Save the dragon!"

The crowd roared with battle cries and curses. Sebani shouted an order, and the Protectors tightened ranks, clamoring together at the entrance. A handful drew their swords. The roaring grew louder and more fervent.

Kainon unleashed a sharp whistle.

Fira swiveled her golden head, looking torn between the wild adulation of the crowd and whatever Kainon said in her mind.

The crowd surged forward with a terrible roar. The Protectors stood firm, shouting warnings before rushing forward to meet the attack.

Pilgrims raised swords, staffs and random sticks. An arrow flew over the crowd and struck a Protector in the neck. She fell, and her companions surged forward. The Protectors and pilgrims met with a thunderous crash.

"Protect the dragon queen!" a pilgrim shouted.

Kainon ran for Fira, who watched the melee with curiosity. Kainon obviously shouted at her with his mind, his hand reaching for her.

Fira hesitated, wings slightly outstretched as if uncertain whether to take flight.

Too late, for the pilgrims were upon her. They grabbed her wings and neck, pressing her down into the dirt. Others fought to keep the Protectors at bay, throwing their bodies against shields and armor.

Matteo sprinted, fearing Fira could get badly hurt in the scrum. She shrieked in fright, flapping her wings desperately. Pilgrims clung on, shouting as more piled onto her.

Kainon punched and kicked with desperate abandon. It

seemed to hardly make a difference. Fira bucked and tried desperately to take flight. Smoke billowed from her nostrils, but a pilgrim grabbed her by her chin bristles and shoved her snout hard into the dirt, cutting off whatever angle was necessary for her to unleash her flame.

Matteo sprinted to help Kainon. He yanked loose a pilgrim who clung to Fira's tail and barely escaped a dagger to the belly.

"You're hurting her!" Kainon yelled.

The pilgrims appeared not to hear him, desperate to keep hold of Fira. Her frantic thrashing only invigorated them more. Now that Tlalam was gone, they had no other dragon hope to cling to.

Matteo wrested another pilgrim off Fira, but it wasn't enough. He searched desperately for a Protector, but they were too busy fending off the rising tide of pilgrims.

Suddenly, Matteo was hauled off his feet. For a heartbeat, he expected a dagger to slide between his ribs. Instead, a blade pressed against his throat, and a thickly accented voice hissed in his ear, "Knotbinder."

The voice was vaguely familiar. Then Matteo saw the man's face.

Matteo froze.

"Make no fuss," the Rhun growled. "Your companion may yet survive us."

Matteo locked eyes with Kainon, who saw what was happening and tried desperately to reach him. The pilgrims buffeted the man back.

From the corner of his eye, Matteo saw more Rhuncavari. They wore the pale travel garb of pilgrims, but their expressions held none of the fanatical gleam apparent in the crowd. One watched Kainon for a few heartbeats before turning her back dismissively.

Kainon appeared caught between Fira and Matteo. He yanked a pilgrim off Fira's neck and hesitated.

The crowd surged, and Matteo lost sight of Kainon. The distance between him and Fira grew as the sea of bodies pushed him and the Rhun past the gate and onto the pebbled shore.

The Rhun buffeted and manhandled him toward a small rowboat pushed up against the shore. Matteo stumbled on the treacherous stones and was lifted toward the boat even as he bucked and kicked. The Rhun would surely kill him in the next few heartbeats.

Kainon suddenly barreled into the back of Matteo's captor. They all hit the ground hard. Kainon rolled to his feet, blade in hand and teeth bared. "Get behind me, Matteo," he ordered.

But another Rhun, a young woman, raised her fist and spat guttural words. Lines of dark blue light spewed out.

"Look out!" Matteo shouted.

A ball of magic crackled through the air and smashed into Kainon. Slammed off his feet, Kainon hit the rocks with a groan. The skin on his arms appeared to blacken momentarily.

The woman bared her teeth in a vicious grin, but her expression quickly soured when Kainon pulled himself up to his knees, panting. The braid in his hair flashed white-hot before steam rolled off his arms and revealed healthy skin beneath. Kainon shook his head as if to clear it.

Matteo tried to reach Kainon but was pulled back when someone grabbed a fistful of his tunic and wrenched him around. Matteo froze as a blade pressed against his throat. "Don't—!"

The Rhun sorcerer raised her fist again, light crackling.

Kainon appeared too dazed to notice.

Matteo didn't think he could survive another hit of magic.

"Nadiya. Enough." An older man with thick grey hair stepped into Matteo's line of sight and frowned fiercely. "The Protector should have fallen the first time."

The young woman, Nadiya, lifted her chin, eyes bright with insult. "My magic remains pure, Master Latan," she hissed.

"And yet he lives." The man, Latan, strode where Kainon knelt trembling and gasping for breath. He gripped Kainon by the back of the head and fished out the braid in Kainon's hair, running a thumb over the knots. Kainon appeared too dazed to notice.

"Your thoughts, Craise?" Latan said.

Another Rhun stepped forward, and Matteo's gaze fell to the bejeweled blade at his hip. Cold ran down Matteo's spine.

Craise's face turned contemplative. "It's rudimentary, done by someone poorly trained in knotbinder ways." He looked curiously between Matteo and Kainon. "Still, a heartfelt effort."

Matteo set his jaw. The fighting between the Protectors and pilgrims spilled down to the water's edge. He briefly saw Sebani in the melee.

"It's believed you offered the dragon a braid, knotbinder," Craise said, seemingly unconcerned by the fighting. "You'd only do so if you're certain your masters still live. Where are they?"

Matteo sneered. "We'll never tell you."

Craise smiled. "We?" He looked at Kainon. "The dragon told his secrets to both of you?"

Matteo's gaze fell helplessly to Kainon.

Kainon shook his head grimly. "Say nothing," he gritted out.

"Just end them both, my lord," Nadiya growled to Latan. "Let's be done with this wretched place."

"They both know where the remaining knotbinders cower." Latan made a two-fingered motion to the woman. "I'm sure we can encourage them to speak. Nadiya, please make our new companions comfortable."

"Yes, my lord."

Nadiya muttered something under her breath. A fresh ball of light burst from her and crackled over Kainon.

Kainon convulsed, a cry wrenched from deep in his throat.

Matteo leapt with his hand outstretched. Something struck the back of his head, and his vision spiraled into darkness.

24

ICY WATER SLAPPED Matteo violently awake.

Submerged, he flailed as his knees and elbows struck against river stones. His wrists were bound in front of him, making it difficult to reach the surface. Dirty lake silt filled his lungs, and he kicked until he emerged, gasping and coughing.

Cruel laughter came from the shore.

Before he could gain any footing, Matteo was dragged through the water and onto the muddy bank. He fell onto his elbows, gagging until his ribs ached.

Kainon stumbled to his knees beside him, drenched and gasping.

Matteo sagged with relief. "You're alive."

The braid in Kainon's hair was now impossible to ignore, bleached stark white by the enchantments working to keep him safe. Matteo didn't know how the braid withstood so many attacks when his other workings quickly turned to ash.

Splashing behind them made Matteo turn to see Nadiya jump from the rowboat. She sloshed out of the water, knocking hard against Kainon's shoulder as she passed.

Four strangers in dark livery stood in the shadow of the trees. Horses waited with them, their reins tied to low-hanging branches.

Kainon glanced about quickly, assessing. "Nine Rhuncavari," he whispered. "It's the entire hunting party."

"Get the boat out of sight," the grey-haired Rhun, Latan, ordered from the beach.

One of the men saluted crisply. "Yes, my lord."

He and his companions dragged the small boat out of sight amongst the trees.

Still catching his breath, Matteo glanced over his shoulder and saw they had reached the very far side of the lake. The Sanctuary appeared scarcely more than a grey-green dot in the distance. Smoke plumed from the island and the chapter house on the opposite shore.

No other boats disturbed the lake.

Matteo wondered if the Protectors still dealt with pilgrims rioting on the island.

"Fira," he whispered, remembering the dragon's shrieks of pain.

Kainon set his jaw. "She lives," he muttered, voice barely noticeable over the waves lapping the shore. "She's sore and furious, but she lives."

They both knew it had been a near thing.

But Matteo's relief was tempered by the thought the pilgrims imprisoned her somehow. "What if—?"

"Sebani will do her duty," Kainon said. "The dragons come first." His gaze turned briefly skyward. "We must escape before Tlalam thinks we're avoiding his quest."

It was easy for a dragon to assume, given Kainon's reputation for prioritizing those he cared about.

Before Matteo could absorb what was happening, the rope tied to his wrists tugged him forward. Cursing, he stumbled to his feet, tripping over dead branches that had washed ashore. One of the Rhun, a dark-haired, thin-lipped man, tied the rope to a saddlebow and mounted. The rubied hilt of the flame blade sparkled. Matteo remembered the man's name.

Craise.

The man scowled but seemed unhurried.

Kainon glared at their captors as a newcomer tied his rope to another horse's saddle. "Rhun soldiers," he muttered under his breath.

Matteo looked at him sharply before looking at the strangers anew. The four soldiers maintained a respectful distance but cast sidelong glances at Latan and the four other Rhun. They seemed particularly wary of Nadiya, who selected from the waiting horses and mounted.

Matteo subtly checked the rope binding his wrists. When he'd first begun training as a knotbinder, he'd found unravelling the knots easier than weaving them. These knots were simple but tight and would only worsen once they dried. He glanced at Kainon's wrists, noting the same knotwork.

"I expect you to try, knotbinder," Craise said, leaning his elbow against his saddlebow, his eyes cold and dark. "But I know you'll disappoint."

Matteo glared up at him. "What makes you so certain?"

"*Matteo,*" Kainon hissed, giving a warning shake of his head.

Matteo knew it wasn't wise to antagonize the Rhun, but he couldn't help it.

Craise smirked. "The ability to weave the knots drains from you like water. My blade still wants you, but its interest isn't so—" He paused, his cold smile deepening the crinkles at the corner of his eyes. "Zealous."

Matteo swallowed and looked again at the smoke rising from chapter house in the distance. If Tlalam spoke truthfully and his teacher was not far away, the distance between them increased with every heartbeat. Perhaps that was for the best, considering.

"Maybe there are no other knotbinders," Matteo said. "Ever think of that?"

"Say nothing," Kainon hissed urgently.

Craise bared his teeth in a sharp grin. "I see the braid in your hair, the one showing your *ka-shi*—your connection to Dar's knotbinders."

Matteo felt the blood drain from his face.

"If you were the last knotbinder, the braid would now be ash."

"How—?" Matteo glared. "No knotbinder would teach you to read the knots."

"Ten summers is a long time," Craise said. He smiled again. "All sorts of secrets spill out from the hunted."

Matteo stared up at him in horror.

Latan nudged his horse beside them. "Torment him when the Protectors aren't so close, Craise," he said mildly. He nodded to the waiting soldiers. "Lead the way, sergeant."

A stocky man with pockmarked skin saluted. He took one of the remaining horses and led them to a game trail leading deep into the forest.

Matteo took a last, desperate glance over Bone Lake through the trees, but no Protectors rowed to their rescue. Did Sebani even know they were captives?

He'd imagined meeting his fate at the end of a Rhuncavari blade countless times, but as the trees closed around them, Matteo now feared that whatever the Rhun planned would be much worse.

KAINON STAYED quiet and watched his captors. His first instinct was to assume the one with the flame blade, Craise, was the leader. But he appeared wholly focused on Matteo. His hand rested on the hilt of the flame blade as if weighing up killing Matteo now or biding his time—for what, Kainon didn't know, but for now he'd settle for being grateful that Matteo was unharmed.

Schooling his face blank, Kainon had carefully listened and learned their captor's names.

The white-haired man, Latan, ignored them with a cold, bemused detachment, looking bony and hawkish on his horse, and Kainon wondered if he was the most dangerous of them all. He appeared to indulge Nadiya, the young woman who took the lead ahead of the Rhuncavar soldiers. Her suggestions were thinly veiled snarls, teeth bared in a vicious grin.

The man riding beside Kainon showed no interest in his companions, looking dark and brooding with caged violence held back only by order. Kainon remembered his deadly accuracy with a bow but had yet to learn his name. Matteo trudged as far from the man as the rope would allow. The boy occasionally rubbed his side as if pained.

Taking up the rear was a middle-aged woman who covered their trail; Craise had called her Alize, and scoffed because she preferred her own company.

Craise's obsession with Matteo set Kainon's teeth on edge. The man frequently looked back or took more difficult paths through the trees to ensure Matteo stumbled or struggled to keep up. The skin around Matteo's wrists already appeared rubbed raw. The knotbinder withstood it with a stoic kind of anger.

Kainon reached out to Fira. It hurt to sense her, buffeted as he was by her rage. Had she been a full-sized dragon, Kainon feared nothing could stop a new razing. As it was, Kainon expected Fira to destroy things in her anger. Reaching out to her felt like putting his hand to a flame. He jolted back, unable to tell if the Protectors had her or the riots had gone in the pilgrims' favor. His only comfort was that Fira lived.

The party avoided the roads and pilgrim trails, travelling deep into the forest. Kainon judged their direction as southeast, following the corridor of forest fingerlings used from the Breeding Sands to reach the Dragon Plains. Sebani must have noticed his and Matteo's absence by now, even if it meant searching the water and the ruins of the Sanctuary temple. It wouldn't take long for her to discern what had happened and muster a contingent to take chase.

They stopped for the night in a grove of pines shielded from the wind. A storm had harried them for most of the afternoon, and the soldiers set up awnings in preparation for rain. They left Kainon and Matteo tied to a tree opposite the picket line for the horses.

The Rhun death sorcerers sat on freshly chopped logs around the campfire. They spoke softly in Rhuncavari, and Kainon cursed himself for never bothering to learn their language. He noticed the older woman, Alize, was not among them.

A soldier dropped a strip of jerky in the dirt beside Kainon. Kainon wasn't so foolhardy as to refuse it. With the fingerlings avoiding them, he couldn't confirm their location but knew the Rhun took them further from the Breeding Sands. He resisted a flare of frustration.

Kainon glanced at Matteo's sullen face. Every passing candlemark took them further from the possibility of finding a new teacher for Matteo. The boy scarcely had time to process the loss of his gift before the Rhun captured them.

He nudged Matteo's knee with his boot. "You should eat," he said quietly. "We'll both need our strength."

Matteo looked set to argue for a few heartbeats before he sighed in resignation. He picked up his jerky and chewed without any enthusiasm. He watched Craise seated at the campfire with blue eyes darkened by loathing.

Kainon nudged him again. "There's more than one enemy here. Don't forget that."

Matteo looked at him sharply. "So many Darshians have died. How many do you think Craise and his cronies have killed?"

Kainon shook his head. It was a useless question.

"What Craise said earlier—do you think they know I can't remember how to weave any knots?"

Kainon rather expected they did. "You'd have broken fingers otherwise. It seems even the Rhun know the price of speaking with dragons."

Matteo looked dismayed. "I suppose so."

After a time, Craise left his seat at the campfire and crouched in front of them. A waterskin hung loosely in his grip. "Thirsty?" he asked.

Matteo looked away, his teeth clenched.

Keeping their strength was more important than their pride. Kainon nodded.

The Rhun smirked and handed the waterskin over. In doing so, the firelight caught on the hilt of his blade on his hip. The large sapphire on the hilt appeared dark and sullen.

Noticing Kainon's gaze, Craise smirked. He drew the blade and turned it about. "Beautiful, isn't it?"

It glowed in a way that seemed to consume the light around it.

"It belonged to the greatest death sorcerer of Rhuncavar. She gifted it to me. I've always been a promising student." Craise whispered an unfamiliar word, and the blade flared all the brighter. "A decade of feasting, and my blade is almost full." His voice took on a dream-like quality.

Kainon resisted the urge to lean back. "I don't understand. What do you mean that it's full?"

Craise smiled coldly. "This isn't the only flame blade forged in Rhuncavar, but it's special. Focused. It has feasted only on my chosen enemy, and when there are no more knotbinders, I'll be the most powerful sorcerer in all of Rhuncavar." He raised an eyebrow at Matteo. "There aren't many of you left. Did you know? I suppose you do, considering how messy your braids are. Not well trained, I see."

Matteo clenched his teeth. "You don't know anything about me."

Craise smirked. "I know more than you'd like, knotbinder. We're more similar than you'll ever want to admit."

Matteo turned his face away.

"You'll figure it out, boy. Right when I slip my blade between your ribs."

"Why wait?" Matteo asked sourly, turning back to glare at him.

"Matteo!" Kainon hissed, almost kicking him.

Craise grinned. "Oh, I am very tempted, knotbinder. My

blade yearns for you. Perhaps I'll grow weary of waiting and let it feed." He set the tip of the blade against Matteo's knee. "I can taste its hunger."

Matteo didn't move, balefully holding the man's gaze.

Chuckling, Craise tapped the blade twice on Matteo's leg before snatching back the waterskin.

Matteo glared at Craise as the man stalked away. The boy muttered something foul in Darshian.

Kainon leaned his back against the tree, thinking. Given the Rhun had hounded Matteo across two kingdoms, it was strange they held off killing him. There had been other opportunities, too, where the Rhun had stayed their hand. Kainon didn't know why, but he resolved to find out.

And use it to his and Matteo's advantage.

25

Matteo woke to garbled sobbing.

He bolted upright, heart in his throat, for one moment fearing something had happened to Kainon. But his companion stirred awake with a low curse, rolling to a crouch and reaching for a blade that was not there.

The camp was quiet, the Rhun having retired to underneath the awnings. The storm had mercifully circled wide of them but still made its presence known with flashes of lightning and the low boom of distant thunder.

Branches cracked underfoot as the Rhun hunter, Alize, emerged from the forest with a scrawny, bound man in tow. By his clothing, the captive was Linnian, likely kidnapped off a road or village miles from the camp. He was gagged, eyes wide and frightened as Alize manhandled him into the grove.

"Curse you," Kainon spat, clambering to his feet to pull at the rope tying him to the tree. "Let him go. What use could you have for him?"

Craise emerged from under one of the awnings, taking

in Alize's quarry. He grinned with relish. "Light the torches," he ordered the soldiers.

The camp quickly brightened, making Matteo squint. None of the Rhun showed signs of sleep, all fully dressed and waiting for Alize's return.

Craise pointed to a spot a few feet from Matteo and Kainon. "Put him there."

A cold rush of dismay hit Matteo's guts. Kainon stood protectively before him, his stance ready for a fight.

Latan presented Alize with a sword bearing a sapphire pommel.

If Matteo didn't know better, he'd think it was the flame blade, but Craise had it already sheathed at his hip.

Craise smiled humorlessly. "I told you that my flame blade remains pure, Matteo. It hardly means we didn't bring another for lesser work."

Matteo rasped, "What are you going to do?"

"Alize will show you." Craise tilted his head in mock contemplation. "I expect it's been some time since you last saw a feeding."

"I remember," Matteo blurted.

Craise smiled again. "Your Protector will benefit from a demonstration, yes?"

Kainon's lip curled. "Cut us loose first. Let's make things interesting."

Craise tilted his head, looking tempted, but then Alize kicked the back of her captive's legs. The villager fell to his knees and stared helplessly at Matteo and Kainon as Alize pressed the blade to his throat.

"It's not necessary, I promise you," Kainon spat. "We both saw what you did outside Briarfall."

"Ah, no surprises for you, then," Craise said, his tone disappointed. He nodded to Alize.

She lowered the sword by a handspan and dragged it across the man's chest. He unleashed a gurgling scream, eyes bulging in terrified pain. The stink of burning flesh made Matteo gag. The villager wrenched loose of Alize's grip and rolled desperately as if on fire. Alize pressed a boot hard into his shoulder to force him down flat.

Craise suddenly grabbed Matteo by the arm and wrenched him forward. He cut away the rope and shoved Matteo to the dying man. "Heal him," he ordered.

Matteo stared up at him in confused horror. "I-I can't. I don't know how." Even if the knowledge hadn't been taken from him, he remembered his failure at Briarfall. Injuries by a flame blade were beyond his abilities.

"The enchantment in the Protector's hair says otherwise."

Kainon tugged on the rope anchoring him to the tree. "Leave him out of your sick games, sorcerer!"

"My companions think you're liars," Craise said. "No matter. Knotbinders have a weird compulsion to heal. So, do it, boy. Weave the knots to spare this man from suffering," Craise said.

Matteo clenched his fists. The villager sniveled and trembled before him, but no golden magic stirred within.

"Matteo doesn't know how, curse you!" Kainon yelled.

Craise shrugged, eyes on Matteo. "If you wait too long, boy, we'll have to test your abilities on your Protector."

Wishing Dar would strike the Rhun all dead, Matteo grabbed a fistful of the man's hair. The man flinched as if expecting another blow.

Matteo's hands remained unmoving. Normally, his fingers began turning the knots, his heart instinctively knowing which braid most suited the injury. He'd never considered where his magic emerged from; it had always pooled in his palms unbidden. He remembered how it felt, warm and golden like a summer day. Kainon said the magic remained, but he wasn't so certain. The ability to create knots that sang with life was gone.

Beside him, the villager whimpered and curled in on himself.

"I'm satisfied," Latan said. He nodded to Alize.

Before Matteo could blink, Alize shoved him aside and drove the lesser flame blade to the hilt through the villager's throat. The blade briefly glowed sickly green. The villager gurgled, eyes bulging in shock as blood spurted across the ground.

Kainon yelled something, but Matteo barely heard over the buzzing in his ears. He scooted back, bile rising as the man died a scant foot away.

Latan appeared unmoved. "You may interrogate the prisoners, Craise, but I expect finesse."

Craise smiled coldly. "Of course, my lord."

Matteo edged backwards, closer to Kainon. The Rhun hunter squatted in front of them, the blade sheathed at his hip glowing brighter now that he was close to Matteo.

Craise smirked when Matteo minutely pulled away. "Where are the other knotbinders?"

Matteo shook his head, his mouth dry.

"The dragon told you where they are," Craise pressed. "You didn't pay a high price for nothing."

"You'll never know what Tlalam said," Matteo swore.

A sick sort of pleasure bloomed in Craise's eyes. "I will," he promised. He motioned to Alize to hand over her flame blade. He turned it about with a flourish before stalking toward Kainon. "Careful, Protector. The slightest prick could be your undoing," he warned as he pressed the tip against Kainon's ribs, though not enough to pierce the skin.

Kainon didn't flinch, though his expression turned murderous.

Craise hummed. "People will go to extraordinary lengths to survive," he murmured. "But I'm always astounded by what people do to save those they truly care for." He looked over his shoulder at Matteo.

Matteo felt the blood drain from his face.

"Give him nothing, Matteo," Kainon said, even as sweat gathered on his temples. The blade had already pierced his tunic.

Matteo pursed his lips. He had no way of knowing if the braid in Kainon's hair could withstand a flame blade.

Craise smirked.

Matteo suddenly dove for the blade, smacking it away from Kainon. His hand somehow found the hilt.

Craise reacted scarcely a heartbeat later. They tugged back and forth as Matteo struggled to maintain his grip. Snarling, Craise punched him hard in the jaw.

Matteo fell back, and Craise was on him, landing more blows about Matteo's head and ribs before suddenly grabbing a fistful of Matteo's braids and wrenching his head back to expose his throat.

Kainon shouted and wrenched violently on his bindings.

White teeth bared, Craise pressed the flame blade against Matteo's throat. Its sudden brightness seared his eyes.

"Craise!" Latan said sharply.

Craise froze, his breath hissing between clenched teeth.

"Don't forget your mission, Craise," Latan warned.

Matteo held still. Each breath made the blade scrape against his skin, causing a low burn. Gazing up, he saw the hesitation in Craise's eyes before the man coolly decided. Matteo's eyes widened as he felt the blade press down.

Suddenly, Kainon slammed into Craise, knocking him aside. The Rhun tumbled before rolling to his feet. The blade lay discarded on the ground. Matteo scrambled for it.

"No!" Latan yelled.

A soldier leapt onto Matteo's back, another kicking the blade away before Matteo could reach it. Matteo kicked and squirmed, but the soldier's weight held him down and grinded his face into the dirt.

With difficulty, Matteo turned his head. Craise had Kainon pinned to the ground as well, with his knees on Kainon's arms. Tangled as he was in the frayed rope, Kainon could barely move. The Rhun hunter bent and whispered something, making Kainon buck furiously.

Latan stepped forward and blocked Matteo's view. "That's quite enough. Craise, with me."

Craise punched Kainon to the side of the head, rocking his face to the side. The Rhuncavari got up and kicked him multiple times. Kainon groaned and attempted to curl protectively into a ball.

Matteo struggled to pull free. "Stop!"

Latan made a two-fingered motion at Nadiya, who watched with sick fascination. Nadiya wove something in the air before making a throwing motion. It struck Craise and knocked him away. He tumbled and lay amongst the pine needles, breathing hard and scowling up at the trees.

Latan stood over him. "You forget, Craise. The Linnian's braid could be your undoing."

Blood was evident on Craise's teeth as he grinned. "I serve Rhuncavar as always, my lord."

"It would be a shame to see you fall so close to the finish," Latan observed, frowning.

Craise's face twisted as if he tasted something sour. "Yes,

my lord," he said, although nothing in his voice indicated submission.

Latan hummed, observing, before letting Craise stand.

The soldier let Matteo go with a shove. Matteo rolled onto his back and touched his neck. To his relief, there was no blood, though he knew it had been close.

Kainon uncurled and rose to his feet. He took slow, testing breaths, nursing his side. With an effort, he straightened as if the healing braid in his hair was already doing its work.

Craise spat something in Rhuncavari and stalked away.

Latan stood in front of Matteo. He ordered a soldier to bind Matteo's wrists once more. "Temper your attitude, lostling," he said once Matteo was secured again to the tree. "We're not done with you yet."

"Why did you stop him?" Matteo asked, unable to help himself.

Latan smiled. "You're *nakono*—useful prey."

Matteo frowned.

Latan's smile deepened. "What knotbinder can resist trying to rescue one of their own? Especially someone who bears the weight of Darsha's future on his young shoulders?"

Kainon cursed softly under his breath.

"They'll die for you, my dear boy," Latan said. "But take some comfort. When you're the very last knotbinder, we'll kill you, too."

26

THE RHUN CONTINUED to take a cautious route through the forest, avoiding towns and roads. The following two days bled together for Kainon in a series of difficult tracks through muddy terrain. To Kainon's enduring frustration, the fingerlings skittered away at the mere sound of the horses. He wondered if his fear about what the Rhun would do to a little serpent made them even more unwilling to help. Fingerlings were driven by instincts of survival. He couldn't blame them for wanting to live.

Craise remained smugly satisfied, but for the most part, the Rhun left Kainon and Matteo be. Even food and water from the Rhun was scarce, but Kainon showed Matteo the plants whose leaves collected rainwater, and quickly harvested the wild peppercress and sorrel for them to eat as they trudged behind the Rhun.

Matteo was uncharacteristically quiet, deep in thought while pulled along behind Craise's horse. The previous day, the knotbinder had tried to apologize for the villager's death, but Kainon was having none of it.

"It was a ploy," Kainon muttered. "They already knew you'd lost the ability to weave."

Matteo nodded, but his blue eyes remained dark with guilt.

Kainon was surprised Matteo had made no fatalistic attempt to rile Craise into using the flame blade. "You're not going to lure Craise into doing something stupid, are you?"

"Of course not," Matteo muttered, glaring at the back of Craise's head. "I need my gift back. All of it. Then there'll be an accounting these bastards won't expect."

Kainon grinned. He'd always admired Matteo's stubbornness. It was what had gotten the boy across the mountains in the first place.

Kainon wondered if the Rhun intended to take them into Rhuncavar, though it was more than a month's journey across the mountains. Eventually, the forest would fork, with one broad arm reaching the ocean and the other taking them close to the Uhur Mountains. Both were a far journey from the Sanctuary.

He thought of Fira and cautiously pushed his mind towards her. The simmering anger lingered, and Kainon gleaned no words from her. He had a vague notion that Fira remained on the Sanctuary island. In his mind, he glimpsed workers sifting through the temple's rubble, collecting broken bits of stone and putting them in wheelbarrows to take away. Others hammered a new roof and eaves. A woman in pilgrim robes cautiously approached Fira, throwing a slab of meat onto the tiled ground in front of her. The woman was too scared to draw closer, and Kainon felt Fira's rage deepen. He wondered what had happened to the Protectors.

He returned to himself and swore softly.

"What is it?" Matteo asked quietly so the Rhun couldn't hear.

"Fira's still at the Sanctuary. I think the pilgrims have her captive."

Matteo stumbled a step. "Where's Captain Sebani? She'd never allow Fira to be taken prisoner."

"I know," Kainon said. He nudged Fira's mind again, but the distance worked against him. He sighed. "Fira will find a way to make the situation work to her benefit. She always does."

But his unease continued to gnaw at him as the afternoon progressed. By his judgement, they headed progressively east. To the south and several weeks' ride was the Breeding Sands. The east was just more forest until they reached the ocean.

"The Rhun seem to know where they're going," Matteo observed, trudging beside him.

It didn't bode well. It was possible Latan and his riders had been in Linnia before, perhaps part of hunting parties rounding up Darshians. Kainon wondered how many Darshians had been hounded through these very forests.

Perhaps that was what disturbed the dragons, although it was late in the hunt for the creatures to grow upset. There were so few of Matteo's people left.

Kainon pushed his mind toward the Breeding Sands. It sat like a dull, heavy weight in the distance. He could not sense how many dragons were on the Sands. At this time in the season, there should be dozens of nesting females.

The need to investigate the Sands had to be tempered by the real possibility of being eaten.

Alize emerged from the forest while the sun pitched high overhead; it was early for her to show herself. Kainon recognized her as a skilled tracker and hunter. She could disappear like a ghost, barely stirring a leaf, and sneak up beside them unawares. Every morning, Alize was gone before anyone else awoke and tended to remain unseen throughout the day unless something caught her attention.

Like now.

Alize spoke to Latan in Rhuncavari, her voice low and urgent.

Kainon craned his neck. Whatever Alize said made Latan give a curt order, and suddenly the party sharply turned south, guiding the horses into more difficult undergrowth.

Kainon felt hope stir. Chances were that a party of Linnians were nearby.

They stopped in a gully overrun with vines, and Latan ordered the riders to dismount.

Craise gave an oily smile as he swung down from the saddle with a jaunty bounce. "Kneel. Both of you."

Matteo's expression soured.

Craise raised an eyebrow, obviously hopeful that Matteo would defy him.

Kainon gave Matteo a look, hoping the boy would save the fight for another time.

Clenching his fists until his knuckles turned white, Matteo knelt.

Kainon followed suit and let himself be pushed onto his back by one of the soldiers.

The man put a boot on Kainon's chest and growled, "Quiet."

Craise drew a plain dagger, the flat of the blade used to tip Matteo's chin up. The boy glowered up at him. Kainon was surprised Craise didn't use the flame blade to taunt Matteo but realized its glow could give them away.

A short time later, Kainon heard hooves thumping in the

undergrowth. He tilted his head but couldn't see past the foliage.

The strangers continued riding at a steady, unhurried pace. Kainon counted several horses, perhaps as many as a dozen. They seemed to have no inkling that a Rhun party hid amongst the trees a few hundred feet away.

A short while later, the riders moved out of earshot.

Alize stepped out from the branches and wordlessly nodded.

"Get them moving," Latan ordered.

Craise gave Matteo a push, toppling him into the ferns. The Rhun hunter smirked and mounted his horse.

Matteo clambered out with red spots on his cheeks and murder in his eyes. He spat a curse in Darshian.

Kainon rolled to his side and froze when his gaze met pale, slitted green eyes. The little creature clung to the underside of a vine. Even looking at it, Kainon almost mistook it for a leaf. Unlike other fingerlings of its size, this one didn't scamper away at being noticed. Its snout twitched as it sniffed.

'*Hello,*' Kainon said gently, expecting it to scurry into the leaf mold.

It blinked its oversized eyes.

Kainon received a nudge of curiosity in his mind. It really shouldn't have been possible, not when fingerlings this tiny were scarcely more than bug eaters with the ability to spit fire.

'*Oh, you brave little thing,*' he marveled.

It reminded him of Fira when she'd first arrived at Bone Lake. She'd stubbornly persisted in ignoring the dangers of being too small to be around humans safely. Judging by its size, this fingerling must have hatched in the last summer or two, but its mind was far too mature for that. Kainon wondered if it could understand complex concepts, such as chewing on the rope until it snapped.

Curiosity spiking again, it dashed along the vine and backflipped onto the dead leaves by Kainon's elbow. He resisted the urge to move and draw attention to it. But he needn't have worried, for the fingerling leapt onto his forearm and slipped unseen beneath his sleeve. Its hot belly and tiny claws pressed against his skin.

Kainon got to his feet slowly. *Very well*, he thought, letting a plan slowly form.

"I WAS THERE, DID YOU KNOW?" Craise asked.

Matteo walked slightly to the side of the man's horse, close enough that the rope didn't yank on his wrists but out of Craise's easy eyeline. It made no difference when the man was in the mood to torment, but at least Matteo walked beside Kainon. His companion wavered between sending Matteo calming looks or appearing ready to haul Craise off his horse and bludgeon him with the nearest branch.

"Are you listening, knotbinder?" Craise prodded.

"I can hear you," Matteo said stonily.

Craise turned in the saddle and grinned down at him. "Fortunate for you that I didn't find you at the temple of your god, Matteo of Darsha."

Matteo tried to concentrate on his footing, but Craise's words rang in his ears.

"We'd marched for seventeen days to get there. Your precious knotbinders were so unprepared. How does a kingdom even survive being so weak?"

Matteo felt tension ripple down his spine.

He smiled. "It was the first time my blade fed. Did you see it, boy? It awakened at the temple."

Matteo glared up at the man. "What's the point? Why attack Darsha at all?"

"I don't expect you to understand a glorious purpose, though you should know there are many flame blades. Their power depends on what they feed upon. Who knows, maybe one will feed upon dragons." He threw a smarmy smile at Kainon.

Kainon snorted. "I'm certain you'd wholly fail."

Craise licked his lips. "Well, it's not my concern. I've chosen my quarry and dedicated my life to the hunt." His voice took on a dreamy quality. "When the last knotbinder falls, I'll carry my blade to the great stone and give it up to Rhuncavar, and he will reward me most fully."

"With what?" Matteo asked. "What would you possibly get out of slaughter?"

Kainon huffed. "It's boring and predictable, Matteo —power."

Craise ignored him. "I'll be Rhuncavar's loyal acolyte, touched and guided by his hand." There was no fanatical gleam in Craise's eyes, which unsettled Matteo even more. Craise believed his actions were rational. "You're weak and ill-prepared, even maybe unworthy of being the last feeding. But I have proven to be most loyal, and I don't mind if my final steps come easily."

Matteo looked away, thoughts skipping about wildly. There'd been no prior warning before the Rhun came, no indication of what they wanted. They simply swept through Darsha, cutting down everyone. Matteo assumed the Rhun sought to expand their territory and steal the wealth in Darsha's mountains—particularly the iron needed for weapons. Maybe they invaded as part of a larger plan to battle other kingdoms.

Matteo never got the opportunity to ask other Darshians; he simply fled for his life, only to end up as bait.

Kainon snorted loudly. "If gods are remotely like dragons, you're just a worm underfoot, Craise."

The satisfied smile on Craise's face grew twisted. "Careful, Linnian. Alize's flame blade has just started to hunger. You're just the sort to feed it."

"Your master seems to think otherwise," Kainon said.

Craise's gaze briefly slid to the braid in Kainon's hair. He snarled and suddenly kicked his horse. It jolted forward a few steps, causing the rope to yank Matteo forward.

Matteo kept on his feet. The raw skin around his wrists burned, but it was worth it to see Craise annoyed. He grinned back at Kainon.

The murderous expression on Kainon's face eased.

The thick undergrowth made for slow going as the day progressed. The Rhun occasionally dismounted to navigate the warren of burrows and boltholes left by fingerlings. The party paused to water the horses at a stream.

Kainon sat and stretched his legs, patting the damp dirt beside him. "Let me see." He motioned to Matteo's wrists.

Matteo knelt. He glanced at the surrounding Rhun, who mostly ignored them. Craise spoke in heated Rhuncavari to Latan, who listened with polite attention. It reminded Matteo of parents who begged the knotbinders to retest their unchosen children. He wondered who Latan was back in Rhuncavar. A lord, for certain, and likely a powerful one considering the wary respect the soldiers afforded him.

Kainon carefully turned Matteo's hands about to check the underside of his wrists. "Not as bad as it could be."

It had bled earlier, but most of the redness would be gone by morning.

"Knotbinders weave healing braids to keep ourselves reasonably healthy, but we can't be self-indulgent."

"Ah. Hence why you're scratched and bruised, and I have scarcely a mark on me."

Matteo shrugged and avoided Kainon's gaze. "I had to be thorough after the green dragon hurt you." There'd been a few heartbeats after Sebani and other Protectors carried Kainon into the chapter house when Matteo felt the red call of a killing braid. It made him determined to weave the healing knots.

"There's something different about my braid, isn't there?" Kainon asked quietly. "What Craise said earlier—if all knotbinders wove as you do, Darsha might not have fallen."

Matteo shrugged. "Healing braids don't come easily to me." He glanced briefly at Kainon. "Maybe intent has to do with it. I have to concentrate so that other knots don't slip through."

Understanding flared in Kainon's eyes. "I was badly hurt, wasn't I?"

Looking away, Matteo said, "Yes."

"Thank you, my friend."

From the corner of Matteo's eye, he saw a tiny green fingerling peeking out from under Kainon's sleeve.

"Ah. Pretend you don't see it," Kainon murmured. He turned his gaze back to the drinking horses. "It doesn't quite understand what I'm asking of it yet."

Matteo smothered a frown.

"It doesn't understand concepts like enemies or escape. I'm trying to convince it that rope is tasty."

Matteo raised an eyebrow. "I believe in you," he said. "Maybe tonight, luck will be with us."

Kainon looked at him sharply and smiled. "Perhaps so." He looked up at the foliage rustling in the wind. "The further the Rhun take us from our task, the harder it'll be to convince the dragons that Linnia still honors the Treaty."

It was difficult to think about dragons with Craise standing on the banks, hands on his hips.

"How far away is the Breeding Sands?"

"Days from here," Kainon said. "But I also want to know what's going on with Fira and rescue her from the pilgrims."

Matteo bit his lip. Fira had been unfailingly loyal; it wasn't right for her to be alone and amongst strangers. "Why haven't the Protectors freed her?"

Kainon shook his head. "I assume Tlalam's absence has caused a lot of fear. If rioting happened at Bone Lake, it's likely also happening elsewhere. Protectors may have their hands full. If Sebani has any say in the matter, she'll get Fira out of danger."

Matteo resisted mentioning it had been days since the pilgrims took Fira; perhaps he was wrong to believe Protectors would do anything to free her. He knew Kainon would upend half the world to keep Fira safe.

Matteo knew he'd be there, too, if Kainon asked him.

"We can't let the Rhun take us any further," Matteo said.

Kainon pulled down his sleeve to hide the fingerling. "Tonight," he promised.

27

DARKNESS SETTLED HEAVILY over the forest, with a thin sliver of moon barely visible through the thick canopy. Crickets and bugs sang confidently in the absence of fingerlings.

Kainon curled on his side, his eyes half-lidded as he studied the camp. The fire had reduced to glowing embers, occasionally brightening when a breeze stirred through the bracken ferns.

Fira lay awake, also. Kainon sensed she still remained at the Sanctuary. Cracked tiles irritated her belly, but much of her attention lingered on the dull, throbbing pain in her left wing. Torn ligaments, perhaps, or, worse, something broken. Her wing was tucked awkwardly against her side.

Kainon's anger stirred. The Protectors should be tending to Fira's every comfort, applying poultices and fire-warmed dressings while awaiting the arrival of healers from Pelan's mage guild. Fira's rage had simmered down, replaced now with morose confusion and loneliness.

He swallowed at discovering the last. It was his fault. He should have shielded Fira from the pilgrims. Or, wiser still, never let her get near the Sanctuary in the first place. He should have encouraged Fira to fly over the Uhur Mountains. But he'd selfishly wanted her to stay.

Pushing his mind toward her, he promised, '*I will come for you.*'

Fira made no indication she heard him.

Returning to himself, he noted the camp remained quiet. The deep shadows were in their favor; dragons knew he and Matteo could use a bit of luck.

Kainon nudged the fingerling awake.

It gave a querulous chirp loud enough for Kainon to glance worriedly across the camp to the Rhun sleeping under the awnings. He watched them carefully. Nadiya and two soldiers were on sentry duty, hidden amongst the trees. Kainon was vaguely aware of their location and knew at least one of them was tasked with watching over him and Matteo.

All the same, Kainon knew this would take time. '*Rope,*' he nudged the fingerling, sending an image of his bindings.

The fingerling sniffed dismissively, content to stay in the warmth close to his ribs.

'*Rope,*' he sent again.

He sent an image of himself trying to pull free, unable to escape. The little creature gave a softly disgruntled hiss and burrowed deeper, concerned that Kainon's jostling disturbed its warm sleeping place.

Kainon tried again, imagining being a fingerling, small and delicate, wandering along a branch in the silvery moonlight. He imagined the branch snapping and him falling into a tangle of creepers, wings ensnared. '*How to get free?*' he asked.

The fingerling gave an annoyed hiss and bit Kainon's side. He flinched at the unexpected bite.

'*I see,*' he sent, chagrined. He showed an image of his wrists again. '*Tangled.*'

With an unimpressed air, tinged with surprise over the stupidity of humans, the fingerling left its warm sleeping spot and slid out from the bottom of Kainon's tunic. It paused atop Kainon's thigh, and he turned slightly so the fingerling remained in the shadows.

Matteo breathed slow and deep, tucked into a ball beside him. But Kainon spotted slight movement of Matteo's eyelashes as he watched.

'*No flame, please,*' Kainon said, sending an image of vines catching alight and blazing out of control. The last thing he wanted was for a tiny spit of flame to expose their activities to the Rhun.

With a disgruntled air, the fingerling set its sharp tiny teeth to the rope around Kainon's wrists. Kainon sent it warm encouragement.

"Over there," Matteo whispered, scarcely audible over the soft grinding of fingerling teeth.

Kainon turned his head slightly and spotted the younger woman. Nadiya wasn't as quiet or skilled as Alize and didn't share the older woman's talent for blending into her surroundings. She sat atop a fallen tree outside the camp area and rested her chin on her hand. She stared into the camp instead of watching for unexpected visitors. Kainon wondered why Latan indulged her, but her ability to throw magic made her very dangerous.

He felt his bindings loosen slightly.

One of the sentries emerged from the trees behind Nadiya. He offered the young woman a smoking pipe. She grinned, holding it while the soldier used a small flint to set it alight. Nadiya took a few deep puffs, cheroot glowing, before handing the pipe back.

The rope around Kainon's wrists fell away with a soft snap. He remained still.

A smoky, sweet scent drifted over the camp. Kainon glanced at the darkness under the awning but no one stirred at the smell. He shuffled just slightly toward Matteo and carefully lowered the fingerling onto his bindings.

'*He's my friend*,' Kainon said when the fingerling squinted balefully up at him. '*Please help him.*'

The fingerling gave a disgruntled huff and bit hard on the rope as if it was Kainon's bones.

Amused, Kainon sent promises of hearty meals and the best, most luxurious treasures for its hoard.

Matteo held still as the fingerling worked.

"We don't have much time," Kainon whispered.

Nadiya and the sentry sat close together with their backs to the camp to hide the glow of their shared pipe.

"I can't see the other soldier," Matteo whispered.

Kainon nodded, mouth drawing tight. The third sentry was somewhere amongst the trees but they couldn't wait to be sure. The sweet smell of the pipe grew stronger; the camp would soon stir.

The bindings unraveled and hit the dirt with a soft thump. Kainon signaled for the fingerling to quickly leap up and find purchase on his tunic.

Matteo crouched, his pale eyes locked on Nadiya. He motioned with his chin, and they backed quietly into the undergrowth, careful not to snap any fallen twigs. The quiet of the night threatened to work against them if they weren't cautious.

Kainon eased through a wall of vines, their tendrils springing back into place behind Matteo. A few more steps and they might risk bolting into the woods.

The missing sentry suddenly stepped out in front of them.

"Ha!" he shouted triumphantly and swung his sword.

Kainon ducked and pushed Matteo to the side. Rolling, Kainon came up against the sentry, ramming his fist into the man's throat. The sentry choked and took a wild swing, but Matteo swung a lump of wood into his guts.

Shouts came from the camp. Nadiya sprinted past the campfire, her hand upraised.

"Run!" Matteo yelled, already jumping over brush and crashing through the undergrowth.

Bolting after him, Kainon felt something static and cruel sizzle past his shoulder. Nadiya cursed and threw another spell that struck a tree. It shattered in an explosion of splinters and large chunks.

Kainon tumbled, tripping on debris before righting himself, his concentration narrowing on momentary flashes of pale hair amidst the trees. The fingerling clung to the neck of his tunic, frightened breaths hissing against his throat. Kainon's legs burned as he raced to catch up beside Matteo. They ran headlong, unsure of their direction.

The thudding sound of horses chased them.

"The knotbinder is mine!" Craise yelled from somewhere to their left.

Kainon caught Matteo's sleeve and steered him toward a stand of sedges. Patches of bare earth scarred the landscape beyond. *Fingerling burrows*, he realized.

The fingerling leapt off Kainon's shoulder and scrambled up a tree trunk, pausing at head height. Kainon had no time to wish it well, barreling through the undergrowth before hitting treacherous footing amongst the burrows. He barely slowed, jumping over deep holes and feeling the jolt in his bones when he hit divots and uneven soil.

Matteo miscalculated his pace and stumbled into a hollow. Breath rasping, he pulled himself out and thankfully kept going. He ducked and weaved between the trees, leaping over burrows like a rabbit.

The Rhun wrenched to a stop at the edge of the warren, horses pawing nervously at the ground. Latan yelled something, and the riders kicked their horses to circle wide and cut them off, but Kainon knew fingerling warrens could spread for miles. He and Matteo needed to get far from the Rhun before finding a hiding place to regroup and catch their breath.

Kainon felt a sudden spark of defiance from the fingerling. In his mind, the little one leapt from tree to tree, scuttling into position as riders galloped toward it.

He had no time to warn it away.

The fingerling spat a gob of fire as a pair of riders charged past. The horses shied in fear, but the fingerling was too small for its attack to have any real effect. The riders fought their rearing horses for only a few heartbeats.

One rider turned about. In Kainon's mind, he saw it was Latan. The man drew his blade and swiftly swung. He cut deep and true.

A white-hot stab of pain brought Kainon crashing to his knees.

No...

He searched blindly, desperately for the fingerling.

Emptiness met him.

Latan pulled his blade out from where it bit deep into the tree.

Matteo grabbed Kainon and hauled him upright. "Are

you hurt?" he asked, running a quick gaze over him. When he was slow to answer, Matteo shouted, "Kainon!"

"I'm not—the fingerling."

Matteo's expression tightened. "We can't stop, Kainon."

"I know." Kainon sucked in shaky gulps of air and forced himself to keep moving. His stinging eyes rivalled the burn in his lungs.

The warren of burrows continued to spread out in front of them amidst the night-covered trees. They tumbled into a stream, splashing over to the other bank.

"The horses have to go around," Matteo gasped, pulling Kainon along.

They scrambled up the side of a gully and lost sight of the riders for the first time.

The woods grew thicker the deeper they went across the warren, with massive trees having adapted to fingerlings exposing their roots and occasionally setting them on fire in territorial disputes.

Distant shouting came from somewhere to their right. Kainon grimly hoped the horses refused to enter the warren, and perhaps some were even injured when the Rhun arrogantly tried to force them onwards.

Kainon allowed himself a moment to hope as he followed Matteo's lead deeper into the warren.

28

MATTEO WATCHED water drip off the fern fronds protecting the entry of their burrow. Dawn filtered palely through the woods, the air earthy and damp. Birds trilled in the absence of fingerlings.

The Rhun hunted somewhere to the east of them. Occasionally, Matteo heard footfalls or a branch snapping, and his heart leapt into his throat, but no one found their hiding place.

Kainon sat pressed in against the rich dark earth at the very back of the burrow, his gaze turned inward. The fingerling's death had hurt him, but not in a way that Matteo's braid could heal, so Matteo kept watch. He knew they couldn't stay for much longer, not with Alize's tracking skills.

The loosely packed floor of the burrow had countless claw marks raking the soil. Hints of gold and silver indicated a fingerling had abandoned its hoard and scurried off to wherever the serpents now gathered.

The forest brightened with each passing moment. Alize would soon find their trail.

Matteo nudged Kainon with his boot. "We need to move."

Kainon blinked with an effort, returning to himself. His eyes were red-rimmed. "I know."

"Do you have any idea where we are?"

Kainon leaned back, turning his gaze to the woods. "We must be near the Heldon River. There are wards along the river that will stop anyone from crossing into the forest bordering the Breeding Sands. The only entry point into the Sands is through the twin chapter houses at Raffal."

"Can we follow the river to safety?"

"There'll be pilgrim roads and villages when we're close to Raffal. But it'll take a good week to get there."

Matteo scratched the streaks of dirt from his arms. "Craise will expect us to head for Bone Lake."

"And so we should," Kainon muttered. "Fira needs us."

Matteo studied him. "She's still not speaking to you?"

Kainon sighed. "I can barely sense her. We've never been this far apart, but Fira's anger could be clouding things, too. She may think I've abandoned her."

Matteo couldn't ignore Kainon's downturned mouth. "I'm sorry about the fingerling."

Kainon's eyes watered. "Damn them," he whispered. "It could have been Fira's sibling. It was so strong-willed."

"It chose you, just like Fira did," Matteo said.

"Aye." Kainon rested his head against the dirt wall, his throat working hard. "

The loss in Kainon's voice brought a lump to Matteo's throat. "I don't know how to help."

Not anymore. Matteo remembered what it was like to weave the braids, how he'd sat on the tiled floor of the Temple of Dar with fronds of grass or cloth, practicing the knots while the sun warmed his back. He remembered stepping into the Temple for the first time with his parents anxiously hopeful behind him. But now, there was only a deep, hollowing blankness. Even the names of the knots were gone.

Kainon's gaze sharpened. "That doesn't matter, Matteo."

Matteo shook his head. "Of course, it does. If I could, I'd tie a killing braid around Latan's throat."

"And I'd be there to hold him down while you do it." He gentled his gaze. "Your magic sleeps; it's not lost."

Matteo's gaze dropped to his hands. The callouses on his fingers were a mocking reminder of what he'd lost. He'd never contemplated a life without the braids. Should he happen to find a knotbinder to train him now, they'd likely view him as too old to start again. And many knotbinders would find his inherent leaning towards killing braids hard to stomach.

A thick lump formed in his throat.

Kainon suddenly grabbed him and pulled him close. "Let's not lose hope, Matteo. Tlalam might have hobbled you, but he still chose you for a reason," he said. "He wants us to succeed."

Matteo sighed regretfully. "Craise won't stop until he has me. The Rhun will forget about you once their mission's complete. You can rally the Protectors and get into the Breeding Sands."

"No, our best chance is together. I know we didn't start off well, but I'm glad to be with you now."

Matteo smiled despite himself. It didn't make sense. Kainon had others to rely on, including an order of Protectors whose duty aligned with the dragons. But Matteo couldn't ignore the hope and relief at not facing the Rhun alone.

"Alize won't make it easy to reach help," he said, pulling back. "She's good at what she does."

Kainon sat back, eyes running over the burrow as he thought. His gaze caught on a delicate gold chain abandoned by the burrow's former inhabitant. A smile formed. "I have an idea, but I'm not sure we'll get much out of it."

Matteo bit his lip but nodded determinedly. "I trust you."

Kainon led the way, carefully easing back the ferns protecting the entry and listening for a few heartbeats before leaving the burrow. He made for a wide gully thick with undergrowth, trekking halfway down where a round boulder poked out of the earth. Kainon pulled back the mossy overhang, revealing another burrow. The opening was wider, the ground inside hard-packed and dry.

"The dominant fingerlings often take the prime spots," Kainon said, settling on his belly and squirming inside. His voice became muffled as he added, "They also tend to steal more sizeable items from Linnians."

He shuffled back, revealing a bone hairpin as long as his palm with a decorated head shaped like a sitting dog. "Never thought I'd steal from the dragons," Kainon muttered, grimacing slightly.

"Tlalam already wants to crunch your bones," Matteo said, squinting as he tried to peer over Kainon's shoulder. "I'm not sure this transgression will seal your fate."

Kainon's mouth quirked. "Thanks for the reminder." He cleaned the hairpin with his tunic. "These woods are ancient and far from the Queen's Road, so we're not likely to have rich pickings, but if we're lucky, we may find a short blade or farmer's hammer."

Matteo took the offered hairpin, testing its weight before

tucking it in his hair. Craise was likely too arrogant to see it as a weapon. Matteo's jaw hardened.

"I just hope the fingerlings see we're taking from them so we can uphold the Treaty," Kainon said, peering over the boulder in search of other burrows. "

As far as Matteo was concerned, it was worth the risk. He pointed to a particularly dark patch of undergrowth. "There's another burrow."

Kainon met his eyes and nodded with grim determination before leading the way.

THEY WASHED their finds in a stream that forked off the Heldon River. The main river was close enough for the roar of churning water to filter through the trees. Kainon warily studied the woods and thick undergrowth. The Rhun could easily come upon them, and neither he nor Matteo would be aware until it was too late.

Kainon quickly assessed their haul of pilfered items. They'd found the remnants of a shield that looked cleaved in two from an ancient battle. Kainon imagined multiple fingerlings had bickered and fought over it while dragging it under fallen trees.

More importantly, they now had three daggers and a trapper's snare that turned his stomach a little. Though rusted, the snare looked no more than fifty summers old and of a size to get curious fingerlings in trouble. Kainon knew that wasn't the device's intent, but he wondered what else the Protectors in the region had missed. Trapping in the woodlands was forbidden.

He wordlessly snapped the pin holding the snare

together and handed the better dagger to Matteo, knowing they had their work cut out for them this time.

"I hoped we'd find something more substantial," Matteo said, tucking the blade away.

"Same. The fingerlings around here are too small to build a decent hoard. We'll make do." Kainon washed his hands in the cool water.

He glanced again toward the river. Straying too close could leave them trapped on the banks should the Rhun find them, but using the river to travel downstream could quicken their journey to Raffal. Kainon knew the wards stopped people from crossing and gaining access to the Breeding Sands, but he was unsure if the river itself was beyond their reach. It felt unwise to try.

"Fira lived here, didn't she?" Matteo asked.

"I suppose she did," Kainon murmured, taking in the trees with renewed interest. "Likely for decades."

Strange that there seemed to be no sign of Fira in the forest when she'd undoubtedly carved out part of it to suit herself. Now that he thought of it, she'd arrived at Bone Lake without so much as a jewel for a hoard.

Kainon smiled. "She came up to me at Bone Lake like a stray cat, all noise and demands."

Matteo snorted, clearly imagining the introduction.

"There's not much known about golden dragons. They find their purpose as they mature, which is why Fira still has black and bronze on her. She's figuring herself out."

Kainon looked up at the sunlight dappling through the leaves. An ache formed in his throat from thinking of her.

"That's why you were allowed to go with her," Matteo said.

Kainon grunted. "Tlalam mistook her for someone

malleable and thought he could curry her favor. He wouldn't have shared otherwise."

"Sebani told me Fira collects people for her hoard."

"Fira's learning to ask first," Kainon said, but he suspected Fira indulged him only because it suited her. Having a dragon's regard was a rare and dangerous honor. She'd made her intent clear about Matteo, though Kainon wondered at her response now that the boy had no new braids to offer her.

Something tugged at the back of his mind, and he sent hopeful, loving thoughts toward Fira.

A furious, brooding mind answered from far closer than Bone Lake. '*Thieves. Brazen, sacrilegious thieves!*'

Blood thundered in Kainon's ears as he stumbled to a halt. The Breeding Sands stretched below him, sand bleached white but with streams of iridescence from generations of crushed shells. The dragon's shadow glided over the dunes.

Five other dragons followed, compelled to take flight. Invaders—stinking *humans*—neared the border of their most sacred land.

'*It is time,*' another voice whispered.

Kainon grabbed his head with both fists, his face tightening with pain. The dragons either didn't know or didn't care that he heard them. He felt their intent to hunt.

"Matteo," he gasped with an effort. "Hide. Quickly."

They found a burrow, one that pushed deep under tree roots. Kainon urgently manhandled Matteo inside. It wouldn't be enough to protect them from flame, nothing would, but the urge to be small and quiet pressed down hard, smothering all else.

In Kainon's mind, the desert turned suddenly to forest, the green momentarily hard on the eyes. A tract of trees only a few miles wide was easy to glide over, and then came a river with spells that promised fire and death to the humans who crossed.

Arrogant humans rode beneath the trees in a V-shape toward the river. There were nine of them, so relaxed and confident in their trespassing. They trampled and smashed the paths made by lifetimes of countless hatchlings.

Easy enough to snatch one human to crunch and roast, to turn them to bone dust across the forest floor.

'*A warning,*' one dragon whispered.

'*A reminder,*' another agreed.

Linked as he was to the lead dragon, Kainon plummeted from the sky, tucking forelegs and wings in tight as she smashed through the branches. Talons snatched and dug deep into flesh, her speed slamming rider and horse to the ground.

Kainon felt momentary disappointment that it wasn't Latan or Craise under her talons but rather one of the soldiers whose neck snapped on impact.

The Rhun scattered amid screaming horses and curses.

Hot, acrid blood filled Kainon's mouth, together with a hint of sourness that reminded the dragon that humans did not make for good eating. Perhaps the ones that had grown soft and plump in their walled fortresses were tastier.

'*Not yet,*' a dragon hissed. '*Let there be a Proving first.*'

Annoyance vibrated through Kainon's bones, together with sulky acceptance. The dragon chomped down on horseflesh, finishing her meal in rapid bites. Then, turning her long snout skyward, she shot out of the trees with a few powerful wingbeats. She immediately wheeled north, falling in with her hovering companions. The mountains called, along with the sweet waters and hunting grounds beyond.

Kainon felt pulled along by her yearning, reveling in the rush of cold wind across her scales, the beat of her wings, and the sun warming her back.

A tug called him back. He ignored it, wanting to skim under the clouds.

A more insistent yank pulled on his scalp. Golden heat bloomed across his skin, drawing him back to his own body. Kainon blinked back into awareness. He drew a deep, shuddering breath, his lungs aching as if he'd been underwater for an age.

Matteo's face was mere inches away, blue eyes searching. He had Kainon's braid wrapped around his fist and appeared ready to yank hard once again. Golden light leached from the braid.

Tasting blood still, Kainon turned and retched heavily. He pulled himself upright with an effort, wiping his mouth with the edge of his tunic.

"Are you back with me?" Matteo asked.

Kainon grimaced. Without Matteo's intervention, he'd have abandoned his body and travelled to the Uhur Mountains. Taking another gulping breath, he gripped Matteo's and held fast as if his companion was the only anchor capable of stopping him from being dragged away on dragon wings.

"Thank you," Kainon whispered.

29

THEY FOUND the Rhun soldier's remains a mile from the river.

Kainon eyed the blood splashed halfway up the trees, noting there was very little left of either the soldier or his horse. All dragons, no matter their size, were messy but thorough eaters.

Matteo looked decidedly pale as he stepped over wet ground. "There's not even a bone or saddle here."

"Or a sword, unfortunately." Kainon sighed. "We can't let the Rhun get any closer to the Breeding Sands, not when their presence here is enough to upset so many dragons."

"Maybe the dragons sensed the flame blades," Matteo murmured.

"Or that five death sorcerers are only days from their nests."

Matteo sighed. "Pity only one of them fell." He glanced at Kainon. "You're certain it was one of the soldiers?"

"I know you would have preferred it to be Craise."

With a shrug, Matteo said, "Not really. If he's to die, well —" He stopped, looking uncomfortable.

"You want it to be by your hand," Kainon surmised.

Matteo nodded, mouth turning thin.

"No small thing, considering everything he's done to your people."

Glancing into the trees, Matteo said, "We have to go after them, don't we? Draw the Rhun away from the Breeding Sands."

It relieved Kainon that Matteo understood. "There aren't many other choices."

Matteo studied the forest, gaze contemplative. "I'm tired of running, Kainon. Ten summers is a long time."

Kainon looked at him curiously. "It's possible the Rhun are still spread out. It'll be hard for them to manage their horses when one's just been eaten."

Matteo nodded. He glanced at Kainon, his eyes questioning.

It was risky to go after the Rhun when they had all the advantages. He and Matteo had only a few weak blades and no magic capable of battling against Craise's flame blade and Nadiya's tree-shattering curses. Kainon realized they hadn't discovered what Latan and Alize were capable of, as well as the silent man whose name Kainon didn't know.

"Several Rhuncavari went this way," he said carefully, recalling where the riders scattered as the dragon smashed through branches and trees.

"Okay," Matteo said, straightening his shoulders determinedly as he stepped over a fallen tree.

They tracked through the undergrowth, following smashed branches and sprays of mud from galloping horses. It appeared to take quite some distance for the Rhun to get their mounts under control.

Kainon and Matteo tracked one rider that broke off alone—if they had to pick the Rhun off one by one, so be it.

A fallen branch snapped in the distance.

Kainon instinctively ducked, pulling Matteo down with him. They took cover amongst the ferns, careful not to break any fronds. Kainon held his breath and waited.

Matteo crouched beside him, his blue eyes staring intently through the undergrowth.

There.

Movement between the trees in the distance, vague shadows that some might have mistaken for wind-stirred branches.

To Kainon's surprise, two figures strode along a ridge of pines. Kainon waited until he made out their features, realizing it was Nadiya and the soldier she liked to flirt with and taunt.

Matteo tensed beside him.

For a terrifying moment, Kainon thought the Rhun had their trail, but the pair came from the east, opposite where the soldier had fallen. Nadiya stalked with a self-satisfied air, her cheeks flushed and a smirk on her face. Meanwhile, the soldier looked rumpled and dazed as he straightened his jerkin and pulled sticks from his hair.

By Kainon's guess, the pair had satisfied their dalliance and now made their way to join the other Rhun. It could only mean the enemy was not far away.

The pair continued with their direction unchanged, traversing within fifty feet of Matteo and Kainon but appearing unaware of their presence. Kainon stayed still, Matteo barely breathing beside him.

Nadiya and the sentry moved beyond their line of sight, crunching through the undergrowth. They continued unabated until the sound of their passage faded.

Kainon pressed a finger to his lips, motioning for Matteo to wait before they carefully eased out of the bracken.

Kainon peered cautiously out from the undergrowth, but the forest had settled again with bird life.

"They won't expect us," Matteo whispered.

The woods were predictable enough that Kainon expected more gullies ahead. If they ambushed Nadiya and the soldier in the depths of a ravine, there stood less chance of other Rhun discovering them should the fight turn noisy. It was time they used the Rhun's arrogance against them.

"If there's the slightest chance they overrun us, we retreat," Kainon said. "We can't let Nadiya use her magic."

Matteo set his jaw but nodded.

Their purloined blades would hardly hold them in good stead in ordinary situations, but it was better than nothing.

Kainon and Matteo left the safety of the undergrowth, forging a path that ran parallel to the Rhun. Nadiya appeared confident with her surroundings, striding with purpose through the trees.

To Kainon's surprise, they reached a dirt road scarcely wide enough for a wagon. Kainon had little idea where they were, but he allowed himself a moment to hope.

Nadiya and the soldier marched along the road, and Kainon wondered if it was a farmer's path leading to a village.

The road was muddy and quiet. Through the trees, Kainon soon spied hints of thatched, flat roofs of a handful of huts. Nadiya and her companion made no show of slowing down

Kainon's heart sank.

Tearful cries and sobs rose from somewhere within the village.

Matteo looked sharply at Kainon and whispered, "They've taken prisoners."

"Come on," Kainon whispered.

They quietly skirted the edge of the village before leaving the trees to press up against a hut.

The village had a few dozen homes, all simple and made of mud and thatch. The Rhun had herded the inhabitants into a pigpen, where they huddled together in the dirt beside the squealing animals.

As Kainon and Matteo watched, the tall, silent Rhun and another soldier dragged out an older man who sagged between them. Alize took up position before them with her lesser flame blade drawn.

"Where are the Protectors?" Matteo whispered urgently.

Kainon shook his head, mouth dry. The village looked furtive and new, and was too deep in the forest to draw a Protector patrol. "The village shouldn't even be here," he whispered, wondering what else the Protectors had missed.

Craise paced before the pen with his flame blade clenched in his fist. "Where have you been?" he snapped after spotting Nadiya and the soldier on the road.

Nadiya swaggered to a stop and arched her eyebrow as she looked over the prisoners. "Someone has to check the perimeter while you have your fun."

"My tastes are more refined than Linnian peasants." Craise sneered.

She smiled toothily and flicked her hair. "But your little pet slipped away while you slept with your member in your hand. What happened, Craise? You should have killed him days ago."

Craise took a step toward her, teeth bared.

Nadiya didn't flinch, eyes narrowing with dark promise.

"My lord," Alize called out.

Latan sat astride his horse, expression mildly interested as he watched Craise and Nadiya. He turned his horse about and inclined his head toward Alize. "Very well, my dear. You have patiently waited your turn."

At Alize's nod, the captive was laid out on the road leading into the village. He was an older man with sun-browned skin and broad shoulders from a life of heavy labor. Sobs came from the villagers.

Craise paced like a caged animal outside the pigpen, throwing Alize sneering looks.

The old farmer suddenly wrenched free of the soldier and rolled to his feet, bolting with surprising speed.

Latan raised a hand and stopped anyone from giving chase. With an indulgent smile, he pointed at Alize and motioned for her to wait, letting the villager almost reach the furthest hut.

"Come on," Matteo whispered, gaze fixed on the running villager.

Kainon wasn't sure what they'd do once they got hold of the man. Get him into the forest, certainly. If luck sided with them, Latan would split his forces, leaving some behind to guard the remaining captives. In the forest, Kainon and Matteo would use their little dragon hoard as best they could.

At Latan's nod, Alize smoothly leapt onto her horse and kicked its sides. A few short strides and it was at full gallop. Alize ran the man down, using her horse to barrel into him.

The villager tumbled wildly and lay wheezing and moaning on the ground, his leg at an odd angle. Alize slid off the horse and drew her flame blade. It didn't glow the way Craise's blade did.

Kainon pushed off the hut, dagger in hand.

But Alize's flame blade momentarily flashed white as she drove it deep into the villager's chest.

The remaining prisoners cried and screamed.

Matteo pulled Kainon back into the shadow of the hut, cursing under his breath. "It's too late," he hissed. "You can't help him."

Alize pulled out the blade, giving it a firm flick to clear the blood. She left the body like he was mere refuse on the road.

Alize pointed her blade at another villager.

Craise sniffed and entered the pen to drag a woman out. She wept as she slipped in the mud but glared hatefully at Alize.

"May dragons eat you and shit you out," the woman spat tearfully.

Alize swung the blade, beheading the woman. The flame blade glowed again. Sweeping his gaze across each Rhun, Kainon calculated which of them he could get to first. Ironically, it was Nadiya, who leaned against a newel post watching the proceedings with a bored twist of her mouth. Easy enough to slip behind her and drive a dagger between her ribs.

Craise returned to the pen, stalking backwards and forwards as he looked over the quailing villagers.

Latan raised a hand. "That'll be enough for now."

Nadiya looked disappointed. "My lord, she's barely started."

"Leave the bodies as they are," Latan said, looking about the village. "Our quarry will realize our intent soon enough."

Kainon felt a cold rush of understanding as he nudged Matteo out of sight. The bait was set, and it was only a matter of time before he and Matteo were forced to show themselves. As a Protector, he had no other choice.

But as he glanced skyward, Kainon decided the Rhun's mistake was to think he and Matteo would arrive alone.

HURRIEDLY MOTIONING for them to retreat into the woods, Kainon found a woodcutter's path that took them about a mile into the trees. Satisfied they were far enough from the village, he turned to Matteo, whose face was like a thundercloud.

"Alize's flame blade is starting to hunger," Matteo said, pacing. "The Rhun plan to destroy Linnia as well."

It only settled the resolve coiling in Kainon's guts.

Matteo paced. "It's my fault. If I hadn't come to Linnia, or if I'd just let Craise—"

"I need you to remove the braid." The words fell from Kainon's mouth unbidden.

Matteo looked at him sharply. "No—*why?* It's the only thing that's stopped the Rhun from killing you."

"I need to send a Calling to the dragons," Kainon said.

Matteo's scowl deepened. "I don't know what that is and I don't care. The dragons like to hurt you."

"It means speaking with dragons even if they wish to ignore me." It wasn't a compulsion, for no magic could do that to a dragon, but it was close enough.

"But Fira's trapped and needs our help," Matteo argued. "What can she do now that she couldn't do before?"

Kainon pushed aside the sudden guilt at Fira's name. '*Soon,*' he thought toward the dragonling but knew she could not hear. "I mean the nesting dragons. They'll help us if I convince them that the Rhuncavari are a threat."

"The dragons don't care about human problems."

"They will if they believe the Rhun intend to disturb the Breeding Sands. We need their help to either take on the Rhun or warn the Protectors."

"What does that have to do with the braid?" Matteo asked.

"The dragons won't believe me if there's magic protecting me. They'll think there's some sort of trap."

Color drained from Matteo's face. "The braid is the only thing stopping your mind from being destroyed just like Tlalam did to Amela."

"I don't expect you to understand," Kainon said. He could think of no other way to warn the Protectors of the risk to Linnia.

"Damn right, I don't!" Matteo spat. "What happens when the dragons find out Fira's trapped and hurt at the Sanctuary? The Protectors have done nothing to save her."

"We don't know if that's true," Kainon argued.

"The dragons won't care. They'll punish you all the same."

Kainon turned to him. "Matteo—"

"No! They'll kill you for the presumption of asking them to meddle in human concerns. You know they will!" Matteo folded his arms. "I won't do it so you can satisfy your guilt over a fingerling's death."

Kainon swallowed. "That's not what this is about."

"It's not?" Matteo's face twisted. "Then tell me."

"Alize's flame blade feeds on Linnians. You know what it means."

"Your death solves none of that!"

Kainon scrubbed his hands through his hair. "I need you to trust me, Matteo. I can't remove the braid myself."

Matteo's eyes watered. "Once it's gone, it's over. There's no more healings left in me to fix what they'll do to you."

"It's a risk we have to take."

Matteo clenched his teeth and looked away.

"Matteo—"

"It's the last braid, Kainon." Matteo's voice broke. "Tlalam took everything after that."

The silence stretched between them.

"I know," Kainon said.

Matteo cursed violently in Darshian and grabbed fistfuls of his own braids as he paced. "Fine," he spat, not looking at him. "Let's get it done. The longer we wait, the more time the Rhun have to torment those villagers."

Kainon let out a shaky breath. "Thank you."

Matteo directed Kainon to kneel. He drew close and eased forward the braid tucked behind Kainon's ear.

Their eyes met for a moment.

Kainon gently caught his hands, cupping them in his own. "We'll get through this, Matteo."

"You don't know that," Matteo said.

"No, I don't, but we can't do this alone."

Grim-faced, Matteo first unraveled the thin strip of leather that tied the end of the braid. Knot by knot, he separated blonde hair from dark brown.

To Kainon's surprise, he felt the magic begin to dissipate. Small aches made themselves known, and a large bruise where he'd smashed his knee against a fallen branch now gave a dull throb. Not for the first time, Kainon marveled at how badly he underestimated Matteo's powers. He mourned for the loss of an entire kingdom whose greatest strength lay in the healing of others.

Matteo bit his lip as he reached the last knot. He hesitated, their eyes meeting once more. His dark blue eyes held the hope that Kainon would change his mind.

Kainon squeezed Matteo's forearm, urging him to continue.

As the final knot unraveled in Matteo's hands, Kainon felt the last glow of the knotbinder's magic fade away.

30

Kainon sat with his back against the rough bark of a tree. He closed his eyes, aware Matteo wavered between watching him from his vantage point upon a branch in a nearby elm and keeping an eye out for any Rhun sneaking through the woods.

"Come back in one piece," Matteo whispered down to him.

Kainon listened to the breeze gently disturb the foliage before he sank his mind down into the cool earth.

Releasing a slow breath, he stretched his mind outwards.

On instinct, he felt lured toward Fira. She remained closed off and insular, barely more than a flickering presence in the distance. Kainon nonetheless sent her a pulse of comfort and strength, hoping she sensed him. Frustration and anger stirred at her situation, but Kainon couldn't focus on that right now.

He forced himself to withdraw from Fira. He needed to sink deep and follow the flow of the wind across the forest, drift along as it swept in from the distant ocean, stirring the tree tops overhead before heading south towards the heated

Breeding Sands. Dragons still remained there; they pulled at his mind like dark stones on white sand. They were far south, further away than Fira, but Kainon hoped their adult minds would notice him, though he suspected he was little more to them than a gnat on their claws.

Kainon took another deep breath and flowed across the terrain. The forest to the west was quiet and still, barely trampled by Linnians. Deep, cool ponds and groves of ancient trees called to fingerlings. He wondered if Fira had traversed this forest on her way to the Sanctuary for their first meeting. He hadn't sensed her approach but she'd seemingly made her decision long before arriving at his door. Fira once said he called her, but he still didn't know what she meant.

Frustrated by his wandering mind, he sank his mind through the foliage and wandered the undergrowth scarred by countless generations of squabbling and territorial fingerlings.

He needed to turn south to reach the explore the Sands. Once again, he felt called to the clear pools where rainwater dripped from thick glossy leaves. Almost against his will, Kainon sank beneath the surface. It was cool and dark in the pool, where fish swam amidst submerged logs and golden pondweed. Kainon was tugged down to the muddy bottom, pulled deeper until his lungs constricted.

Something big and ominous slept in the darkness. Kainon's mind skimmed over it and felt the passage of time. It was something that rarely ever stirred. It drowsed in the quiet and solitude, lulled by dripping water and sunlight dancing across the surface of the pool. It felt ancient, older than Linnia. Kainon tried to draw back but found himself entangled.

A presence rolled over him like a wave, turning him over

to examine him. He held his breath as something raked through his mind, sifting. Unbidden, a memory of Matteo weaving the knots came to the surface, and Kainon wrenched his mind back. But the presence seeped through as if his protections were nothing. It burned across his thoughts and memories, skipping over people, history and time. Kainon struggled to yank free, feeling his body clench. Its interest stirred as it paused to observe his and Matteo's conversation with Tlalam, and Kainon felt its cool amusement at how pampered Tlalam had become.

'*Have they all become like this?*' a presence raked through his mind.

Kainon mentally lurched in pain. '*Who?*'

The soil vibrated. The creature hissed something unintelligible and then scoured through Kainon's mind, searching for dragons. It flicked through his time with fingerlings, spending a little more effort dallying with his memories with Fira before dismissing them. It mined his memory for the Treaty and Linnia's duty to protect the Sands. It spent little time on humans, uncaring of the Rhun and Amela's fate, vaguely disinterested in Matteo's plight.

'*The People have grown fat,*' it rumbled. '*Needing humans to protect what's ours.*'

Kainon's mind ached. '*Linnia honors the Treaty.*'

'*The People need no treaty.*'

'*You're wrong,*' he countered before he could stop himself.

Its interest sharpened and stabbed at his thoughts. '*You spit like a hatchling who has yet to discover its fire.*'

'*I mean no disrespect, ancient one. But our two lands prosper through our unity.*'

'*And yet you disturb me with your desperation and fear.*'

Kainon's body quivered. '*I seek a trade.*'

Amusement roiled through his mind. '*You already belong to another.*'

Kainon thought of Tlalam, his stomach turning.

'*I did not awaken after a thousand years of slumber for your blindness, human.*'

The presence tightened around Kainon. He struggled to breathe. '*I ask for your aid.*' Kainon's thoughts went to the murdered villagers and Matteo's blue eyes turning dark with fear and anger.

'*I could close my eyes and sleep for millennia and you would be nothing but ash. What do I care about your problems?*'

Kainon struggled to hold firm. '*It's true our lives are fleeting but they are to honor you and all dragons.*'

'*The People need no honoring if it means growing fat on gifts from those we are meant to rule. I have slept too long if this is how the People have fallen.*'

The water in the pond trembled.

Kainon mentally stepped back.

The pond bulged and splashed before suddenly draining away. Something massive emerged from the mud. It dwarfed Tlalam, its black scales sloughing off the soil as it rose.

Kainon resisted the urge to cower.

'*It's time the People remember who they are.*'

Kainon sensed fire and battle. '*Honored dragon—*'

'*Your troubles bore me, human.*'

Kainon sensed the creature's intent to fly over the Uhur Mountains, but not before detouring over a small village where Linnians hunkered fearfully in a pigpen.

'*But I appreciate the awakening. For that alone, I will reward you.*'

It rose out of the forest on massive, powerful wings. Kainon felt fire gathering in its guts.

Buffeted as he was, Kainon felt ensnared by a vision of fire exploding across roofs and shattering huts and people alike. Great swathes of burned land spread before him, where the very soil melted into blackened glass.

The creature had razed villages before. It would do it again for Kainon.

Kainon opened his eyes to the tranquility of the forest and shuddered in realization. "What have I done?" he whispered.

31

"You're an idiot," Matteo muttered tersely, using a damp rag torn from his cloak to clean up the blood dribbling from Kainon's nose. "But I'm glad you're alive."

Kainon made a soft groan of agreement, sagging forward as Matteo wiped his cheek. He opened bloodshot eyes. "It's a black dragon, Matteo. They thrive on chaos."

Matteo grunted but made no rush to move from the shady grove. He suspected Kainon's ears still rang.

The man was pale and looked ready to collapse. "There's been war in its lifetime, possibly even against other dragons. It doesn't like Tlalam."

"Seems reasonable," Matteo muttered. The back of his hand brushed a few loose strands of Kainon's hair as he pressed a cool, clean rag to his forehead. His fingers twitched, but the weaving of a braid never came. A great abyss now cut between his mind and hands.

Matteo sat back with a sigh. "How long do we have?"

Kainon massaged his temple. "A candlemark, maybe less. It draws closer by the moment."

"But the dragon spared you."

"I think it was indulging itself rather than having any concern for me. I'm not sure how to use that to our advantage."

As long as the Rhun felt the dragon's wrath, Matteo cared very little about what else it did. He grimaced a little, reminding himself the villagers needed to be kept safe from whatever was about to befall their homes.

Kainon climbed to his feet. He rocked a little before Matteo rose and steadied him. He smiled slightly. "I'm glad you're here, Matteo."

Matteo smiled despite himself. "Same, strangely enough. Are you up for this?"

"A dragon-speaker's life is tied to pain." He stretched, his spine creaking. "For all his faults, Tlalam was skilled in quietening his mind to save dragon-speakers from the worst effects of talking with him."

"You're basically saying that causing pain is a dragon's choice."

Kainon tilted his head. "I suppose that's true." He motioned in the direction of the village. "We can't dally any longer."

Matteo watched him dubiously as he stumbled through the undergrowth before steadying. Kainon appeared to rally as they returned to the woodcutter's path.

They took a careful route back to the outskirts of the village, staying low in the brush. Matteo knew they were done for if Alize hunted them.

He took position behind a large boulder that fetched up close to a stream, a dagger clenched in his fist. "Maybe they want us in the village," he whispered.

Kainon looked at the branches overhead, green eyes dark with worry. "We've got our own ambush to worry about. I'll come in from the eastward side. Remember," he murmured as they prepared to separate. "Don't enter the village until after the dragon's gone. Flee if you have to. It won't care about half the forest catching fire if it plans to raze the village. But afterwards, the fire and smoke will be to our advantage."

Matteo nodded. "Will the dragon listen to you if you ask it to attack only the Rhun?"

Kainon grimaced. "I don't think it sees a difference, but I'll try."

Matteo tightened his grip on the dagger. "Be careful."

"You, too." Kainon ducked low and disappeared into the undergrowth.

After a few steps, Matteo no longer heard his footfalls. He settled behind the boulder, wondering if Craise would bolt at the sight of a dragon or hold firm. Matteo hoped for the latter. He imagined himself emerging from the smoke, dagger in hand. Craise might have a flame blade, but Matteo had the weight of a destroyed kingdom propelling him forward.

Matteo hesitated. He'd agreed to wait until Kainon had sent the dragon away. But the thought of Craise slinking off into the forest to escape the dragon set his teeth on edge.

Before giving himself time to reconsider, Matteo pushed away from his hiding place and crept up the embankment towards the nearest hut. He paused, waiting for an outcry.

Sprinting across the exposed tract of grass, he then pressed hard against the rough mud wall. Bored voices spoke in Rhuncavari on the other side of the hut.

Blood pounded in his ears as Matteo edged closer toward the Rhun.

One way or another, there would be an accounting.

KAINON REACHED the far side of the village, where game trails led into the woods. Baskets of smokeweed hung from the branches to dry. He had some hundred feet between himself and the nearest hut. Goats roamed unfettered, busily destroying reed fences and climbing roofs, while wild rabbits took over the gardens.

Kainon settled on his haunches and resisted massaging his temples. He felt wrung out but had no time for self-misery. The dragon loomed as a dark presence in his mind, so giant that he couldn't tell how far the creature ranged from the village. It could still be miles or just heartbeats away. Kainon cursed himself and tried to concentrate. Pressure built behind his eyes. His nose dripped and he hastily wiped it clean.

He looked over the village. Craise leaned against a post close to the pigpen, his face sour. Nadiya rode with one of the soldiers on sentry duty, making a slow, lazy circle around the outskirts of the village.

Kainon crouched low and waited for the two riders to pass. The remaining Rhun were nowhere to be seen, and Kainon assumed they must be taking their ease in one of the huts. The most prominent building looked like two huts strapped together with an enclosed walkway in a hodgepodge semblance of a town hall.

There was little sign that the village could house a Protector contingent—or that they even wanted to. Trapping and hunting in these forests were strictly forbidden. Regardless, one look told Kainon that the people here rarely flourished even in the best of times.

He rubbed his temples as the pressure in his head grew more insistent. The dragon seemed determined to take advantage of their discussion. Kainon swore under his breath. He should have known better than to think Tlalam was the only dragon who liked to misconstrue words for their own benefit.

He needed to get the villagers out as quickly as possible. Waiting for a dragon to attack seemed folly.

A sudden sharp point suddenly dug into his back.

"Don't move, Linnian," an accented male voice rasped in his ear.

Kainon held still.

"Where's the knotbinder?"

Kainon turned his head slightly. One of the remaining soldiers stood over him, lips curled in a sneer. The man lifted his gaze, appearing ready to call out to the village.

Kainon took his momentary distraction to twist and tackle the man into the ferns. They thrashed noisily, fighting for the blade. Kainon grabbed the man's wrist and squeezed hard while jamming his elbow into his throat.

The soldier coughed but still fought.

A voice called out from the village.

Using the distraction to his advantage, the soldier scored a solid punch to the side of Kainon's temple. They rolled, and Kainon got the man under him and wrested the sword from the man's grip. The soldier yelled but Kainon slashed him deep in the chest. The man howled and collapsed. Kainon rolled to his feet, sword clenched tight.

Thudding hooves alerted him to Nadiya as she galloped toward him with a delighted grin. She raised her hand.

Kainon dove.

The tree trunk behind him exploded into splinters. He scrambled back, hoping to draw Nadiya into the forest. Out of all the Rhun, she'd proven the most dangerous and eager to kill. Even Craise, obsessed with Matteo, mainly remained focused on their mission. Kainon only hoped it would be to his and Matteo's advantage. He got to his feet, stumbling from the growing weight in his mind.

Nadiya's horse crashed through the undergrowth.

Kainon instinctively leapt to the side but not fast enough to avoid branches shattering about him. Splinters lodged deep in his arm.

"Time to feed Alize's blade, Protector!" Nadiya yelled.

Gritting his teeth against the hot spears of pain, Kainon ducked between the trees, hoping not to give Nadiya a clear advantage. He ran parallel to the village and saw Latan, Alize, and the silent fifth Rhun emerge from a hut.

Latan spotted him and smiled, turning to speak with Alize.

But a flash of blond hair drew Kainon's attention to the shadows behind the pigpen.

Matteo!

He smothered a shout of frustration. Matteo was supposed to wait until the dragon had passed!

Nadiya was almost upon him, and Kainon's skin flinched in expectation now that there was less cover to protect him. He tripped, luck saving him as a surge of energy flew over his head.

He rolled to face Nadiya, who pulled up her horse with a wide grin. "There's nowhere to hide, dragon lover," she said, hand lifting to weave magic.

Kainon braced for pain.

But then the sky above her exploded into flame.

32

THE PIGPEN SAT to the side of a rudimentary bakehouse. Matteo peered around the door hanging half off its hinges to glance inside. The ovens were dark, the smell of burnt and abandoned bread turning the air stale. He crept past a flour-covered table and observed the pigpen through a broken window.

By his count, perhaps two dozen villagers crammed into the pen—certainly not enough to account for the whole village. Maybe others had escaped into the woods.

Or the Rhun had already fed them to Alize's flame blade.

Matteo's stomach turned.

Someone leaned their back against the pen's fence, ignoring the villagers.

Matteo recognized the arrogant angle of the man's jaw.

Craise.

Matteo's feet took him to the door without his volition. The dagger felt was a comforting weight in his hand. Matteo had no qualms surprising Craise and sliding the blade across his throat. His fist grew hot from the tightness of his grip on the hilt.

A sudden shout made Matteo flinch back. *Have I been discovered?*

But then Craise launched from the fence, his gaze fixed on the forest on the far side of the village. A flash of movement pierced the trees, a figure being chased by another. Nadiya bolted toward them on her horse.

It took long heartbeats for Matteo to realize Kainon was in the area.

He left the bakehouse but scarcely took a step before someone suddenly grabbed him from behind.

A muscled arm grabbed him around the throat and wrenched him against a tall body. Matteo twisted and saw the fifth death sorcerer's stoic face before the man hefted him past the pigpen. Matteo glimpsed the villagers huddled together, so terrified they seemed to pay no attention to either him or the commotion in the forest.

Matteo dug in his feet to no avail.

"Excellent work, Hass. Put him there," Craise said, appearing suddenly before them. He pointed at the ground at his feet.

Hass kicked the back of Matteo's knees, and he fell to the dirt. Hass grabbed a fistful of his tunic and held him still.

Coldly smiling, Craise drew his flame blade. It brightened as he pressed the tip just under Matteo's chin. "Stupid boy. They're not even your people. What were you going to do?"

Matteo gritted his teeth. "Kill you," he hissed.

Craise's smile brightened. "You would have had a place among the Rhun had you been born on the right side of the mountains."

Matteo frowned, tensing as Craise pulled back the blade as if to stab down.

"Craise!" Latan snapped, striding toward them with Alize in tow. "You have your orders!"

Craise appeared not to hear, his gaze fixed on Matteo. Hass made no move to obey Latan, either.

Latan motioned at Alize to draw her bow. The man seemed not so offended by Matteo's impending death but rather by Craise's disregard for his leadership.

A strange 'whomp' drew Matteo's gaze skyward.

Grey clouds suddenly turned a brilliant orange.

Hass' reflexively tightened his grip on Matteo's neck as the sky shifted and roiled.

Then a massive dragon dropped through the flames.

Craise half-lowered the flame blade, face slack-jawed.

The dragon made Tlalam seem insignificant in every way possible. Its scales were a solid, oily black, crowned by bristling black spines that spread from snout to tail. Its forked tail snapped back and forth as it dove from the clouds.

The dragon shot over the village with one wingbeat, dispersing the air and making the thatched roofs shiver. Matteo felt the vibration in the dirt beneath his knees.

Fire blasted across the village and struck a hut, flames exploding.

Matteo used the roaring noise of flames to ram his elbow into Hass' guts. The man grunted, the grip on his hair loosening enough for Matteo to yank free. He rolled to his feet, slipping past Craise while the man stared fixated at the dragon.

Horses shrieked and whinnied. Matteo spotted Kainon leaping away as Nadiya fought her horse.

The mount bucked Nadiya from the saddle, but the woman nimbly landed on her feet. The horse bolted down the road with a shrill scream as roofs caught alight.

Heat pressed against Matteo's back as he launched over the pigpen's fence. The villagers huddled together, trembling and gasping but making no attempt to flee.

"Run!" Matteo shouted at them. "Come on!" He gripped the nearest villager and shook him violently. The man paid no attention, almost as if a trance ensnared him. Matteo looked about and noticed immobile expressions on all of the villagers.

Then Matteo saw the strange knotting that bound the man's wrists. A wave of disorientation swept over him. The knots were both strange and familiar.

Matteo sank to his knees and gripped the rope. Power zapped his skin, and he snatched his hand away with a gasp.

Alize sprinted down the road with her flame blade held aloft, shouting something at the burning sky.

As if hearing her challenge, the dragon swooped low, its massive jaws opening to reveal burning orange in its depths. A stream of flames burst free.

The bakehouse suddenly shattered. A flaming shower of mud, brick and thatch rained down.

Matteo ducked as debris landed around him. He looked for Craise, but the smoke blocked his view. He spotted Hass outside the pen. His hands wove about in a series of circles, face blank with concentration. Hass lifted his gaze to the dragon. A bolt of purple lightning erupted from his hands and shot into the sky.

"Watch out!" Matteo shouted.

The dragon swiveled in the air as the bolt brushed over its side. It shrieked in outrage.

Matteo's mouth dropped. He'd thought Nadiya was the most powerful among the Rhun, but Hass stood in the middle of the road as if confident his magic could kill a dragon.

The dragon wheeled around, head rearing back and its ribs expanding as it drew air for another explosive burst of flame.

Hass was ready with another bolt.

It struck the dragon on the delicate underside of its wings.

The dragon careened wildly through the air and smashed into a row of huts, demolishing everything with a fiery boom.

Stillness fell, broken only by the crackle of flames.

Matteo quickly turned back to the captive villager and grabbed his bindings. A nasty bite of power singed his fingers, but he tightened his grip. "Trust me," he told the man.

The man's eyes appeared glazed, and Matteo was unsure he heard him.

Shouting and clattering debris outside the pen pulled at his attention. The dragon emerged from the smoke as thatched roofing and muddy walls sloughed off its black scales. A low, deep rumble vibrated from its throat before the dragon opened its mouth. An orange glow came from the depths.

Matteo shoved the villager down and threw his body over him, but the blast of flame never reached them. The dragon instead turned to an adversary down the street, spewing fire that scorched across the ground. A hut blocked Matteo's view, but a shrieking horse told him the flames had reached their target.

Smoke and sweat stung his eyes. He looked for Kainon to no avail.

Gritting his teeth, Matteo returned to the villager's bindings and grabbed tight. The rope seemed to buck and twist under his fingers, biting and snarling like a living thing. Matteo gripped one of the knots and instinctively twisted.

The binding froze as if surprised.

Matteo twisted again, getting his fingers deep into the rope as it loosened and pulsed. Red leaked from his fingers, burning through whatever strange enchantment gripped the villager.

Killing braids, Matteo realized. The knowledge to heal might be gone, but the most inherent part of his knotbinding remained.

But the red magic leached toward the villager, hungry to take a life. Matteo quickly nudged it toward the enchanted rope, willing it to consume and kill. Heat built within his hands as if the dragon had reached him after all.

The rope suddenly turned black and collapsed into ash.

The villager blinked into awareness before settling his attention on Matteo. His eyes widened and he fell back, raising his arms with a shout of terror.

Matteo closed his hands into a fist and fought down the swell of power that threatened to leach down into the muddy ground. It hungered for the villager and was angry at having been quiet for so long.

He took a slow, calming breath. Tlalam had left him with something after all.

"Get away, demon!" the villager shouted.

Matteo raised his hand in a quelling motion. "Easy—"

The villager flinched as if expecting to be struck before he scrambled backwards on all fours until his head hit the pig pen's wooden fence.

Matteo rose, caught between the urge to calm the man or turn his attention to the other captives. The man scrambled over the fence, tripping over himself in his haste.

A thump came behind Matteo, with boots squelching in the mud of the pigpen.

He turned.

Craise held up the glowing death blade and grinned.

33

KAINON BARELY KEPT his feet as the world tumbled over itself when the dragon crashed into the huts. For precious heartbeats, destroyed beams, cracked tiles and mud consumed his vision. The dragon's outraged confusion threatened to consume him.

By instinct, Kainon ducked as a blade whistled overhead. He blindly parried a strike to the guts and shoved Nadiya back. His vision cleared enough to see her grin viciously. He wondered why she didn't use her magic and quickly realized she was playing with him.

The stoic, tall death sorcerer edged closer to the dragon, purple light crackling around his hands and casting his face in a sickly glow.

The dragon clawed out of the debris, thatch and shattered furnishings tumbling free of the black spines along its back.

"Show it your power, Hass!" Latan called out, a hectic light in his eyes.

Kainon's mind scattered under the onslaught of the

dragon's outrage, but underneath the promise of death was a flare of curiosity over the Rhun's magic.

'*Don't*,' Kainon gasped.

The dragon lowered its head and sniffed the air, nostrils flaring as it examined the death sorcerer.

Kainon fought off another blow from Nadiya and shouted at the dragon, '*The Rhun will never serve you!*'

The dragon's curiosity brightened when the tall death sorcerer, Hass, remained unflinching under its appraisal.

'*They'll make any promise so they can steal your hoard,*' Kainon pressed desperately.

'*Death is my hoard,*' the dragon hissed.

It snaked forward with incredible speed, maw open. Hass raised his hands, undaunted as he weaved a new spell. He flung it into the air as the dragon snapped down and chomped his body in two.

Bones crunched, and Kainon grimaced and turned his head.

Nadiya laughed manically.

To his dismay, Kainon discovered that magic carried its own spice in the blood—a gingery tang that made him reflexively spit even as the dragon took its time savoring the bites last of the dead sorcerer.

Its interest piqued, it swiveled its giant head toward Nadiya.

"Ha!" Kainon shouted as she took a step back.

Sickly green light dragged Kainon's attention to outside the pen, where Alize stalked with the lesser flame blade. A villager toppled over the edge of the fence, scurrying away from whatever had him frightened in the pen. He was unaware of Alize striding up from behind.

"Get out of the way!" Kainon shouted, torn between racing to the man and keeping Nadiya at bay.

The dragon decided for him, teeth snapping at the air where Nadiya had been a heartbeat before. She rolled, a tight grin on her face as she splayed out her hands. Light crackled across her fingertips.

'Pathetic,' it hissed, offended. It gnashed its teeth and snapped at the air above Nadiya's head.

Nadiya threw a ball of light from clawed fingers. The magic crackled and spat across the dragon's snout.

It shook its head, a couple of scales beside its nostril looking raw.

Its outrage stirred anew and threatened to shake Kainon's mind loose. Nadiya was just a gnat, one that dared think she could smite an ancient dragon.

It opened its maw, showing the furnace building within.

Focused as she was on the gathering inferno, Nadiya missed the sweep of its blade-shaped tail. Huge and muscular like a snake, the tail swept her off her feet and catapulted her through the air. Nadiya shot across the village and crashed into the corner of a hut. Her body crunched on impact.

Kainon grimaced, shaking his head vigorously to clear the smug amusement from the black dragon. He sprinted for Alize, intent on bodily slamming her away from the villager.

A flash of blond hair drew his gaze to the pigpen, where Matteo stood protectively before the cowering villagers. Craise stalked toward him, flame blade alight.

"*Craise!*" Kainon roared.

A horse barreled into Kainon and sent him tumbling. Sharp pain stabbed his ribs. Wheezing, he got to his feet as Latan wheeled his horse about.

"Where's your braid, Protector?" Latan called out. The

white-haired sorcerer seemed not to care about the dragon stomping and smashing its way through the village.

With an effort, Kainon sent to the dragon, '*The glowing blades have power worthy of you.*'

It wasn't convinced, considering the poor showing of the Rhun magic-users.

'*They are born from death,*' Kainon pressed, even as he forced himself to straighten and face Latan. He pleaded for the dragon to go for the blade that glowed brightest, but the smoke marred its view of Craise.

"I do not say this lightly, Protector," Latan said, kicking his horse into a trot. His control over the animal was astonishing, given the dragon was only a few dozen feet away. "Tell me the location of the knotbinders, and I'll spare you."

Kainon stepped out of the way. "But not Matteo?"

Latan smiled. "His fate is already decided."

"Why don't you come down and convince me?" Kainon spat.

"Very well."

Latan swung down from the saddle and leisurely unsheathed his sword.

Sweat beaded Kainon's temples as he breathed through the fiery pain chomping at his side.

From the corner of his eye, he saw the dragon go for Alize. She was fleet-footed and nimble, leaping over shattered beams and collapsed walls to avoid the dragon's fire. If she reached the forest, she stood a chance at escaping.

Kainon sent a warning to the dragon.

Annoyance flared in response. It did not need advice from a potential meal.

"Your responsibility toward the knotbinder is a surprise,

Protector," Latan said, spinning his sword with a flourish. "Considering your Order's stance on outsiders."

Kainon raised his sword, hoping that the oncoming fight did not involve magic, otherwise it would be a short fight indeed. "Pretty sure you know nothing about Protectors."

Latan tutted softly as if disappointed. "Not every knotbinder who entered Linnia had to be hunted."

Kainon frowned.

"Your Order has been very accommodating, rounding them up for us and dumping them right where we want them."

Kainon felt his lip curl. "You're lying," he snarled.

Latan gave a regretful look. "A few knotbinders slipped the noose, of course. Tell me where they are, and Rhuncavar and Darsha will no longer impose on your precious kingdom."

Bile rose in Kainon's throat. He'd initially been no different to Matteo, so confident in his right to use the knotbinder as bait to keep the borders pure. What had the Protectors done?

Latan read something in his expression. "The boy will never know. Just name the location and we'll be done with this wretched serpent's den."

That was a lie; Kainon needed only to look at Alize's flame blade. "Why's it so important that all the knotbinders die? What's got you so scared?"

Latan smiled pityingly. "Death and rebirth go hand in hand, Protector. Now, I must have your answer."

Kainon raised his sword. "Happy to disappoint."

"I figured," Latan said.

Power illuminated his eyes as he strode the distance between them.

MATTEO TOOK a step back for every stride Craise took towards him. There was only so far he could retreat. He stopped in front of the bound villagers and willfully planted his feet.

"It's just us now, boy," Craise said as if there were no prisoners in the pen. The blade pulsed like a living thing.

Eyes on the glowing blade, Matteo felt heat pool in his fingertips. The prisoners' bindings had awakened something he'd thought was lost. "The knots," he said. "What did you do?"

Craise smirked. "Your people are quick to trade Dar's secrets for their lives."

"That's not how knotbinding works," Matteo countered. One had to be Darshian, for a start, and be born with inherent power that stayed dormant until a knotbinder took up the role of teacher.

Craise swung the flame blade in a mocking strike.

Matteo ducked easily and sidestepped, drawing the Rhuncavari away from the villagers.

Following with lazy confidence, Craise said, "You think I'm not like you."

"You're not Darshian."

"Dar disagrees with you, not that it matters. The Temple didn't welcome me, either, even though I was born in the same valley as you."

The smoke rolled in thick plumes as the dragon lumbered through it, searching.

"That's a lie," Matteo spat.

Craise bared his teeth. "No teacher stepped forward after the testing because I lacked your sallow skin and pale hair."

Matteo shook his head. The Rhuncavari was trying to unbalance him.

"So I made myself a new home among the Rhuncavari, but I never forgot how the beloved knotbinders of Darsha treated me." Craise swung again, the blade whistling inches from Matteo's skin. The man was taunting him. "They ignored me until they had no choice."

Matteo looked him up and down. Craise couldn't have been much older than Matteo was now when the Rhun invaded. There was no conceivable way the Rhun would have entrusted Craise with a flame blade if he was telling the truth.

"Oh, I had to prove myself to the Rhun. They appreciate vengeful sorts." Craise tilted his head. "Is that why you cling to the old ways, Matteo? You want revenge in the name of Dar?"

It was too inconceivable that Craise was Darshian, much less a knotbinder. But the enchantment binding the villagers had sparked *something* in Matteo, an echo of familiarity that was impossible to ignore.

Craise flicked his wrist, the flame blade snapping out so close that he'd have nicked Matteo's chin if he hadn't twisted aside. The man grinned.

Matteo spat back, "If a knotbinder taught you anything, it's how to be weak." He motioned to the bound villagers. "The enchantment fell apart the moment I touched it. An infant could weave better."

Craise sneered.

"That's why you need the flame blade. Because you're nothing without it." Matteo edged toward the thickening smoke. "Ever think that's the reason why no knotbinder chose you?"

Craise trailed after him, mouth tightening with murderous intent.

"You're just a sulky child indulging in a temper tantrum," Matteo taunted. "Even the Rhun can barely stand you."

The ground shook under the weight of the dragon stomping through the smoke. It hunted something in the grey pall—hopefully not Kainon. Matteo moved deeper into the smoke, trusting the sickly glow of the flame blade would be a beacon.

"I'm surprised you have such a simple view of the world, considering how loss has shaped you," Craise said, his voice pitying. "None of that will matter when the flame blade is full. Pity you won't be there to see it."

"You're too late," Matteo countered. "The knotbinders are already out of reach. That's what Tlalam told me."

"If that were so, Matteo, your *kha-shi* braid should be dead."

Matteo reflexively grabbed the braid in question, feeling the knots thrum with warmth and connection with the other remaining knotbinders. It steadied him a little, reminding him that hope was not lost—if he survived this.

"I told Latan you were a waste of time," Craise muttered. "Now he's indisposed, and I can finally take what's mine."

Knowing Craise meant to kill him, Matteo launched over the pen fence and ran toward the darkest smoke. It cut into his lungs, and he covered his mouth and nose with his tunic as he sprinted past pockets of fire.

The glowing flame blade sliced through the smoke.

Matteo ducked, stumbling over debris. He took cover behind a crushed hut, his eyes stinging. He needed surprise and luck to be his friends now.

At least the flame blade made the Rhun easy to track.

The man spun about, searching, before violently kicking something out of the way.

"Coward!" Craise yelled into the smoke. "You snivel and hide just like your dead brethren!"

That was hardly going to draw Matteo out.

But it did catch the attention of something far larger and ominous. The smoke billowed before splitting apart as the dragon's massive head appeared. Its forked tongue flicked out, tasting the air. Its slitted pupil had flecks of gold that reminded him of Fira.

Craise brandished the flame blade like a warning, saying something that made the blade flash searing white.

The dragon flinched at the sudden brightness.

But Craise didn't attack.

He doesn't want to taint the blade, Matteo realized. The man was so committed to his cause that he'd risk being eaten by a dragon.

Snarl caught in his throat, Matteo picked up a burning paling and ran at Craise. The paling smashed down on Craise's wrists in a shower of sparks. Craise lost grip of the blade with a startled curse. It clanged somewhere amongst the burning debris.

Matteo swung again, embers shooting in every direction as he struck Craise in the shoulder and care. The man stumbled backwards, hitting the ground hard, but a heartbeat later he kicked out and knocked Matteo's feet from under him.

Matteo hit the ground with a hard grunt.

Craise leapt on top of him, his weight slamming Matteo down as hands closed around his throat. Craise squeezed, teeth bared in a rictus of a snarl.

Choking, Matteo frantically scratched at the man's

hands before tearing at the man's eyes. Pressure built in his lungs.

"The blade will resent me for this," Craise hissed, using his weight to bear down. "Oh, but it's worth it."

Black spots danced in front of Matteo's eyes. His fingers raked down Craise's face.

"No!"

Craise's grip loosened in surprise, just enough for Matteo to draw a desperate breath. He rammed the heel of his hand against Craise's face to no avail.

Craise gazed to the side, attention locked on a sudden brilliant light piercing the smoke. "Stop him!"

Matteo's vision cleared to see Kainon step through the haze with the flame blade held aloft.

34

Instinct told Kainon to run.

The dragon was an ominous presence in his mind, and he dove behind its flanks, hoping it wouldn't take offence over him using it as a shield against Latan. It appeared distracted, hunting the smoke for a dull glow—Alize's blade. Its eyesight was better suited to smoke and fire than a Linnian's, but its centuries-old sleep had dulled its senses.

Hunkering low, Kainon trotted past the dragon's hind leg.

The dragon had no interest in Latan, so Kainon had no way of tracking the man through the smoke. With no braid to protect him, Kainon knew he would not survive whatever enchantment the sorcerer threw at him.

He pressed on, heading in the vague direction of the pigpen through thick bands of spoke. To his dismay, Matteo was no longer there, though the villagers remained huddled together in the muddy far corner. He debated herding them away from the smoke and fire before it could consume them. But where was Matteo? His absence surely meant Craise gave chase.

Turning about, he observed that every hut was alight. And yet, Kainon had the unsettling notion that the dragon held back the worst of its destructive power.

But then he spotted Matteo as little more than a furtive flash of movement between the rolling smoke. The knotbinder leapt with a blazing length of wood, smashing the flame blade from Craise's hands.

Kainon mentally cheered even as Matteo struck again, but then the boy was on the ground and Craise was on top of him. Kainon sprinted, leaping over fire to reach them.

The flame blade lay under some shattered beams. Without stopping to consider his actions, Kainon reached for it.

"*No!*" Latan shouted behind him.

The sudden onslaught of screaming voices was worse than the dragons. Kainon screwed his eyes shut even as bile flooded his mouth. The flame blade had gorged on hundreds of knotbinders, feeding on their anguish and terror. Kainon trembled and resisted the urge to throw the sword away.

"Stop him!" Craise roared even as Matteo fought to get out from underneath him.

Something struck Kainon in the back, but it washed over him as if made of gossamer.

Latan shouted a curse and tried again.

The dragon swiveled its head, interest piqued, though not with Latan. It spun, viper-quick, shattering another hut. Latan disappeared amongst the dust and debris with a choked cry.

Kainon hardly cared. Incandescent rage filled him. Without his volition, he strode toward Matteo and Craise. Something gripped his movements, making him take the blade in both hands and raise it in readiness to swing.

The sword felt insistent, and Kainon felt an ancient hunger stir in his belly. The blade yearned to be finally unleashed. It was *so close* to fulfilling its purpose.

Craise's mouth dropped, his face turning pale as Kainon drew close.

Matteo left off trying to scratch and gouge his way free. He reached into his hair and pulled free the fingerling's purloined hairpin. He jabbed once, twice, and again into Craise's shoulder with frantic rapid stabs.

Craise roared and rolled away, but that was his undoing.

Kainon stepped close and swung, beheading the Rhun sorcerer with a single blow. Power rushed over Kainon in a wave.

MATTEO SCURRIED BACK from Craise's body, his breath wheezing through his bruised throat.

Dizziness gripped him. Everything felt bruised or burning.

Kainon stood over him, his green eyes glazed as if in some internal battle.

A sense of wrongness swept over Matteo, and he instinctively grabbed the *kha-shi* braid. Its edge darkened and turned brittle with every passing heartbeat.

"No," he whispered, staring at Craise's decapitated head. "No, no, no."

Unbidden, Tlalam's words came back to him. '*What you seek is closer than you think...*'

The braid linking him to the last of the knotbinders crumbled to ash between his fingers.

Matteo screamed his realization and loss.

35

KAINON FOUGHT THE BLADE. It wanted just one more life, then it would be whole and full and the world would be his. No bowing to Tlalam's riddles and demands, no navigating the Protectors and their rules. No having to see betrayal on Matteo's face when he discovered what the Protectors had done to Darsha's people.

Kainon's hands quivered on the hilt.

Anything Kainon wanted was within reach. The blade was insistent. It belonged to him now.

Just feed it one more knotbinder.

It coiled about his mind like a vine, sinking in its barbs. Something lurked in the shadow behind the blade, out of focus.

'*How fascinating,*' the dragon hissed in his mind. It emerged fully from the smoke and loomed over Kainon. It tasted the air, finding potential and portent.

Kainon ached from being pulled in multiple directions. With an effort, he asked, '*Will you take the blade?*'

Avarice flooded his mind. But caution and knowing quickly followed.

'*That is no gift, dragon-speaker,*' the dragon chided.

Kainon raised the blade in offering. '*Will you destroy it?*'

The dragon swiveled its head, studying Kainon with an unblinking eye. '*And what fun would that be?*'

Kainon shuddered.

The dragon felt done with this little diversion. There were more important matters on the other side of the Uhur Mountains.

It lumbered past Matteo, who kneeled curled over himself beside Craise's body. Despite every step rattling through the destroyed village, the boy did not notice the dragon.

Muscles bunching, the dragon launched upwards without any of Tlalam's ungainliness. It circled overhead as if to admire the carnage before wheeling north.

Kainon removed his cloak and wrapped the flame blade as tightly as possible. The separation eased some of the tension charging across his skin. Setting it aside, he went to Matteo.

"Matteo," he said, gripping his shoulders and pulling him upright. Tears streaked the lad's face. "Come away; it's over now."

Matteo's blue eyes were dark with despair. "Craise was a knotbinder," he whispered, mouth trembling.

Kainon's guts clenched. He knew as much, considering the flame blade's exaltation when he'd deprived the sorcerer of his head. But to hear it said aloud was something else.

Kainon cupped Matteo's jaw. "I'm sorry."

"He—he was the last," Matteo choked out.

Kainon drew Matteo in tightly. "No, Matteo," he murmured, his eyes burning with tears as he rested his cheek on Matteo's head. "You are."

36

THE VILLAGERS TREATED Kainon and Matteo with distrust, despite being released from Craise's enchantment following his demise. Many recalled very little after the Rhun rode into their village at nightfall and now had to contend with their destroyed homes and two strangers in their midst.

"They blame us," Kainon explained to Matteo, who appeared resentful of the villagers and their complaints when he had his own loss.

Matteo threw a length of charred wood onto a refuse pile. The ash on his face gave him a distinctly mournful air. Mottled bruises showed darkly across his throat.

"They're lucky they weren't all fed to Alize's blade," Matteo said.

The blade in question was worryingly absent, along with Alize and Nadiya.

"I don't like that we haven't found the women's bodies," Kainon said, looking across the rubble.

Matteo shrugged, though a shadow crossed his face. "Maybe the dragon ate them."

It was possible, though the dragon's feasting had been

thankfully perfunctory rather than with any real appetite. Kainon did not want to consider the chaos wreaked by a dragon with a taste for humans and destruction.

They'd stopped the fires from spreading into the forest, but little was left of the village. It was a relief to Kainon, as the village should not have been there in the first place. He wondered how Protectors patrolling in the forest had not come upon it. It looked several summers old.

"The Protectors don't care about what we do here," a woman told him.

Kainon hadn't the energy to tell her he was a Protector. "Maybe so, but the fingerlings must have a safe, unblocked path through the forest."

She shrugged. "They can go around. We're not hunting them, not that it matters," the woman continued. "We'll be moving on now that a dragon knows about us. It could come back."

You're not that interesting, Kainon wanted to say, his gaze tracking toward Matteo.

The boy moved around the ruined huts like a ghost, pale and bruised. The villagers avoided him, noting him as an outlander.

In the evening, Kainon pulled Matteo under an awning at the edge of the trees away from the villagers. They'd taken blankets and packs from the dead Rhuncavari, though Matteo seemed to loathe using them.

"Talk to me," Kainon murmured.

Matteo sat with his knees tucked close to his chest, his mouth downturned. "What do I say? Tlalam took my abilities, and there's no one left to teach me," he said bitterly. He picked up a stick and broke it into small pieces before throwing them into the small campfire.

"You're not the last of your people," Kainon said.

"Like that matters."

"Of course it does."

Matteo sniffed and wiped his nose. "I know there's other ways to fight; I just thought I'd always be a knotbinder." He looked off into the trees, his eyes distant. "The Rhun are afraid of knotbinders, and I wanted to be their undoing."

Kainon rubbed Matteo's back, fingers brushing the warm ends of his braids. His gaze slid toward the tree hollow where he'd hidden Craise's flame blade.

Something waited within the blade, something dark and ancient, and it was far from fearful of knotbinders. It had set its previous owner on a seemingly impossible task of killing all knotbinders, and now it was mere feet from success.

I have to destroy it, Kainon knew, though he had no idea how to go about it.

The dragon hadn't wanted the blade, but it hadn't said that destroying it was impossible. Keeping it close to Matteo in the meantime was dangerous.

Then there was the added mess of telling Matteo the Protectors had essentially given his people to the Rhun.

Kainon sighed and tugged the back of Matteo's tunic. The knotbinder resisted, his back a long line of tension. "Matteo..."

Matteo looked over his shoulder at him, his eyes dark and brimming.

Kainon tugged again, gratified when Matteo went lax and settled beside him.

They stared up at the awning together.

"Despite everything," Matteo murmured. "I really thought Darsha stood a chance."

Kainon wished there was something he could do to heal Matteo's pain. "I know."

MATTEO WOKE to the crickets still chirping in the darkness. The air had grown chill, with the chance of frost come morning. He lay still for precious heartbeats, listening to Kainon's slow and steady breaths beside him.

A lump formed in his throat. What was he going to do now? Everything that had kept him going was now gone. The Rhun had won.

He touched his temple where the braid had once been, feeling short bristly hair under his fingers. He'd been so proud when his teacher had first woven the braid, feeling a rush of warmth that told him he was part of something bigger than himself.

Not only was it now gone, but Matteo was irreparably weakened. Useless. The Rhun had won in every way that mattered.

"Whatever you're thinking, Matteo," Kainon murmured in the darkness. "You're wrong."

Matteo debated lying still and pretending to sleep but pushed himself up and sat cross-legged. He looked down on the panes of Kainon's face in the starlight. "How can you say that?"

Kainon shrugged minutely and tucked his hands behind his head. His eyes were clear, like he'd been awake for some time contemplating matters. "You're alive despite the Rhun's best efforts. And now they've lost the flame blade."

Matteo's gaze tracked toward the grove of dark trees nearby where he'd seen Kainon disappear during the day.

"We'll destroy it, Matteo," Kainon promised. "We'll hide it someplace safe until we figure out how."

"The other flame blade is still missing," Matteo said.

"Yes, we must accept that Alize is likely still alive."

"Nadiya, too."

The young woman was likely badly hurt, given how the black dragon had thrown her halfway across the village. It would slow Alize down.

"We can find them," Matteo said.

Kainon hesitated. "We could, but I'd prefer you were safe first. Hiding the flame blade will help."

Matteo returned his gaze to Kainon. "My safety's not important anymore."

"We have different views on what's important, Matteo," Kainon said. "I know this isn't what you intended when you entered Linnia. I certainly didn't expect to become friends with an angry outlander I pulled out of some bushes."

Matteo couldn't help but snort at that.

"But I'm glad I did," Kainon continued. "Now, I understand if you want to be done with Linnia and our proclivity for dragon quests. Say the word and we'll turn east and I'll get you to Erania."

Even in the dark, Matteo could read the earnestness in Kainon's expression.

"But if you think as I do, then our best chance of dealing with our individual and shared problems is together. I don't have the faintest idea where to go from here, but we can do this."

It had been a long time since Matteo last dared to hope. There was very little reason to do so now, but whatever happened next, he no longer had to face it alone.

"Okay." Matteo felt the tension leave his shoulders as he nodded firmly. "Together."

37

SEBANI and two dozen Protectors rode into the village the next day.

The Protectors eyed the destroyed huts with dismay, perhaps seeing a dragon's touch. The villagers looked caught between fleeing into the bushes or resigning themselves to the Protectors being in their business.

Matteo sagged in relief when he and Kainon spotted Sebani. He stopped dragging a charred wooden beam toward the refuse pile and waved.

Sebani swung down from her horse and strode to them. "Dragons balls, you've both got more lives than a cat stealing a fingerling's hoard!" she laughed as she clasped their forearms in turn.

Kainon chuckled. "It's about time we saw a friendly face."

"Dragon lords, I expect so," Sebani grinned. She turned and ordered the Protectors to check the villagers for injuries before critically examining Matteo and Kainon. "Didn't expect to see you both in one piece. We lost the Rhun's trail days ago, curse them."

That would have been Alize's handiwork. Matteo couldn't tell if she was exceptionally stealthy or whether magic was also at play.

"How did you find us?" he asked.

"The smoke alerted us to something afoot here." Sebani gave the ruined village a squinty-eyed look. "I didn't expect to find this!"

Matteo grimaced in agreement. The scorched earth crunched underfoot, and he'd found several glass-like crystals where one of the dragon's fireballs had exploded a hut.

"There'll need to be more forest patrols," Kainon said. "Other villages could be out here that we don't know about."

"In time, my friend," Sebani promised. "First, tell me about the Rhun. I suspect they didn't simply let you both free. Where are they?"

Matteo and Kainon quickly shared what had befallen them since parting ways to speak with Tlalam.

"Never thought I'd be pleased to hear of a dragon eating people," Sebani said with a shudder. "Good riddance, I say."

"There's one or two Rhun still on the loose," Kainon said. "One's an exceptional hunter, and she may have a flame blade that's just started to feed on Linnians."

Sebani cursed. "She'll find the whole of Linnia against her, then. No offence meant, Matteo, but Linnia can take on the Rhun. Our mages come from a lineage born from fighting dragons."

"No offence taken," Matteo said, more worried about what could happen if the lesser flame blade got a taste for Linnian mages.

"I don't like that there are flame blades in Linnia," Sebani muttered.

Matteo resisted shifting from foot to foot. He'd slept

better than expected last night, though he'd woken from a dream of Alize emerging from the trees to finish what Craise had started.

"Any idea on how to destroy them?" Kainon asked.

Matteo glanced at him carefully. Kainon had hidden Craise's blade from the villagers, though tracking the dragon-speaker's gaze toward a pine grove near the road was easy.

"Afraid not," Sebani said. "Killing its bearer might help, but then the task passes to the blade's new owner. The mage guild may have answers."

Kainon's calm mask slipped a little. He hadn't told Matteo he possessed Craise's flame blade, but a shadow in Kainon's green eyes spoke of a new burden.

"Maybe Fira can help," Matteo said.

"Fira likes Kainon well enough," Sebani agreed. "She may not even demand anything in return."

It felt strange to hear Fira spoken about as if she were no different to Tlalam. Having Fira's company was not solely about keeping her fed and happy; she genuinely liked Kainon and the people in Briarfall.

"Is she okay?" Matteo asked, glancing briefly at Kainon.

Kainon sent him a warm look for the asking.

"She was hurt, but the Protectors have matters in hand," Sebani said. "I rallied a contingent to chase after you as soon as we regained control of the Sanctuary."

Kainon frowned. "There are still pilgrims at the Sanctuary. Fira's trapped at the temple."

"That doesn't sound right," Sebani said, frowning, too. "The commander ordered the pilgrims away after they rioted."

"What about Fira?" Matteo asked.

Sebani hesitated, her brow creasing. "If she's at the

temple, she went there after my contingent left. She could have chosen to go there rather than return to the chapter house. She's maturing rapidly, so her way of doing things will become less predictable."

Kainon gave a worried grunt. "Even if she chose, Fira's deeply unhappy."

"Well, you'd know best. We can't have yet another dragon angry with us," Sebani said as she studied the collapsed and smoldering huts. "You did well to have one of them attack the Rhun."

The tense line of Kainon's mouth said it had been a near thing. "It should be nearing the Uhur Mountains by now."

Sebani nodded, her gaze still assessing the wreckage. "A black dragon, you say. Revelers of death and madness." She cursed softly under her breath. "The Treaty demands that they never return to Linnia."

"This one never left," Kainon said. "It doesn't care about the Treaty, but it doesn't have issues with us, unlike the dragons leaving the Breeding Sands."

"That's no comfort at all, Kainon," Sebani said tersely. "What did Tlalam tell you?"

They quickly went over what had happened at the temple.

Sebani's unhappiness only increased. "A dragon's quest, without much to go on." She sighed. "The dragons have some sort of problem with the Treaty but don't care to honor it themselves."

Kainon shook his head. "We can't claim to be sticking to the Treaty, either. Look around, Sebani. This village shouldn't be here, and we found a snare in the forest that was decades old."

Sebani frowned.

"What else are the Protectors missing?" Kainon asked.

"We've been called thieves. Even the fingerlings are hiding from us—possibly to avoid being caught in a firestorm meant for Linnians."

"You've turned into a grim fellow, Kainon," Sebani said, her mouth turned down. "But with good reason. We need greater minds than our own to figure out what Tlalam meant."

"We think the answer's in the Breeding Sands," Matteo said.

Kainon grunted in agreement. "Now that you're here to distract the Rhun, Matteo and I can get close enough to the Sands to see what's afoot."

"Now, *that* would break the Treaty," Sebani replied. "I can't let you go without orders from the Grand Chapter House, Kainon. You may even need a royal decree to enter the Sands."

Matteo glanced at Kainon, who appeared unsurprised but frustrated by Sebani's response.

"Sebani, it's just a matter of time before a dragon leaves the Breeding Sands and takes her anger out on us," Kainon argued.

"I know it's urgent, but my hands are tied. Let's get you both back to Bone Lake," Sebani said, a tinge of an order in her voice. "We'll figure out a way forward from there."

They made plans to leave in the morning, and Sebani turned her attention to the villagers who gaggled at the Protectors. A few still looked ready to run off into the forest, but Sebani promised to help them relocate with as many of their possessions as possible.

Kainon briefly entered the pine grove and returned with Craise's flame blade wrapped within a cloak.

Matteo felt his lip curl at the sight of it.

Kainon acted like holding the blade wasn't a burden, but

Matteo noticed how quick Kainon was to tuck the blade under a saddle he had acquired off one of the remaining Rhun horses.

"Do you really think Fira can help?" Matteo asked.

"I hope so, if she isn't mad at us for abandoning her," Kainon said, worry lacing his voice.

That was a sobering thought. "Fira knows she means everything to you," Matteo replied.

He grunted in agreement. "Thia warned me a long time ago I'd be part of Fira's hoard," Kainon said with a quirk of his lips. "You are, too."

"Me?" Matteo blinked in surprise.

"Of course; ever since you made her a flower crown in the mountain pass."

"That was so long ago," Matteo murmured, remembering how Fira's eyes had whirled and danced. "I didn't think gaining a dragon's regard was so easy."

"Oh, it's not," Kainon said. "And before you start thinking it's because you're a knotbinder—and that she'll change her mind now—many mages try to curry favor with the dragons. It takes a special kind of alchemy to win them over."

Matteo felt his cheeks grow warm. "I like Fira, too."

"Hopefully, she'll join us on our quest."

"Do you think she'll say no?"

Kainon gave a dubious grunt. "I can't be sure of anything with Fira anymore. She's already grown far bigger than I ever thought possible in my lifetime."

"Yet another mystery," Matteo said with a sigh.

Kainon grinned. "No pouting, knotbinder. We're free of the Rhun and soon back with our scaly friend."

Matteo saw through Kainon's attempt at light-heartedness. Tlalam's quest loomed over them both, and with the loss of his gift, Matteo wasn't sure he had anything useful to offer. And if Fira was done with them and refused to help destroy the flame blade, they could quickly find themselves waylaid once again by power-hungry Rhun.

Matteo thought of Tlalam, who'd taken his gift of healing despite knowing he would never accept Craise as his teacher. While Kainon was certain Tlalam wanted them to succeed and repair the relationship between Linnia and the dragons, Matteo wasn't so sure.

That was fine. He'd survived the Rhun and outlived every other knotbinder.

He could play a dragon's game as well.

For a heartbeat, Matteo thought he saw his fingertips glow red.

Wiping his hands on his breeches, he joined Kainon to find Rhuncavari supplies for the ride back to Bone Lake.

THE END OF BOOK ONE

AUTHOR'S NOTE

Thanks so much for reading. Reviews are the lifeblood of authors, so please feel free to share your thoughts about *The Last Knotbinder* on Amazon or Goodreads.

Your support and feedback means everything!

ACKNOWLEDGMENTS

This book wouldn't have been possible without the wonderful people in my life.

The person who helps me the most is my amazing twin sister, Bam, who is always there to beta read and listen to me moan and question every plot point and life choice along the way.

Then there's Lindsay Davis, creative life coach extraordinaire. She can get me back on track with a well-aimed observation, question or task. Without her, I'm pretty sure this book would be languishing in my unfinished folder forever. Thank you, Linz!

Thank you to my family and friends, who have the grace and patience to let me find my feet on my own terms. Thank you for being there during times of heartbreak and healing. I couldn't have written this book without you.

And also a huge thank you to the readers who help make it possible for me to do what I've always wanted to do.

ALSO BY K.K. NESS

ABOUT THE AUTHOR

K.K. NESS is a social worker by day and a writer...also by day. She loves creating stories with a cast of characters whose antics and mayhem make her happy. She resides in sunny Queensland, Australia, with various family and animal friends.

Visit her website to subscribe for the latest releases and updates.

www.kkness.com